A BURNT CHILD

Books by Stig Dagerman
Published by the University of Minnesota Press

German Autumn
Island of the Doomed

A BURNT CHILD

A NOVEL

Stig Dagerman

Translated by Benjamin Mier-Cruz
Introduction by Per Olov Enquist

University of Minnesota Press
Minneapolis

The University of Minnesota Press gratefully acknowledges financial assistance provided for the publication of this book from the Swedish Arts Council and the Barbro Osher Pro Suecia Foundation.

Originally published in Swedish as *Bränt barn* by Norstedts, Sweden, in 1948; copyright 1948 Stig Dagerman.

A different English translation was published in 1950 by William Morrow and Company.

First University of Minnesota Press edition, 2013. Published by agreement with Norstedts Agency.

Published by the University of Minnesota Press
111 Third Avenue South, Suite 290
Minneapolis, MN 55401-2520
http://www.upress.umn.edu

LIBRARY OF CONGRESS CATALOGING-IN-PUBLICATION DATA
Dagerman, Stig, 1923–1954, author.
[Bränt barn. English]
A burnt child : a novel / Stig Dagerman ; translated by Benjamin Mier-Cruz ; Introduction by Per Olov Enquist.
ISBN 978-0-8166-7799-3 (pb : acid-free paper)
I. Mier-Cruz, Benjamin, translator. II. Title.
PT9875.D12B713 2013
839.73'74—dc23   2013007881

Printed in the United States of America on acid-free paper

The University of Minnesota is an equal-opportunity educator and employer.

20 19 18 17 16 15 14 13   10 9 8 7 6 5 4 3 2 1

CONTENTS

INTRODUCTION

Per Olov Enquist

Bränt barn (A Burnt Child) was the first book I read by Stig Dagerman—I think in 1949. It overwhelmed me, and for a long time I
wrote my own school essays in the same style that I imagined was
his. I read everything by him after that, but nothing was like *A
Burnt Child.*

What was so compelling about this novel about a young man
who had an affair with his father's new wife? Surely it wasn't por-
nography. And why has this of all his novels divided critics, even
today? Olof Lagercrantz, for instance, scarcely mentions it in his
classic biography of Dagerman. And the novel has often been ac-
cused of having too much Oedipus complex, psychoanalysis, and
Freud.

Yet even after sixty years I still cannot see why the book has
been overlooked; I must have missed something. I had read, and
still read, a remarkably realistic, clear, and poignant story about a
young man who insidiously resembles myself.

I still do not understand the criticism. *A Burnt Child* is truly
the Modest Masterpiece.

Stig Dagerman had a short life, but his creative life was even shorter. I figure three years and eleven months.

He debuted with *Ormen* (The Snake) in November 1945: we'll consider this the starting point. In the fall of 1946 he published *De dömdas ö* (Island of the Doomed), a powerful, symbolic novel that enchanted critics ("the flying fortress of 1940s literary problems").[1] This was followed by the short story collection *Nattens lekar* (The Games of Night) later the same year. Everyone was talking about Dagerman; he was the genius of the decade. Also in the fall of 1946, he reported on what he saw in bomb-wrecked and famished Germany, where he was on assignment for two months for the newspaper *Expressen*. This report would be published as a book in the spring of 1947 under the name *Tysk höst* (German Autumn). The next book he wrote, in the summer of 1948, was *A Burnt Child*.

It happened fast, an entire novel in six weeks. The time lag between the end of his German expedition and when he resumed writing is particularly notable. A black hole. Nothing for a year and a half. But there was no time to lose! His writing career was so short! Less than four years! Why did he take a break during this frantically prolific period, and what was it that happened?

Apparently nothing. The great success of his German report— still an international classic, as no one else wanted to deal with the horrific reality of the defeated Germans—led the *Expressen* editors to find another assignment for him. He would travel to France and write . . . what, exactly? *French Autumn*? A companion to August Strindberg's *Among French Peasants*?

France was not Germany: France was a closed country and a victorious power. The success could not be repeated. He spoke excellent German, but his French was lousy. France was like a sealed clam, and as he wandered about the French countryside his debts and feelings of guilt increased. But nothing was written. He was sent out, he was given an advance, but he did not deliver. Yes, the spring was awful, but something else was wrong.

What was the problem? He was in the middle of his writing career, which would end on the tenth of October 1949, when he completed his final novel, *Bröllopsbesvär* (Wedding Worries). By this point, his work had essentially reached its highest creative achievement. And yet as a living, breathing person, Dagerman still had five years left before he would take his own life. Even so, he couldn't write. Three years and eleven months as a writer. And no more.

What happened between December 1946, when he returned home from Germany, and July 1948, when he began writing *A Burnt Child* and completed it in just six weeks? Why did his style change, moving away from critically acclaimed abstractions with symbolic characters, as in *Island of the Doomed,* to the caustic, realistic, and spare prose of the summer of 1948? Had reality hit him so hard that he stalled, almost becoming paralyzed?

Lasse Bergström made an observation in his foreword to *Stig Dagerman's Letters* that I find quite telling and that covers the entirety of Dagerman's resumed career—what was left of it:

> It is clear that the German experience of 1946 was a turning point. After that, he could no longer express internal fear as freely and naturally as he did in *The Snake* and *Island of the Doomed.* His fiction now embraced external reality, as in the novel *A Burnt Child.* He seems to claim new literary ground but in the process loses the fear that previously had free rein, like a dark beast, in his fiction and in his heart.[2]

In other words, reality had put the theoretical fear of the forties to the test. What he saw in Germany in the autumn of 1946 were the remains of a war-torn European culture, a landscape in which 660,000 civilian men, women, and children were annihilated by carpet bombs in the final year of the war. He witnessed a state of apathy, doubt, and guilt—not as an expression of intellectual reflection but as, well, simply reality. The young twenty-three-year-old author was jarred out of the typical issues of existential fear, guilt, and culpability facing his fellow Swedish writers of the forties—the group known as the *Fyrtiotalisterna*—to confront a reality where people were starving and dying amid ruins. He was thus barely able to ask fear-ridden questions about the meaning of life—or guilt. He identified with the defeated, something that always came naturally to him. He was also now married to a young German woman, a refugee from Nazism: she and her family had given Dagerman the "keys to interviews" with their surviving relatives in Germany. But they didn't have easy answers to the questions of guilt and responsibility either.

The leap from founder of the flying fortress of 1940s literary problems to witness to the ruins of European misery in Berlin (incidentally, also created by the flying fortress) was great. Dagerman almost didn't succeed. He was sent glowing reviews for *Island of the Doomed* while in the Ruhr region, and forgetting the famine and hopelessness for a moment, he wrote, "I wanted to die of shame—but that didn't work out either."³

He later wrote to his publisher about the years that followed, saying that "after Germany the joy of writing was gone." But that wasn't all: "The foolish year in France may have been devastating. Roaming in solitude from place to place with a journalistic imperative in the backseat and a typewriter in my suitcase that ultimately grew so heavy with failure that I could hardly lift it. Where is the road I'm searching everywhere for?"⁴

He finally gave up, notifying the newspaper that a year of French ambitions produced no results, nothing but debts. He secluded himself in a village in Bretagne for six weeks and wrote what would become his most compressed, simple, and poignant novel, which is now after sixty years still read all over the world, the only one, in fact, by any Swedish writer of the forties that is still so prevalent.

A simple novel about a family in Södermalm in Stockholm. A simple novel about a young two-timer, an angst-filled self-portrait written by a twenty-five-year-old thin-skinned author who couldn't cope with the world's and his own betrayal, expectations, and declarations of genius. It's also possible that part of the unparalleled charge in this novel is due to the fact that everything in Dagerman's life seemed to be falling apart, including his happy marriage. And that he, writing his most personal novel, didn't need to base it on theoretical knowledge of psychoanalysis, Freud, and the Oedipus complex: he had just experienced a shorter intimate relationship with his mother-in-law who had come from Germany by way of the Spanish civil war and who had taught him a lot about reality beyond the literary angst of the Swedish writers of the forties.

In any event, this became *A Burnt Child.*

The following year he was sent to Australia by boat (there was always someone who sent him out, often a film company with a brilliant idea for the newly appointed genius) to write about the conditions of exile—a project he didn't finish either. Then there was his final novel, *Wedding Worries,* a nosedive back into his childhood milieu, a story created nearly in panic as a burlesque and grotesque tragedy in a farming village. Then nothing for five years but new projects that always ended after three pages. Then a garage, closed doors, and a running car. There is perhaps no simple answer to the enigma of Dagerman's career: why did it get so bright, and why did it end so soon?

One could say that his last two novels were about the internal disintegration of the family (*A Burnt Child*) and the village where he grew up (*Wedding Worries*): first he looked inward, then backward.

Then it was over.

A few days before taking his own life, he wrote in a letter to a worried female friend who had probably suspected something:

> Somehow my life has come to a standstill, and I don't know how I'll be able to revive it. I can't do anything anymore: can't write; can't laugh; can't speak; can't read. I feel like I'm outside the whole game. When I'm with people, I have to force myself to listen to what they are saying in order to smile at the right moments. And the last time I read *Steppenwolf* it hit me that I have a connection there, that is, not with the ones who take their own life out of necessity but the ones who always have

death by their side as a matter of precaution, to speak with, to hope for. I don't know why I'm still living. I see no end to the piling up of these senseless days.

I once read something by a Catholic about someone whom nobody could see because he concealed himself in light. If only we had some light to hide ourselves in.[5]

NOTES

1. Quoted in Erik Lindegren's review of *Island of the Doomed* in *Bonniers Litterära Magasin* 9 (1946). Lindegren's review is also reprinted in *40-talsförfattare: ett urval essäer om svenska författare ur 40-talsgenerationen,* ed. Lars-Olof Franzén (Stockholm: Aldus/Bonnier, 1965).

2. Lasse Bergström's foreword to *Stig Dagerman's Letters,* in *Stig Dagerman: Brev,* ed. Hans Sandberg (Stockholm: Norstedts Förlag, 2002), 10.

3. From Dagerman's letter to Axel Liffner in 1946, in *Stig Dagerman: Brev,* 96.

4. From Dagerman's letter to Ragnar Svanström in 1949, in *Stig Dagerman: Brev,* 214.

5. From Dagerman's letter to Inga Landgré in 1954, in *Stig Dagerman: Brev,* 325–26.

A BURNT CHILD

It is not true that a burnt child dreads the fire.
It is drawn to it like a moth to a flame. It knows
that when it goes near it, it will burn itself again.
Still, it gets too close.

BLOWING OUT A CANDLE

A WIFE IS TO BE BURIED AT TWO O'CLOCK, and at eleven-thirty the husband is standing in the kitchen in front of the cracked mirror above the sink. He hasn't cried much, but he has lain long awake and the whites of his eyes are red. His shirt is white and bright, and his freshly ironed pants are faintly steaming. As his youngest sister adjusts the stiff white collar behind his neck and draws the white bow across his throat so tenderly that it feels like a caress, the widower leans over the sink and peers searchingly into his eyes. Then he rubs them as if wiping away a tear, but the back of his hand is still dry. The youngest sister, who is the beautiful sister, holds her hand still at his throat. The bow tie gleams white as snow against his ruddy skin. He furtively strokes her hand. The beautiful sister is the sister he adores. For he adores anything beautiful. The wife was ugly and sick. Which is why he has not been crying.

The ugly sister is standing at the stove. The gas is hissing, and the lid of the shiny coffeepot is bobbing up and down. With red fingers, she fumbles after the valves to turn it off. She has lived in town for twelve years now, but she still hasn't figured out the gas valves. She wears black-rimmed glasses, and whenever she wants to look someone in the eye, she leans in closely and stares awkwardly. Finally, she finds the right valve and turns it off.

Should it be a white tie for a funeral?

It is the beautiful sister who asks. The widower is fiddling with his cuff links. He has long black shoes, and they squeak when he abruptly stands on his toes. But the ugly sister spins around sharply as if someone had come at her.

White to a funeral! I should know after the consul's!

Then she purses her lips. Her eyes blink behind her glasses as if they were afraid. They probably are. She knows all about funerals but almost nothing about weddings. The beautiful sister smiles and continues making adjustments and being caressed. The ugly sister moves a vase of white flowers from the table to the sink. The widower looks in the mirror again and suddenly finds himself smiling. He closes his eyes and breathes in the smell of the kitchen. For as long as he can remember, funerals have smelled like coffee and sweaty sisters.

But a mother will also be buried, and the son is twenty years old and nothing. He is standing by himself under the ceiling light in the room full of people. His eyes are a little swollen. He has flushed them with water after a night of crying and thinks no one will notice. But in reality everything is noticeable, so the funeral guests have left him alone. Not out of respect but out of fear, because the world is afraid of those who cry.

The father stands perfectly still for a while, not even playing with his cuff links or tugging at his mourning band. The golden pendulum clock, a fiftieth birthday present, strikes a thin, thin note. The guests are standing by the windows and murmuring. Their voices are veiled in mourning, but someone from the father's side is tapping a march on the windowsill with his knuckles. The knuckles are hard and he wishes they would stop. But they don't. Then someone who traveled all the way from the country turns on the radio, although it isn't even noon yet. It hums and hums, but no one has the sense to turn it off.

Soundlessly, the January light falls into the room and gleams over all the shiny, squeaky shoes. At the center of the room there is a large and freshly vacant space under the ceiling light, where the son is standing by himself and watching and listening to everything. Although he is really somewhere else. Before his mother died and he ended up alone, there used to be a long oak table where he is standing, but now the table is by the window. A white tablecloth is spread over it and on top of the cloth are glasses, carafes with dark wine, fifteen fragile white cups, and a big brown cake that is sweet but will taste bitter. Today, the mother's portrait is on this very window-table, behind the carafes in a heavy black frame. It is wreathed with greenery, January's precious greenery. As the funeral coffee brews, and the pastor shaves at the parsonage, and the gas tanks of the funeral cars are filled in the garage, the eleven guests gather around the table and the photograph of the deceased. She is young in the photograph. Her hair is still thick and dark, and it drapes heavily over her smooth brow. Her teeth, which are scarcely visible between her round lips, are white and untarnished.

She was twenty-five then, one of them says.

Twenty-six, corrects another.

Alma was pretty when she was young.

Yes, Alma was good-looking, all right.

Yes, when she was young, she was good-looking.

So you can understand why Knut, why Knut . . . um . . .

Then they remember the son, who is standing in the room and listening.

She had pretty hair, someone chimes in. Much too quickly.

She was already expecting the girl by then.

Oh, she had a daughter?

Should've had, but she died.

As a baby?

She was just a year old. And then they had the boy, but they were married by then.

Then they remember him again, and this time they stay quiet. Someone pulls out a big white handkerchief and blows his nose. The radio is finally turned off. Then they step aside with squeaking steps because the coffee is coming. The nice aunt, whom he likes because she has been crying behind her glasses, is carrying the pot. She carries it high and dignified like a candlestick, and she is sweating through her tight, black dress. The younger aunt comes in behind her. She has black silk stockings, and the men in the room forget the occasion and admire her beautiful legs. She smiles at someone briefly. She has not been crying.

The father comes in last. Slowly and with a dejected gaze, he walks toward the son. Everyone has now turned around and stopped talking—even the one tapping the march has fallen silent. The father is silent, too. Silent and alone, they come together in the middle of the room. Their hands meet, and their arms meet. Then their chests meet. Finally, their eyes meet. Not long, yet long enough for both to see who has been crying and who is dry-eyed.

Don't cry, my boy, the father says.

He says it quietly, but everyone still hears it. One of the guests lets out a sob, much too briefly, however. Shoes are squeaking and dresses are rustling like footsteps among leaves. The father's arm is as hard as stone.

Don't cry, my boy, he says once again.

Then the son gently frees himself from the man who has not cried. Alone, he walks all the way from his spot underneath the light to the table with the steaming cups and brimming glasses. Someone standing in the way bashfully steps aside. Without shaking, he picks up a cup, then a glass, and slowly turns around.

The father is still standing there, his stone arm hanging, as if wounded, on his right side. Slowly, he lowers his head and bends one of his red ears down. But it isn't until the sun starts to beam through the windows that the son notices how unexpectedly bright the father's eyes are. Then he spills a few drops of the dark, bitter wine on the floor between his shoes.

Before the cars arrive, they stand around in groups in different parts of the room. Four are standing under the chiming pendulum clock with glasses in their hands. They take sips when no one is looking. They are the widower's relatives from the country, the ones you only see at weddings and funerals and whose clothes smell like mothballs. They look at the expensive clock. Then at each other. They look at the expensive encyclopedia with its leather bind-ing glistening behind the glass of the bookcase. Then they glance at each other again and take another sip. At once, they are whispering with lips moistened by coffee and wine. They have never cared for the deceased.

Underneath the ceiling light, the sisters are standing with four of the father's friends who took a Monday morning off to attend the funeral. Perhaps there could have been more, but not even the ones who came cared for the deceased. Nevertheless, they talk about her for a moment with subdued, muffled voices. Then they change the subject, but their voices remain the same.

The widower and the son are standing by one of the windows with three of the next-door neighbors: two women happy to experience a little variety and a man on sick leave. The son is standing closest to the window and has put down his glass and cup on the windowsill between two flowerpots. He knows that the neighbors disliked his mother, so he doesn't care to listen. Still, the one who is sick talks about his illness. The two female neighbors talk about other illnesses. And the widower talks about the deceased's illness. She had had a bad heart and had been bloated with water. In low voices, they talk about frail hearts and water.

Meanwhile, the son is looking out the window. He knows they will also be looking out the window soon, so he hurries to see as much as he can. He sees the blue tracks of the streetcar line, white with ice and salt along the bend. He sees freezing little snowflakes floating down to the street. He sees blue smoke rising from the chimney of a warm shelter. Some workmen, who had been tearing up the pavement with a drill and some picks, put their tools down, blow white smoke into their hands, and take a break. A cat is creeping through the snow, and directly across it a straddle-legged dray horse is peeing yellow and violently into the gutter.

The entire time, the sun is gleaming on a gilded bull's head above a butcher shop. Everything is as usual in that shop. The door swings open and shut by people with vaporous breath. Meat is on display on white plates in the window, and the shop assistants raise their sharp cleavers behind the marble counter. Like so many times before, he leans against the window so closely that it fogs up from his hot breath. Like so many times before, yet not like those first few days—for it was worse in the beginning. In those days, the entire windowpane fogged up after only a moment, and he had had to grab his hand and pull it down to his pocket so that it wouldn't break free and shatter the pane. He also had to bite his lips so that his mouth wouldn't fly open and shout, Why haven't you closed? You, down there! How could you! Why don't you hang sheets over your windows? Why don't you lock up your doors? Why are you letting your vans still deliver meat when you know what's happened? You butchers! You ruthless butchers! Why are you letting everything go on as usual when you know that everything has changed?

He is calmer now and merely leans forward and watches. Merely leans forward and breathes. Merely shifts his gaze like a telescope toward the gilded bull's head and the tall display window with its heaping mountains of meat. Merely presses his thighs painfully hard against the windowsill. Merely thinks, My mother died in there. My mother died in there while my father was sitting in the kitchen shaving and while I, her son, was sitting in my room playing poker with myself. In there, she fell off a chair without one of us there to catch her. It was in there that she lay on the floor amid the dirt and sawdust while a butcher stood with his back to her, cutting up a sheep.

Maybe he isn't so calm, after all. Maybe he has said something, too. He might have even given a start. In any case, he feels a stone arm around his shoulder. In any case, he sees a stone hand rubbing and rubbing the misty glass. No, a large cold eye. He feels it with his fingertips and shivers. But the stone hand is still rubbing, and once it is finished, the eye is cold and clear, but the back of the hand is wet with tears. He wipes it off on his sleeve and then lets it fall.

Don't cry, my boy, he hears the father whisper.

But he continues to cry. Someone presses a handkerchief into his hand, and as he is drying his eyes he can hear through the silence of the room that everyone is listening to him cry. Out of shame, he quiets down. Then he forces his eyes to comply and then rolls the little yellow handkerchief, which smells like pungent perfume, into a ball and proceeds to hand it to the nearest woman. That is when the father says:

Keep it. I have another.

The ball has grown heavy in his hand. He leans in closely against the glass, but it doesn't fog up this time. The father gently presses his cheek against his. It is a cheek of stone.

Look, he whispers.

And the son looks. He sees the cars pulling up around the corner in a long procession. Five black cars in bluish snow. Five black cars relentlessly gliding up to the entrance and gently stopping with snow on their roofs.

Three would have probably been enough, the aunt with glasses whispers so that no one will hear, yet so that almost everyone does.

And three certainly would have been enough, but there had to be at least five black cars for it to be eye-catching. The father adores things that attract attention, and he adores things that are beautiful. So he ordered five.

They have to walk down four flights of stairs to reach the cars. They descend very slowly as if for the last time. The father goes first, then the son, and then the thirteen others. Through the staircase windows they can see the snow falling more and more heavily and draping the hangers on the carpet-beating rack in gray clouds. And if it doesn't clear up, the cars won't be visible at all. Now all fifteen of them are silent, no sixteen, for the son's fiancée meets them on the third flight. She is thin and pale and had trouble getting time off from the clothing shop in Norr Mälarstrand. She has snow on the front of her black coat, snow on her black gloves, and snow on the veil of her hat, so that only her eyes are visible. And she was probably crying. But who knows why?

The black procession glides silently down the stairs. Neighbors open their doors and look on in grave silence. It is a beautiful performance with fine roles. A child begins to cry and cleaves desperately to the wall as though it were looking at death itself. Once they have passed, all the doors close in compassionate silence. The son goes first, followed by the son's fiancée, then the father, and finally the thirteen others. The stone steps are hard, and the clanging of their heels and the rustling of their black clothes are dreadful. Dreadful is the snow outside as it falls silently and heavily, burying all the living and the dead. Dreadful, too, is the length of the steps. They walk and walk but never reach the bottom. The son reaches for the fiancée's hand but only finds her cold, wet glove. He squeezes it hard, harder, but only to feel how cold she is. He peers down the stairs and continues walking on and on. The grooves are deep in the steps of sorrow and full of salt and sand.

Most dreadful is the sight awaiting him at the final step. Beautiful yet dreadful. Without realizing it, he has let go of the fiancée's hand and walks alone through the dark entrance to the street door. But just before he opens the door and meets the patient cars glowing dimly like shadows through the snow and glass, it strikes him how still and gloomy it is behind him. He slowly turns around on the doormat and catches a glimpse of something he will never forget, because it is so beautiful and so dreadful. All fifteen of them in black have stopped halfway down the steps. They are obscuring the window with their bodies, making it very dark. The women's faces glisten as hard as bone through their thick veils. Everything else is gloomy: the stairs, the walls, and the somber clothes. Only their faces are white, as well as a single gloveless hand pressed against a coat. For a moment, they stand completely still, as if waiting for an invisible photographer. Then they drift slowly down to him like one giant shadow. The steps of sorrow have ended.

Snow is falling outside. An unseen streetcar jingles as it rolls by. The streetlights glow dimly over some roadwork. They climb into the cars with snow on their clothes. With sixteen people to five spacious cars, they are forced to sit far apart from each other and freeze. Just as they are about to leave, the snow begins to subside enough for people to see them depart. They pick up the pastor at the parsonage. He is waiting for them, bareheaded, in the vestibule. He climbs into the car of the immediate family and sits in the front seat, next to the chauffeur. He shakes their hands through the window, drawing out his solemn gaze at each one of them. His eyes are clouded with tears from the biting wind, but for a brief moment they almost think he is crying.

On the way he asks them about the deceased. What her life was like, what she died of, and how she died. The father answers for the four of them: for himself, for the son, for the son's fiancée, and for his pretty sister. He doesn't like priests. He just thinks it's nice to have one. So he answers sullenly that she lived like poor people do. When she could, she went off to clean, and when she could no longer do that, she stayed home, lying around mostly. Had a bad temper. Otherwise, she was nice, nice for the most part. At least she meant well. She was bloated in the end and had trouble with stairs.

The son is sitting by the window, gazing out. It's clearing up outside, and the sky over Södermalm is as clear as ice. The street they are on is cold and rough, and the wind's fierce broom sweeps over the sidewalks, taking a hat with it, a new black hat. There is a pale man in a butcher shop with a saw in his hand . . . she had trouble with stairs . . . yet they still let her go. They drive over the bridge. The canal is frozen. Thin ski tracks zigzag across it. At the dock, a boat is paralyzed askew in the frozen water.

In which hospital did Mrs. Lundin pass away? the pastor asks.

They are all taken aback by this and look down at the floor of the car. For a long time, the father explains what she died of, for a really long time, almost until they can see the gates of the cemetery. But how she died is nobody's business. The pale fiancée turns around and looks at the son. But he is looking out the rear window, watching how the other cars are rolling up, one after the other, along the long white curve. It's really quite beautiful with so many lined up, and someone stops to look.

She died at home? the pastor asks.

Yes, says the beautiful sister, exactly. She died at home.

Then they arrive.

They walk down the long path to the chapel. The wind slashes through veils and whips tears from their eyes. The pastor and the father go first. Then the son and the fiancée. Then the aunts, hand in hand. Then the father's relatives from the country. Then the four fake friends. Then the two female neighbors. Lastly, the sick neighbor, who is only thinking about his illness.

They do not take up a lot of space in the chapel. The father plops down on the first pew with his black hat in his hand. He looks over his shoulder to see if anyone else is coming, but there is no one in sight. Actually, as soon as everyone sits down, two women appear with a flag. Before the deceased became ugly and bloated, she had once belonged to a women's club. They have all but forgotten, but the club has not forgotten. And as the woman carrying the flag proceeds down the aisle with the banner valiantly raised, the widower, too, remembers it painfully well. He didn't mean any harm by it, but one evening he snapped at her for dashing off to the meetings, and she never went again. Regardless, the banner is beautiful with its black mourning veil, and the one carrying it isn't so bad herself. Her face was already red because of the wind, but now it turns crimson on account of the eighteen sets of eyes on her. Some of the relatives from the country in the second pew are somewhat upset by the red banner, but as someone whispers, At least it has a crepe, a mourning crepe, that is.

The yellow casket is in the middle of the room, and although they have tried to avoid looking at it, they are ultimately forced to acknowledge it's there. It's there on its bier and looks magnificent with its eight wreathes. And if they tilt their heads, they can read what it says on the ribbons.

A final farewell from the Carlsson family, a woman reads quietly into her husband's ear. Then she suddenly begins to sob. It is their wreath. And it is beautiful.

The music begins. A violin and an organ, and as they play in the gallery, the son looks down at his fiancée's hands, which are quivering rhythmically like a leaf inside her gloves. Then he looks at his father's hands. They are resting heavily and motionless on his lap. But suddenly they pull out a watch and begin opening and closing the watchcase, over and over again until the music stops. The pretty sister is fiddling with a ring, twisting and turning it. Then she takes it off and seems lost. But the ugly sister cannot see the casket very well, so she huffs on her lenses and wipes them with a large white handkerchief. Now she can see better. And at the very front, nearest the casket, the woman holding the banner is standing stiffly, but they can tell from the fluttering of the veil that she is shaking.

The pastor begins to speak. It is a speech about a good wife to a good husband and a good mother to a good son and a good daughter. So the pastor thinks the son's fiancée is the daughter of the deceased. This makes everyone annoyed with her, but they look in her direction anyway. She, for that matter, is biting into her glove and crying—she cries easily. The pastor talks about a strenuous life and about the great amount of patience needed to endure an illness. And all the women sob into their handkerchiefs or the sleeves of their coats, because they all have their own illnesses. Finally, the pastor speaks about the good fortune she had to die at home, surrounded by her dear loved ones. Then all the men bite their lips, either harshly or lightly, because they are all afraid of dying. But the son is fumbling after a handkerchief, which is damp and smells like perfume. Then at the graveside the sand starts to rattle and the coffin, with all its flowers, sinks down slowly like a cinema organ. They try to keep it in sight for as long as they can, like a train vanishing with a friend on board. At last, there is nothing left. Just a hole in the ground that smells like flowers and, soon, not even flowers. Now the widower is standing by the hole. He is standing nervously and a little hunched over, and they can see his watch dangling behind his unbuttoned coat. And every time he tries to speak, it swings like a pendulum behind the black coat.

My dear, he says.

But tears overcome him. Suddenly, certainty lashes him like a whip and he gives a start so violent that one of them fears he is about to fall in. But he does not fall in. He merely leans over the hole. Then he takes a step back, his expression frozen with certainty. But when he is back at his seat, the pastor lays his large hand reassuringly over the father's until it stops trembling and becomes as still as a stone.

The son reads a poem at the graveside. It's on a little sheet of white paper that had been in the same pocket as the wet handkerchief. Now the poem smells like perfume and the ink has smeared to the edges, but this isn't why he is reading so poorly. It is because he is crying. He knows the poem by heart, and the last verses, once he has settled down, go very well. His voice is steady and calm now, and he sounds perhaps even a little pleased with himself.

The father is also pleased because he appreciates anything beautiful. He appreciates beautiful poems at beautiful funerals. He looks at the pastor, but the pastor is merely listening. But he is listening beautifully. After all, he's accustomed to listening gracefully to funeral poems. It's a long poem even though the paper is small, and once it is read, several of them shift their gaze toward the pastor to see what he thinks of their service.

But for the son the page is instantly blank. He is standing in front of the hole with a piece of paper in his hand, and his hand is trembling. He looks at the white empty space and can't make out a thing. So he looks over the edge of the paper, and his eyes sink lower and lower. The edges of the grave are gray and smooth. The coffin's lid is yellow and cold. The flowers gleam red.

It isn't until then that he finally understands. And it's difficult to understand. One step forward and he is crying. One step more and he knows this is the end. A handkerchief firmly against his eye and he senses there is no more delay. No more death announcements to compose. No invitations to write up. No poem to think about at night when he's unable to sleep. No solace and no sanctuary, and no end and no beginning. Only a certainty, as empty as the grave, that his mother is lying down there and that she is dead, irretrievably gone. Beyond prayers and thoughts, flowers and poems, tears and words. And with a handkerchief pressed against one eye at a time, he cries with emptiness, cries and cries, because emptiness has more tears than anything else.

The pastor cautiously guides him back, a stone hand pulls him down to his seat, and then a stone arm wraps around his shoulder. Through a curtain of tears he then sees the woman with the banner go up and lower it three times into the hole, but when the banner comes up the third time, the mourning veil comes loose and floats slowly down to the ground. Then they all walk around the grave one last time. Those with bouquets let them fall. They either bang against the coffin lid or fall rustling onto a wreath. The others just look—a brief glimpse or an extended gaze—take two steps back, and shake the pastor's hand.

But at the edge of the grave, the son frees himself from the stone arm, and with emptiness throbbing in his throat he rips his poem into tiny, tiny pieces. So small that it looks like snow dancing delicately over the coffin, covered by flowers and tears.

They drop the pastor at the snowdrift in front of the parsonage. He is in a hurry, and now no one thinks he was ever crying. It's snowing hard, and on the way back to the city the five cars have lost each other in the snowfall. They became six and then seven in the funeral procession. A butcher's van has joined them as well as a small truck with furniture. And when it clears up on the bridge for half a minute, they can see a cabinet with a mirror from one car and a large slaughtered animal from another. The ride back from the cemetery has been a difficult one. The whirling snow has whipped tears out of the ones who haven't cried. But for the ones who have been crying, it has stripped them of their sorrow and provided empty teardrops instead. They invited the woman with the banner and her companion to ride in the last car, and because the flagpole is so long, they had to leave one of the windows open. Snow has therefore drifted inside, and the man who is sick has complained the whole way, talking about his illness and about how sensitive he is to the cold. But the two women from the club were talking about Alma.

Alma was a good friend, they were saying; you couldn't find a better friend than her.

But nobody has agreed with them; they merely sat in silence without conceding. And when they stepped out at the top of Södermalm, someone hastily rolled up the window, looking forward to a warm funeral meal.

And it's warm in the restaurant. Warm and elegant. It feels a little strange that the waiters are wearing such white jackets and that they bow so low. They probably could have had it at home—the funeral meal, that is. The sister with glasses could have made the food, and the sister without glasses could have served it, and they would have had enough space. But it's a fine restaurant, and the private room, which the widower has rented, is a beautiful and impressive room, since the widower has a taste for anything beautiful and impressive, even if it costs him.

In this regard Alma was cheap, some of them think as they enter the private room, and had dear Knut died first the funeral meal would have certainly been at home—if there would have been any meal at all. At the very most maybe a little coffee at first, then a glass of wine and some cake afterward.

A few minutes of silence pass before they sit down. The table is set for seventeen, and the widower stands between the sisters and starts to count. Counts the small plates and the chairs and only reaches sixteen. But after three tries, he hits seventeen. The light in the room is dim, and the seventeen faces are flushed after the storm and grief. The awkward, silent minutes that pass are saturated with sweet sorrow. At first it's completely silent, then less so because someone is rubbing his hands, rubbing and rubbing as one does before some hard work. Then someone coughs so that the rubbing won't be heard. Then someone whispers something, and someone coughs again so that the whispering won't be heard. Then the widower turns around.

Let's sit down then, he says, almost whispering.

Dresses rustle and shoes squeak. Chairs scrape and purse clasps snap. It is dark and solemn in the room, and all of them, feeling curiously pure where they are sitting, look down at their white plates. Pure, almost like children. And the plates are shiny enough for them to reflect their feelings in them, making a beautiful picture.

But something embarrassing happens to the widower. He is sitting next to the son, and the pretty sister is sitting on his other side. He is looking around for the food and drinks, already raising his hand to wave for them. Then the double doors open, and three white-clad waiters carrying trays enter in succession. They look so curiously at him as they pass by that he squirms and lowers his eyes. This is when he first notices the candle. One by one, they all notice the candle, the tall white candle in the black candlestick that is burning all alone on the table. One by one, they look at the candle and at the large white plate in front of the widower. Then they look at him.

You are sitting in Alma's seat! someone says shrilly.

It is the ugly sister who says it. Her eyes are blinking behind her foggy glasses, and he could have hit her for having said it so loudly. He should be able to get up with dignity, but instead his demeanor is frightened, humiliated and frightened. A used match has been left on Alma's white plate.

Now the son is the one sitting nearest the candle. It is his mother's candle burning down. He looks at it but only feels emptiness. He stares into the flame until he can see nothing else, and, blinded, he tries to think: this is my mother's life burning away. It is my mother who is slowly dying.

But he knows that she is dead and that the candle doesn't change anything. It's just an ordinary candle that is burning, and once it has burned out, nothing else will have happened but that an ordinary candle has burned down to its stick. Looking at the fiancée, he notices that she doesn't dare look at the candle. She can only bear to look down at her lap, where a crumpled-up handkerchief is. Otherwise she would have to cry.

The son watches his father, watches him for a long time. So long that he forgets to eat. His sandwich sits uneaten on his plate and his beer remains untouched because he suddenly has the urge to look into the father's eyes. He still doesn't really know why; he just knows that he has to look into his eyes—if only for a second. But the father isn't looking in the son's direction. The candle is in the son's direction, and he doesn't want to see the candle. It's a beautiful candle, and although he appreciates what is beautiful, he doesn't want to see it. So he looks in the opposite direction, in all other possible directions. He becomes sweaty and red from twisting his neck so much. He nods to the guests across him and to each side of him, tosses a word here and another there, and drops a fork with a piece of herring into his lap. Suddenly, he forgets where he is and starts laughing, laughs as one does at something trivial. Then the ugly sister takes him by the arm, pinches him above the elbow, and says so that almost everyone can hear it:

You shouldn't laugh, Knut!

No, he shouldn't laugh. He realizes this, and icy shame shoots through his body, paralyzing him. He pulls out his handkerchief, which is dry now but will soon turn wet from sweat, the sweat of shame. He hides behind it for a while, composes his expression so that when everyone can see him again he is wearing a beautiful mask, a peaceful and beautiful mask of earnestness, and perhaps even grief. And when the hard liquor is being served, he is able to look at the candle on account of the mask. But the son is sitting in front of the candle, and the son's eyes sink into his own, piercing them so that it nearly burns. This makes it easier for him to look at the candle because it's a beautiful candle, one he can appreciate. But the son's eyes are not beautiful, so he cannot love them. He cannot even bear to look at them.

They have a drink in silence in honor of the deceased. Then someone gives a sigh of satisfaction after finishing, but his wife coughs to cover it up. The widower coughs, too, and then starts tapping on his glass.

A moment of silence for Alma, he says and bows his head.

Then they all bow their heads. And nearly all of them think about the deceased. The candle burns with a tall, bright flame. Outside, the snow is whirling and dogs are barking. Inside, it is silent and warm, and from a distance they can hear sweet music coming from the restaurant. A minute is a long time. A lot can happen. One of them sees the coffin sinking and being swallowed up by a hole. One sees the ambulance with red lights skidding through the snow, and another sees Alma sitting in his yard with her swollen legs on a pillow. One of them sees her when she was young, standing on a flight of stairs with a towel on her head. One hears her voice saying something disturbing through a door. He shakes his head until a better memory comes to mind. One always comes when you shake your head.

But one of them thinks of something else and wishes that the minute would finally end and that the candle would burn out quickly. The silence and the candle frighten him that much. There is someone else who doesn't see her either, because he knows that she is dead and that only a big empty hole is left when someone is dead. For the entire minute, he looks down at his plate, which has two frightened red eyes on it the whole time. For a whole silent minute he thinks, Why is Papa so afraid? And then he realizes that that was exactly what he wanted to know: whether these eyes were mourning or whether they were merely afraid.

After that, there isn't a silent moment for the rest of the evening. They are given a lot of alcohol, suspiciously more than they have a right to, and it tastes good. First, it warms you and gives you beautiful eyes, and then it makes everyone else's eyes beautiful, too. Everything hard becomes soft, and all that is yours becomes theirs. If you give someone your hand, there is someone to take it. And if you say something, there is someone who will listen as if it were worth listening to. You get closer to each other, and it feels good to get closer. Your lips become beautiful, and your mouth becomes gentle and friendly. Everything is warm and all shadows disappear. Sorrow itself takes on the form of happiness.

They look at the candle, which is burning lower and lower and which will have soon burnt out. But they are not afraid of it, or afraid that it's burning so quickly, or that someone's life is burning away with the bright, glaring flame. Bright and glaring? No, it is soft and warm, and the lower it sinks, the softer it becomes. The lower it sinks, the softer the memory of Alma becomes. Then everyone pulls out photographs and holds them up for their neighbors' lovely eyes to see. All pictures become lovely when they are viewed by lovely eyes.

She was kind and patient, says the woman who had stood on the sidewalk and watched the ambulance skid by. She was beautiful in death and so gracious in the mortuary with her hands folded together. You could hardly tell that she fell on her forehead.

And a good friend, that's what Alma was, says the sick man who had shivered in the car.

How she suffered and struggled all the time, says the man in whose yard she sat with both legs swollen.

And how hard she fought, his wife adds.

And we all know what she meant to Knut, and he knows that best of all, says someone who was never her friend.

But it's true. He does know best of all. And that's why he is sitting so quietly. The alcohol tastes good. And no one notices you if you are sitting quietly. Nor will they notice if you are too afraid to look at a candle. It may be true that death is a big empty hole and that sorrow is to know just how empty that hole is, but it's only true if you are sober. If you have liquor, then you can fill the hole up with all the beautiful thoughts you can think of and all the nice words you can find. You can fill it up all the way to the brim and place a stone on it afterward.

But if you can't, then you must have your reasons. The entire time the son sits and talks to his pale and petite fiancée about his dead mother, he thinks to himself, Why isn't Papa saying anything? And why is he so afraid?

As for him, he isn't trying to fill any empty hole, because he knows how empty it is. He is merely talking about the deceased with his fiancée. He isn't doing it because he has been drinking. In fact, he never drinks. Almost never. He is doing it because he loved her. And, of course, you talk about the one you loved—if you talk at all. And he loved her because she loved him. And the one who has loved you should always receive your love in return. Otherwise, you are a fool.

But the flame is sinking lower and lower, and several of them want to leave before it has reached the bottom. The son's fiancée is the first to leave. She is pale and has a headache. She is always pale, and she almost always has a headache. Or else she is crying. She even cries a little when she is laughing. She is just seventeen years old. The son walks her out to the entrance, where a telephone is sitting on a table. An attendant calls for a taxi since it's snowing outside and she is almost always cold. Once she has her gloves on, he squeezes her hand very hard and looks deep into her eyes. She starts to cry. Then the taxi rolls up in the snow, and he gives her three *kronor* for the fare. It's all he has.

He is sitting at the table between the candle and an empty chair. The flame is very low now but it warms him all the more, especially his hands. It feels good to be warmed since he always gets cold as soon as he touches the fiancée. He does care for her, but she makes him cold. So he has never been able to really hold her. He moves closer to the candle to get even warmer. Two enemies of the deceased leave because there is nothing more to eat or drink.

There are now thirteen at the table, and when the relatives from the country notice this, they want to leave, too. The father walks them out. They are his relatives, as the deceased doesn't have any left. Two brothers, twenty years older, had died in America. Her mother died in a sanatorium in Jämtland, and her father died at sea when he was young.

The father's relatives take a taxi through the snow. They don't ride to the station as they say they will but to some richer relatives in Essingen. But they are respectful and don't want to hurt the man who is poor and grieving. And they are a little drunk, too. They only come to the city for funerals and christenings, but when they do, they stay for a long time.

As they are saying good-bye at the entrance, a couple of the father's rivals, two of his colleagues, leave as well. They are in a good mood, and since it's only nine they still have plenty of time for more drinking. But they don't tell Knut, because nobody wants to hurt a man who is recently widowed. Then one of the sisters, the beautiful one, comes out half a minute later. She has a headache and ought to go home. But when the coworkers pull up, she climbs into the same car.

What beautiful legs, one of them says as he brushes the snow from her silk stockings.

He has thought so the whole day. Even in the chapel, he thought it. So he whispers it into her ear. At first she thinks it's inappropriate. Then she thinks it's funny. Eventually, she likes it. She likes anyone who thinks she is beautiful. And because so many people find her beautiful, she likes so many people. But she likes herself most of all.

But back in the private room, the candle is almost burnt out and the ugly sister feels like crying, so she leaves before the tears start to fill her eyes. She knows that crying makes her ugly—uglier, that is. But the father is upset when she leaves. Not because she is leaving, but because she is ugly. Unattractive women usually arouse his contempt.

Why is Papa so upset? the son thinks. Now he is almost sitting on top of the candle. He is warm, and when he's warm, he longs for his fiancée because he wants to warm her, too. But whenever she comes near, he just gets cold. The father looks at him, probably accidentally, but he looks all the same. What's Papa so afraid of? he thinks.

Maybe it's the candle. Now the flame is almost scorching the black mourning crepe as it sinks mercilessly down to the bottom. Only emptiness is above it. The vast emptiness of death. But there is still a piece of candle grease underneath it, and he suddenly finds himself hoping that it will allow the candle to burn for a long time. Even though he knows all about the emptiness, he is still able to hope. Why does he still have hope? Is it because the father is so afraid of the candle going out?

Then the neighbors depart and leave them alone with the candle. No, the father walks them out and leaves the son alone with the candle. The flame is flickering. It's almost dark in the room. And in the darkness the son does something unheard of. Slowly and silently, he leaves his seat and moves over to the mother's. It's so cold that he shivers. So cold is death. So frightfully cold. The flame of life is as faint as this flame now. When someone opens a door and looks in, the flame flickers violently, so he cups his hands around it to shield it. An attendant is standing between the doors.

Mr. Lundin? he asks.

Yes, the son answers.

There is a call for you up front.

For which Mr. Lundin? For Bengt?

Yes, the attendant says, I believe it was Bengt.

The son gets up to speak to his fiancée. He closes the door very carefully so that the candle won't go out. He genuinely enjoys talking to his fiancée on the phone because he can make his voice very warm and then blow his warmth into her cold ear, making her voice warm, too. They are both warm over the phone.

As the son makes his way through the nearly empty restaurant, the three neighbors are sitting in a taxi. They will split the fare among the three of them since they cannot afford it on their own. The snow falls beautifully as they drive up Götgatan, billowing gently like a thick curtain in front of the display windows.

She had a nice funeral, says one of the female neighbors.

The others remain silent because there is nothing more to say. But the man who is sick is sitting in the middle, and suddenly he is no longer sick. He is healthy and strong—and drunk, too. So when the taxi rolls up their dark street, he puts his hand under one of the women's snow-covered breasts. And the other woman laughs.

While the son is still making his way to the phone, the father is in the restroom. He has just washed his hands. Now he is washing them again. He holds them up to the mirror. Yes, they are clean. But he washes them one more time.

The telephone is on the table, and the receiver is off the hook. The son smiles as he sits down. He is grinning at what he's about to say. If she has a headache, he will tell her, Take one pill and think of me. And if that doesn't help, take one more and think of something else. But if she is crying, he will say, Don't you remember what I said at the table? Yes, the same thing Mama told me whenever I was sad—when I was grown up and sad. When I was little, she kissed me until I felt better, but when I was older and sad, she said, Sit down at your desk and write a letter to yourself. It's always good to write to yourself. Almost only to yourself. And when the letter is finished, you won't be sad anymore. But you will have a long letter. A long and beautiful letter.

So he picks up the receiver and says hello.

But it's a woman's voice that he doesn't recognize, and the voice says:

How are you feeling, my dear? Tired?

Tired? he asks. Who is this?

It's Gun, whispers the mysterious woman.

Then she is very frightened. He can tell by her sobbing gasps how terribly frightened she is. He isn't afraid at all.

Who is this? she whispers.

This is Bengt, Bengt Lundin. He spit the *t*s into the receiver.

I'm sorry, she says. And she is gone.

He hangs up. Shortly after, an attendant grabs the telephone and calls a cab for a drunken person. And when the father with clean hands emerges from the restroom, the son is sitting alone on a chair beside the telephone. He is not smoking. He is just sitting. He has the corner of a handkerchief between his teeth. He always chews on something when he is upset, either his nails or a handkerchief.

They walk back to the private room together. It's almost dark now, but the flame will continue to burn for a little while longer. The son is walking behind the father, but once inside he sits on the opposite side of the table. He wants to look him in the eye. He wants to see whether his eyes are afraid. But the father doesn't look at him. The father is standing next to the deceased's cold chair and looks down at her empty plate. But it's no longer empty. The bill is on the mother's plate.

The son waits and waits. If his father's eyes are afraid, he will make them even more afraid. But if they are not afraid, he is going to hurt them, hurt them as much as he can. More than he has ever hurt anyone in his entire life. He gazes at his bowed head and his thin, messy hair. He gazes at the wide, red face, which the light is struggling to illuminate, lighting it less and less. Then he notices that his eyelids are twitching, maybe from fatigue, maybe from fear.

Then he realizes how he can make the twitching worse, so horribly excruciating that every time his eyelids close, they will close to a burning candle. He cups his hands around the flame like a shield. There is only emptiness above the flame and a few centimeters of wax underneath it. But his strong hands surround all of it. You cannot wake the dead. Not for yourself. Because, for you, the dead stays dead. But you can resurrect her for others. You can say to someone else, She's alive, you know. The candle is still burning. The candle will not go out. So she is alive.

The candle is burning inside his hands, which swelter over the flame. His whole body is blistering. It is a scorching heat, but he needs it. He needs to burn.

Someone called, he says.

He has perfume in his mouth, so it didn't sound like he wanted it to. The father looks up from the bill. He is anxious but not particularly fearful. Nevertheless, the candle is blazing. But he can't really see it. The sons' hands are darkening it.

Oh, he answers, who?

A woman, says the son.

I see, the father replies. What did she say?

She only apologized, the son whispers. Her name was Gun.

Immediately, the father's eyes shoot up from the bill and look over the son's head and up to the ceiling. Finally, the mask thuds off, the widower's dismal mask. And behind the mask is joy, a great and terrible joy. After all, joy can look like fear in anyone who is forced to mourn. He is afraid to reveal his happiness, but there's nothing he can do to suppress it. The dead cannot haunt someone made happy by the living. And the son can always keep his hands there a little while longer, but even in this moment he knows that his hands are only filled with emptiness, that there is only emptiness above the candle and emptiness beneath the clump of wax, and that to grieve is to have an empty hole inside of you, a vast empty hole that no tears can fill.

At that moment, the son burns his hands. Someone walks through the doors, someone who wants to be paid, and the flame flutters again. First, to one side and burns his left hand, and then to the other side and burns his right hand. Then the burnt son pulls his hands back. The one who entered has stopped at the door and is silent. The whole room is silent. The whole world is silent. The son's tongue tastes like perfume, so he is unable to say a word. The perfume of the woman he hates is so bitter that he can't even scream. He can only swallow, and swallow some more, and raise his burnt hands up to his parched eyes.

Grinning, the father blows out the candle.

A Letter in February from Himself to Himself

Dear Bengt!

It's been a while since I last wrote to you. Last time, I wrote
that Mama was dead. Now she's dead and cremated. Her urn is
on a shelf in some building at the cemetery. We were there on
Sunday—Papa, Berit, and I. You know what it's like there. Just
a big gray storeroom for the ashes of the dead. Berit cried the
whole time. I for one felt nothing. As we walked out, Papa said
the urn was ugly. So I said it was beautiful. When we got home
Berit made coffee, and the phone rang while we were drinking
it. When Papa came back, he said it was a coworker who called.
He didn't need to say that.

    Berit left early. She had a headache. After she left, Papa said
that Berit was ugly. So I said she was nice. Then he asked me if I
missed Mama. I said that I knew she was dead. Then Papa said
he thought that was good and that I was sensible, but I didn't
understand then what he meant. That evening we drank some
more coffee and ate the rest of the gingerbread from Christmas.
I reminded Papa that Mama had baked it, and he replied that

she had always baked well. Then he went out to buy the paper. It was snowing, and he doesn't like going out in the snow.

He came back at two in the morning. He arrived in a taxi and wasn't sober. He didn't have the paper with him, and he didn't like that I asked him about it. Nor did he appreciate that I was still up studying. Otherwise, he usually likes it when I stay up late to study. He wants me to be something, the sooner the better.

As he got undressed, I asked him about it. You know what about. About whom. Are you spying on me? he asked. I replied that I wasn't spying, but that I still knew everything. Then he shouted that he didn't have to answer to me. I wasn't scared. No, I answered, but to Mama. He grabbed me hard by the shoulders, but I didn't break free. You know Alma is dead, he said. He always calls her Alma when he's drunk. Yes, I answered, but she hasn't always been. Then he asked me if I thought she knew about it. Yes, I said, she knew about it for a while. It was a lie, but he let me go and shut up. She was sick, I added, and you still did it. Then he repeated that he didn't have to answer to me. I asked him why. You're young, he said. I asked him if there was anything wrong with being young. He responded that sons can't hold their fathers accountable. I asked him why not. Because sons are young and fathers are old, he answered. Then I asked whether sons couldn't be better than their fathers. It's not a matter of being better, he said. Then what is it a matter of? I asked. It's a matter of having experience, was his answer. You get that over time. Then I don't want that kind of experience, I yelled, not even if it's thrown at me! Then that's too bad for you, son, he answered and tried to touch me. I didn't let him.

But after I had gone to bed, he came in through the darkness and sat on my bed. After sitting silently for a while, he asked, Do you think she took it hard? Yes, I said after a while, she always cried when you were gone at night. Really? he replied and said nothing more. But as he was leaving, I yelled at him. I don't want to see her, I shouted, ever! Then he replied, She is going to be your mother, so you have to! I didn't sleep that night. Instead, I took her handkerchief from my dark suit and tried tearing it to pieces. But it was too strong. Stronger than I was. So I went back to bed. But I just lay there, hating the scent all night.

And now, dear Bengt, I have a lot to ask you. First, Can anyone hate his own father like I do? I could probably answer you that, yes, you can. You can if your father acts like mine. Then you ask what he's done wrong. My answer is that he has deceived my mother because she was sick and because he thought she was ugly. I never thought she was ugly. Then you ask why it's any of my business. After all, she didn't know about it. To that I say that it doesn't matter whether she knew or not. The fact remains: she was betrayed. And is there anything worse than to be unfaithful to the person who loves you? And is there anything more horrible than to be betrayed? Someone looks into your eyes, Bengt, and you believe that the other person's eyes are your mirrors. Yours alone. But now they reflect someone else. There has to be a bottom, Bengt, but a mirror is bottomless. Papa is a mirror. And that's why I hate him. All that is beautiful can be reflected in him, all that is repulsive and beautiful. And I don't respect fidelity because it's beautiful; I respect it because it's necessary. He who betrays another kills her slowly. Because infidelity makes her sink. Makes her sink down into her shame, which is a deep swamp, and into her hatred, which is even deeper. If Berit cheated on me, I'd never want to see her again. But I would hit her first.

Can anyone hit his own father? Can you answer me that, Bengt? You can need to hate him, you say, but you may not strike him. Maybe we can't hit anyone? Well, whoever is innocent can hit. Whoever is innocent can do anything to the one who is immoral. Because the one who is innocent is right. He's the only one in the world who is right. Purity has such terrible power, Bengt. That's why I want to be pure. If I didn't want to, I'd punch myself in the face.

I never want to see her. I have seen my mother sleeping. I have walked by her in the dark and heard her sleep. So I don't want to see the other woman. I have seen my mother dead. She had a wound on her forehead. So I don't want to see that other woman's forehead. I never want to see her. But if I ever do happen to see her, I'd strike her across the forehead. Don't forget that, Bengt!

It's February now. You know what it's like in February. It snows and it's warm. The days are getting a little longer. So the nights are getting shorter. I haven't seen Berit for a few days. The last time I saw her, I hurt her. I didn't mean to, but I hurt her all the same. We were at the cinema, and afterward when we were sitting at a café she started crying over the film. So I thought I'd really give her something to cry about. I told her about Papa and she stopped crying. She didn't believe it was true, but I wanted her to know it was true. So I said that she was stupid, that she was stupid and immature. Then she started to cry again, but she still didn't believe it. She never believes anything bad you say about others, yet she believes everything you say about her. She started to get cold. She always gets cold when she cries a lot. Then she gets a headache. So she put her hand on the table so that I could warm it, but I was annoyed and pretended not to see it. But then as we were about to leave, I said to her, Don't forget your hand, there on the table. I regretted it afterward, but afterward it was too late. I haven't called her in three days. I know she's just sitting around and waiting, crying and waiting. But she wouldn't dare call. And I do love her. But I always get melancholic when I think of her. Eventually, I want to warm her, too. I would never be able to betray her. Besides, she loves me too much.

My studies aren't going so badly. Not so great either. It's a little hard for me to concentrate right now. A young girl with glasses sits next to me in class, and just the other day she noticed I was wearing a black armband. She leaned over and looked at it. You're grieving, she said. Yes, I answered, my mother has passed away. Then she moved away from me as though I had a contagious disease. Later, I got a question that I didn't really understand. The professor grew impatient and gave it to the near-sighted girl. She can answer everyone else's questions, and one day she'll be able to answer her own. She looked at me when she answered, and I noticed that she felt sorry for me. I don't want anyone feeling sorry for me. There's nothing to feel sorry for, because I know that Mama is dead. Had I gone out that day and gone shopping for her, she'd still be dead. Maybe she wouldn't have had that cut on her forehead, but that's all.

I didn't make it to the exam today. When it was time to go, the telephone rang. I answered but nobody was there. It's incredibly annoying when the phone rings and no one's there when you pick up. I stood with the receiver in my hand and felt how terribly cold it was. Just as I was about to hang up, I thought I heard a voice. I listened again, but no one was there. Then something compelled me to go into the other room. I opened the door and froze. You see, I thought Mama was sitting in the armchair behind the table. Then I realized it was just her dress. Her best dress, the one she never got to wear. Papa had taken it out of the closet and spread it over the armchair. I don't know why. But then when I was about to leave, I couldn't dare turn my back to it, so I opened all the windows in the apartment and turned on the radio. A steamroller rumbled down the street, and a boat sounded from the Hammarby channel but then went silent. I lay in bed instead of going out. It was about two o'clock. When I woke up the radio was hot, and I closed all the windows. Soon after, Papa came home from work and I was glad when he arrived. It's easier to lie when you're happy. I told him that the exam went well, and then he gave me twenty *kronor*. He had a packet of pea soup and pork with him. I put it in some water and boiled it; it made two plates per person. We didn't say anything to each other. We're always silent when we eat, nowadays.

Afterward, I went to my room to catch up on my studying. But then I couldn't study. I just sat around listening to see whether he'd go out. He walked back and forth in the other room for a while. Finally, he went out and by then it was dark and sleeting. I locked both of my doors, both to the hallway and to his room, but I still couldn't concentrate. I just waited for him to come back. He never came. Then I opened my window all the way. It was very cold outside. It was windy and snowing. The neon light on the corner was broken and flickered like fire through the snow. I stood for a long time watching it. I thought about the exams. They would be unbearable if everyone sat around feeling sorry for me. Yet I'd still take them, if I wanted to.

There's no reason to feel sorry for me. But, Bengt! Does a person have to be afraid of the one he once loved? Because I loved her. I really loved her. I did. But I'm not afraid at all. I just miss her. I didn't at first, since you can't miss what isn't there. But now I know she is here. I found that out right before I was to go to class today. It was like a revelation. She is inside me. Because she loved me she is inside me, and that's where I'll let her stay. She's inside Papa, too. Once he realizes it, he will leave that other woman and come back to me. And that's when I will stop hating him.

He just came home, so I'll close now and study for a bit. He won't go out again tonight.

Sincerely
Yours,
Bengt

PRELUDE TO A DREAM

WHEN SOMEONE IS DEAD, there is, on the one hand, a big empty hole. But on the other hand, there is a lot left over. You go up to these things and look at them, twisting and turning them. But you don't really know what to do with them. You start by gently touching them. But after a while, your fingers grow tired. That is why you end up hating them. Dresses are the worst. After that, shoes.

On certain nights, when the father thinks the son is sleeping and when the son thinks the father is sleeping, the father pulls the shades down as far as they can go over the two windows in the room. Then he locks the door to the hallway. But over the keyhole to the son's room, he hangs Alma's black hat. Not because he plans on doing something he shouldn't. He simply wants to be more alone. And when he is more alone, he turns on as many lights as possible: all five lights on the ceiling as well as the lamp on top of the radio. He doesn't do this because he's afraid of the dark. He only does this so that he won't be entirely alone.

When all of this is done, he opens the closet door. It creaked on the first night, so he greased the hinges. Now it no longer makes a sound. The deceased's shoes are on the floor of the closet. He takes them out, pair after pair. There are four pairs, and he puts them all on the table because it has the most light. Eventually, the green tablecloth becomes dirty because he doesn't spread newspaper over it. He used to spread newspaper on the chair where he stood to wind up the clock. Now the chair is also dirty. But the clock has stopped.

Next, he leans over the shoes. Brushes his hands over them. Holds one shoe at a time up to the light. If he ever finds a smudge on an upper, he rubs and rubs the spot against his sleeve until it's dirty and until the leather shines immaculately in the harsh light. If there is ever a little dried mud under a sole, he scrapes it onto the floor with a used match. Then he flicks the match onto the linoleum, since it's no longer good, of course.

There are eight shoes to look at, and he studies each one of them at length. One pair has holes in the soles and cracks on the upper. It's a wide, heavy pair with low heels, and the label inside has been worn away by Alma's feet. She was wearing these shoes when she died. Some sawdust is stuck between the cracks, and there is a streetcar ticket hanging from the broken heel. He takes it off on the first night. And when he scrapes off the sawdust four nights later, the ticket is still on the floor. He doesn't pick it up. With his fingers he feels the smooth interior of the shoes. He thinks it's beautiful. He finds it very beautiful that a woman's foot can polish the inside of a shoe. Otherwise, he thinks the shoes are ugly. Even so, on the first night he spent nearly the longest time on these shoes. He held them underneath the ceiling light and was glad that it was so bright. But even though it was bright, he couldn't help feeling that a dead person had once worn these shoes. He felt this less on the following night. On the third night, he found them exceptionally ugly. On the fifth night, he doesn't even hold them up to the light. He places them by the door. Now they can be thrown away. After all, what use is a pair of worn-out shoes?

Now he studies a different pair for a long time. A pair of bulky walking shoes. Stiff and black, but not ugly. She hardly wore them, had said that they were tight and that they pinched. On the first night, he quickly puts them aside. They aren't particularly beautiful and she wasn't wearing them when she died. But on the second night, he looks at them for a long time. On the fifth night, he looks at them almost the longest. He likes that she barely wore them. He sticks a couple fingers inside the shoe and feels under the toe. There is a nail there, so he bends it down with his pocketknife. It's hardly noticeable after that.

Then there is a third pair. She had worn them to parties, the few parties she had been to, since she never really enjoyed going out. There was a funeral and a wedding now and then and that time he celebrated his fiftieth birthday party last October. It was the biggest party of all—sixty people and damn expensive. He had to take out a loan, so there were no new shoes for that party. Instead, she had old ones half-soled. Good soles but a little rough. She hadn't worn them down much. The last time she wore them was the day after Christmas. They were invited to Mälarhöjden. The heels are also very nice. But she thought they were too high. On the fifth night a thought occurs to him as he holds the heels up to the light. Alma was a good woman, all right. And she didn't go through shoes. The thought makes him happy. So happy that he pulls out a handkerchief. Then he gazes a little longer at the beautiful high heels. A beautiful woman can walk in these, a beautiful woman with beautiful feet.

But on the first night, as well as all the other nights, it's the fourth pair that he looks at the longest. It's a strange pair of shoes. Perhaps not so strange in themselves, but strange because they had belonged to her. Well, belonged and not belonged. The fact is that she had never worn them. He came home with them one Saturday evening at the beginning of December after winning a Soccer League pool. He put the box in the middle of the table and smiled contentedly. She untied the knot, since she never used scissors for knots, and after lifting the lid, she said, Do you think I'm seventeen?

These words were difficult for him to forget. She never wore them the day after Christmas. And they are so beautiful now that he's glad they were never worn, never even tried on. They are black and the heels are high and they have a bold curve. The straps are thin. And meant to be fastened around slender insteps—slender, beautiful insteps. A beautiful woman should fasten them in the evening, and a man should unfasten them at night. Such are these black shoes, shoes for a party. He looks at these shoes the longest. On the fifth evening, he opens up the bookcase and hides them behind an unread Bible.

After hiding them, he is sweaty. So he quietly rolls up the shades and opens the window slightly. But when he looks out, a car turns onto the street and its lights reflect in the windows of the butcher shop. He instantly closes the window and is no longer sweating. He puts the remaining shoes back inside the closet. But he grabs the ones he set by the front door and takes them with him to the kitchen. He plans on throwing them in the garbage, but it's full. So he puts them next to it on the floor. Then he opens the pantry and looks for a beer. But no one remembers to buy beer anymore. So he takes a swig instead, a big swig straight from the bottle of aquavit. He isn't cold anymore.

He locks the door to his room again. Then he stands by the son's door for a while and listens. He doesn't hear a sound, but he lets the hat stay where it is. It's an ugly hat. Alma didn't like hats. So whenever she did buy one, she always bought an ugly one. Alma didn't like anything that was beautiful.

But it's probably worse with dresses. It isn't so painful with jewelry. Because the jewelry poor women get from their husbands is nothing to flaunt. And their husbands know it. And they never dare flaunt the jewelry they get from other men. But their husbands don't know anything about that. This is why jewelry isn't so bad. Dresses are much worse.

There are three dresses. A black one hangs at the very front. He takes it out, along with the hanger, and lays it on the table underneath the lamp. Carefully, he takes it off the hanger. Then he drops the hanger on the floor. He stands in silence for a while and waits, but he doesn't hear anything from the son's room. He is not alarmed, because he is confident that the son is fast asleep. It's a simple black dress. It's quite worn, but it can be turned. The belt that goes to it is missing. It was lost in the ambulance. A button is missing near the neck, but a new one can be sewn on. There is also a little blood. But it isn't Alma's blood. When she was lying on the floor, the butcher assistant cut her coat open. Then he cut the top button off her dress. He had taken a first aid course and thought that she needed air. In reality, however, she didn't need a thing. But it isn't a lot of blood, and if it can't be cleaned, then a collar can cover it up. A resourceful woman could manage it. It isn't a particularly beautiful dress. But it is in one piece.

A green one is hanging farther in. It is quite stunning. She had worn it to his fiftieth birthday party. She wore it to her own party, too. Which, come April, will have been two years ago. Around the bodice is a thin red belt that passes through the dress's green velvet loops. And the bodice is pleated. It has a torn seam, but it can be easily mended. It goes far up the neck and down the back a little. But she usually wore a boa over her shoulders—a boa that he bought for her. It was very cheap, since he was the frugal type, after all. He eventually sold it when he had needed money, but he told her about it afterward. She didn't get upset. And she didn't ask what he needed the money for.

Alma was kind, he thinks to himself. Thinks it completely willingly as he stands under the light and pokes through the loops with his nail. A little below the neckband are two shiny spots with a good handbreadth, the widower's handbreadth, between them. He is a little irritated when he sees them. He starts rubbing and rubbing them. But then he suddenly stops. It feels as if he has burned himself. The area he was rubbing had been stretched out by Alma's breasts. She had large, heavy breasts, and they stretched out all of her dresses. When she was young, they were also large, but in those days they were firm. He used to sink into them headfirst. But later he always felt with his hand first. He thinks breasts should be big and firm enough to provide just the right resistance to a man's hands. That was nice. And beautiful, too. Nevertheless, he burned himself as he rubbed against the memory of Alma's breasts.

Then he hangs the green dress in the closet again.

Finally, he takes out the red dress. He always takes it out last. Because he looks at it the longest and because it hangs the farthest in. But also because it's the worst dress. Because it's the most beautiful dress. Even though he appreciates anything beautiful, he's afraid of the beautiful red dress. When he holds it, he holds it like a man holds a woman, a dainty and beautiful woman. And before he lays it on the table, he blows away as much dust as he can from the table-cloth.

He shouldn't actually feel what he feels when he leans over the red dress and watches the light reflecting on its soft surface. No stretched out breasts have ever left any marks on it. Nor have any bony hips or a protruding backside touched it. The dress is utterly pristine because Alma has never worn it. He bought it for a Christmas present. He didn't have the money for it, but he still bought it. Alma wasn't with him when he did. If she had tried it on, it would have been too tight. And he knew it would be too tight. But he bought the dress anyway.

You couldn't have known, she said on Christmas morning, as she stood barelegged in her thick slip in front of the mirror, trying to put it on. In that moment he wanted to say, Yes, of course, I could have known. I knew, all right. But I still bought it. But instead of saying it, he started laughing. Not a prolonged laugh by any means, but afterward he wished that he hadn't because she asked what he was laughing at. At a story I happened to think of, he answered. She didn't ask which story. She only laid the dress on the table. Don't worry, she said; you'll see, I can let it out. Since I can't wear it as it is now. Then a thought sank deep into his mind like a hot stone. Then it dropped to his tongue, where it stayed and burned impatiently. But he was able to put it out with saliva this time. The burning thought: you weren't meant to wear it anyway.

Now he remembers the thought. He can never forget it because it's such a dangerous thought. On Christmas, he had filled his mouth with spit and put it out. But it came back the day after Christmas. They were invited to Mälarhöjden at five that evening, so Alma got up at five that morning. When he asked why she was up so early, she answered, I'm going to try to let out the dress so I can wear it tonight. Then he pulled her back into bed. Don't do that, he said. Why not? she asked. Then he told her he wanted to exchange it the next day for a larger size. The next day was Sunday. He knew that. But she had forgotten. Nevertheless, she went back to bed. Suddenly, she took his hand and placed it on her left breast. Then, as soon as she let his hand go, he pulled it away. He put it over his mouth instead, as if to suppress a yawn. But it wasn't a yawn. It was a glowing stone that wanted out of his mouth. Something wanted him to spit it out. Something tried to force him to say, I didn't mean for you to have the dress. But I bought it anyway.

But ever since that first night when he took out the red dress and laid it on the table, he has known that the most horrible thing about the thought was not the words he already knew. The most horrible thing is that the words continued. Nobody had forced him to think the words that followed. Or to say them. Yet he knows them like one knows what is said behind a closed door without being able to make out a single word. The knowledge of these lingering words was what had made him so certain that day when the blaring ambulance came closer, block by block—so sure of himself that before it stopped he had already wiped the shaving cream from his face with a towel and put on his jacket. And when they came running up the stairs to get him, it was this knowledge that had made certain he was already ready to go.

Before the fifth night, nobody had forced him to reveal what the rest of the words were. But on the fifth night he is forced. As he fondles the delicate shoulders of the red dress, he hears a faint yet terrifying sound behind him, the sound of something light falling by the son's door. When he turns around, Alma's hat is lying on the floor. It was hanging on the doorknob before it fell. Someone must have turned the knob for it to have been able to fall. Dreadful is the eye now watching him through the naked keyhole. And it's an ugly eye because it's so naked, because it's so merciless, because it's so terrifyingly young. There is nothing more terrifying to a hardened conscience than a young, naked eye. It knows nothing. And therefore understands everything.

But he isn't afraid of his son because he understands everything. He's afraid of him because of what the son's eye forces him to do. For it is terrible. It makes him grab the red dress, which suddenly doesn't have a loop that isn't burning, makes him pick it up from the table, and makes him take it to the armchair. It makes him slowly spread it out into a woman and then makes him bend over the woman who has suddenly appeared out of nowhere. As he hunches over her, it forces him to think so loudly that it drowns out everything inside him as well as everything outside of him: you were never meant to wear this dress, Alma. I didn't buy it for you. I bought it because I knew you were going to die.

Afterward, he is no longer afraid of the son. But he is so terribly afraid of what he has been forced to think that he can't even be in the same room with such a thought. So he leaves the room with all its bright lights. From the kitchen, he rushes out to the entrance. He carries the worn-out shoes downstairs with him. But he forgets to turn on the light before he ventures across the yard to the garbage container. He's afraid that the stairwell light will go out before he can get back. So he flings the shoes into the snow-covered yard and runs through the front door and out to the street. From the street, he looks up at the windows. The son is looking out the father's window. So he walks farther down the street. When he looks back at the window, the son is gone. Then the light goes out in the father's room. And when he reaches the corner, the light goes out in the son's room, too. By the time he comes back, it has snowed a lot. The entire building is draped in darkness. He turns on the yard light and starts looking for the shoes. They are covered in snow, and he can't find them. Then a shift worker arrives on his bicycle. He asks the widower what he's looking for. The widower tells him that he's looking for his key. Then, on the way to the bicycle storage shed the worker rides over the shoes. He picks them up, and brushing off the snow, he says:

There's a pair of shoes here. I'll be damned if they aren't nice. I think I'll take them up to my old lady and get off easy this time.

Then the widower finds his key, and they walk up the stairs together. The worker goes first. He has his tool bag in one hand and Alma's shoes under his arm. When they are four flights up, the widower invites him in for a drink. The shift worker is exhausted. Soon he will be very drunk. And when he leaves, he forgets the shoes. Then the widower empties the garbage on the floor. He puts Alma's shoes at the bottom and buries them underneath the trash. After that, he rinses his hands and has another drink.

He isn't afraid when he goes into the room. He only turns on one of the ceiling lights, and under the light he hangs the red dress back in the closet. He also picks up the hat.

When someone is dead, there is someone left behind to mourn. When a wife is dead, the widower stays behind to mourn. When a mother is dead, a son is left behind to mourn. If they don't mourn, one pretends that they do. This is called decency. To be decent is to leave people alone. And to pretend they are doing what others want them to do.

They are left alone for the first few weeks. And unless they contact a friend, they are completely alone. The son doesn't contact anyone. So he is alone. Sometimes he calls his fiancée, but anytime she mentions that she has a headache, he hangs up. Still, it is true. If the father is lonely, then there really isn't anyone who notices. Sometimes his sisters call. But if the line is busy, they wonder who is calling. Then they tell everyone what they suspect. And everyone believes them because they never liked Alma. Because of this and because he is mourning, no one else calls him.

Sometimes the sisters do get through. This happens more often than not, but they never tell anyone this. Whenever the son answers, they never ask to speak with the father. They only ask what he is doing. Whenever he tells them that the father has gone out to get the paper, they ask whether he left a long time ago. Five minutes ago, he always says. They don't like this answer. They like to be right. They like being right more than they like knowing the truth. Besides, they know the son is lying. They can always tell when people are lying, but never when people are telling the truth.

They live together in a single-room apartment with a kitchen on Hantverkar Street. The ugly one works at the consul's. The beautiful one is a waitress. The beautiful one has been married twice. The ugly one has never been married. This is why they don't like each other. But whenever they call their brother, they always call together. Then they only have one thought and only one ear. Sometimes they put the phone down and start whispering. When they speak to the son, that is. One evening, after they stopped whispering, the beautiful one says:

Do you have anyone to clean for you?

No, he answers, we don't have anyone to clean for us.

Then the ugly one must have yanked the phone away. In any case, she is the one who shouts:

She should probably come and clean. That's the least she could do!

He doesn't ask who. If he asks who, they would whisper for a bit. Then they would lie. So he tells them that they will try to clean for themselves. As best they can. They don't like his response. The ugly sister, whom he considers nice because she had cried, doesn't like the answer because she thinks it's inappropriate. She can tolerate almost anything, but nothing inappropriate. Because such is not tolerated at the consul's. And when she had cried, she did it because it was inappropriate not to cry, not because she was compassionate. Sometimes being appropriate is the same thing as being compassionate. But it can just as often be the same thing as being mean. And now she is being mean. He holds the receiver firmly against his ear as her meanness spits through it. But it doesn't come out the other end. It's lodged inside him and aches.

I feel so bad for you, my boy, she says. Your mother is dead and you have no father. I feel so sorry for you, my boy.

Malice has a tender voice, a silky, flattering voice. Nothing else in the world has such a silky voice. And how it hurts! With pain, he nearly screams into the receiver.

Don't feel bad for us. And we do clean. Papa cleans out the closet every other night.

Now it's silent on the other end. Then the beautiful one speaks. She is not mean. Concerned is what she is.

What's he doing in the closet? she quickly asks.

Then he starts to describe everything that has been going on late at night. He explains about the shoes. Then it's quiet for a while. After that, he explains about the dresses. Then it's quiet for a lot longer. The beautiful sister comes back on the line. She is very concerned now. She has been concerned the entire time. She is beautiful and knows what men do for beautiful women.

We'll come and help you clean, she says. But don't tell Knut. It's to be a surprise.

And it certainly will be a surprise. But not much will be cleaned. The sisters arrive at seven the following evening. The father and son are both home at the time. They had just eaten pea soup. Then they had some coffee. They told each other how good they thought it was. But neither of them really thought that. Which is why they repeated it.

Before the aunts come in, they look behind the door as if they were expecting someone to be there. The father notices and is annoyed. He gets upset with the ugly sister, even though they are both looking.

What are you staring at? he asks and turns on the light for them in the entrance.

Nothing at all, the ugly one answers.

And in a way, it was nothing. In a way, it's also nothing they are staring at when they scan the room with their coats still on. They aren't staring at anything, yet almost immediately they notice that the flowers are wilted and that Alma's portrait is gone. The closet doors are not ajar. But had they been even remotely open, they could have peeked inside. But now they can't peek inside without staring. So they don't look at all. But as they take off their coats in the entrance, the young and beautiful one starts whistling. The other one doesn't whistle. She has never learned how. Nor is it appropriate. The widower is annoyed and asks them why they are whistling. The beautiful one replies that she is simply whistling. Which is precisely what she is doing.

There's a lot of whistling. But there's not a lot of cleaning. Yes, they throw the wilted flowers away, and, yes, the ugly one sweeps the used matches, dried mud, and a white streetcar ticket from the floor, and of course, she dusts here and a little there over the cabinets and the picture frames. But as soon as she's in the room by herself, she puts the rag down and looks at other things for a while. She looks, for instance, at the photographs on the bookcase. One picture is missing. It was one of Alma. But the ones in which she was not alone are still there. Then she tries looking through the dusty glass of the bookcase. When Knut comes into the room, she tells him that the books ought to be dusted. Then the brother says that he has lost the key. He lost it somewhere in the snow in the yard.

Then she asks why the key was even in the yard. He doesn't answer. Instead, he turns on the radio. But no one listens to it.

In any event, they spread a fresh tablecloth on the table. Coffee will be made after the ugly one cleans the kettle. The beautiful sister rinses a cup for herself. The ugly one washes three more. Then the beautiful sister waters the flowers in the room. Not all of them, but the five that the water is able to reach. Then she stands on a chair and adjusts the pendulum clock. He would rather do it himself, but because it is she, he doesn't say anything to her—but also because he had forgotten to do it himself. When she stretches out her body to pull the hour hand down to eight, he tells her that she has beautiful legs. The sister laughs and says that her shoes aren't worth much.

Afterward, when they are sitting at the table in the kitchen, the beautiful one suddenly stretches out one of her arms. Then she stretches out the other one and yawns. The sleeve on the first arm has a torn seam in the armpit. Then she mentions that she doesn't have a single decent dress to wear. The widower takes her arm and squeezes it above the elbow. Then he asks her to go in the other room with him.

When they come back, the son is suddenly terrified. She had come in swiftly and silently through the doorway. His mind knows that it's his aunt, but his fear is quicker than his thoughts. His fear can only see his mother coming. And he imagines this because the beautiful aunt is wearing his mother's green dress. She says that she has to take it in. And when she takes it off, her slip comes off with it. She is standing with glistening teeth between the table and the stove. She is blushing, but her body is as shiny as salmon. The father takes her gently by the hips. Then the ugly one tells him to leave her alone. The beautiful one grows solemn and folds up Alma's green dress. He has kissed her before. She was sixteen then, and she was braiding her hair. Then he kissed her when she was eighteen, but then she immediately burst into tears. Now she is thirty-six. For eighteen years she hasn't cried whenever someone has kissed her. But he has never done it again.

After she folds up the dress, she takes off her shoes. The ugly sister takes off hers, too. Then the brother goes to get the two pairs of shoes from the closet. And the black dress, too. As the sisters try on the shoes, the beautiful one saunters back and forth in the high heels. But the other one sticks her feet under the darkness of the table to see how the shoes fit. She doesn't try on the dress at all. Nor does she thank him for it. But just as they are about to leave, looking at the widower, she says that Alma would have wanted her sisters-in-law to have them. She stressed the word *sisters-in-law*. The question is whether he noticed it.

Then the beautiful sister asks for a bag to carry the clothes in.

There has to be one in the closet, she says. I can go and get it myself.

But it's the widower who quickly leaves and comes back. To punish him, she decides to keep the bag.

You can keep the bag, he says.

It's her reward for not allowing her to look inside the closet. But he doesn't give anything to the ugly sister for not opening the glass door of the bookcase for her. The bag is light, only two pairs of shoes and two dresses. Still, they ask Bengt to carry it down for them. Once they reach the street, the beautiful aunt asks him whether there wasn't another pair. He says that they must be in the closet. Then she asks whether there wasn't another dress, too, a new red one. He denies it and says that his father already returned it. Now the beautiful one regrets that she ever came and cleaned. The ugly one thinks the beautiful one is selfish. She herself feels quite content. Quite content and therefore quite good.

Alma was sweet, she says to her nephew as they cross the street. It's a pity that she left so soon. A pity for you.

Once the streetcar leaves, he doesn't really know why he lied. He walks past a little cinema and looks at the pictures behind the frosty glass for a little while. Then he sees a black dog in the entrance. He still doesn't know why he lied. Then he goes home. But he runs into his father at a corner. They pass each other in the darkness and the snow. After a while, the son turns around and heads after the father. He realizes that he doesn't have his key. Then he realizes that he does have it after all. But he continues walking to get some air. When the father notices that the son is following him, he walks through a door that had just opened at the corner. He walks briskly across the yard and out the other side. But on the next street the father runs.

Inside the building, the son skims through the list of tenants. Then someone comes up to him and asks him who he's looking for. He replies that he must be in the wrong building. Then he runs out. He runs all the way home. But once he's outside the front gate of his building, he turns around and goes back. There was a vending machine in the other building, and he wants to buy some throat lozenges from it. But when he gets there, there is no vending machine. And the door is locked. Then he remembers that there was once an accident in this building. Somebody who was smoking in bed had burnt to death. In the heavy snowfall, he is standing on the sidewalk and studying window after window, trying to remember where it happened. All the lights eventually go out before he can remember. Besides, it's windy and snowing. Signposts are squeaking, and windows are creaking. So he takes cover in the doorway. No one is going in. No one is coming out. When he finally does come home, the father is already there. At once, he finds himself curiously happy and asks him to make some coffee. When he holds out his coffee cup, the father takes his other hand.

I had to give the dresses away, he says.

The son keeps his hand there. Then he lets it be stroked. In the middle of the night he remembers that the accident happened in a different building. A sound from the other room had woken him up when he suddenly remembered before falling back asleep. In the morning, the red dress is spread out over the armchair again.

In the evening the father comes home with a dog. A big black dog. Whenever he goes near it, it growls. So the father gives it a lump of sugar. As they eat their pea soup, the dog sits beside the firewood bin and watches them. Then while they drink coffee, the son chucks another lump of sugar at it. The dog doesn't touch it. Then the son asks him why he bought a dog. The father says it's so that they won't be so lonely. Then he says he got it for a bargain.

Later that night, after the son has gone to bed—because the need to listen to what was happening in the other room had prevented him from studying—he hears the dog come pattering through the hallway. It treads slowly, almost like a frightened human being. It must be very late. He sits listening in silence for a long time because whatever is happening in the other room is lasting as long as usual, maybe even longer. Even though there is only one dress now. And maybe a pair of shoes.

At last, the dog stops. It stops in front of his door. And lingers there. At first, it's almost completely silent. Then it starts to pant, and when it does, it pants like a frightened human being. Frightened people terrify him. And frightened animals terrify him almost just as much. So he gets up and pads through the darkness to lock his door. But then he finds that he has already locked it. As he slips back into bed, the dog starts whimpering some more. It almost sounds like a sleeping infant. Finally, it patters down the hallway again. Then the father drops something in his room. He doesn't pick up whatever he dropped. It becomes absolutely silent in the room. Then, after a long period of silence, the son falls asleep.

He has a dream as he sleeps. He dreams that someone is calling to him. He doesn't recognize the voice. Nor does he recognize his own name. And he is standing in a strange room. It has no windows. No mirrors either. But there are black candles burning along the walls. They burn down very quickly but are constantly replenished as soon as they burn out. The candles make the room dreadfully hot, and he suddenly realizes that he has to take everything off to keep from bursting into flames. But when he looks down at his body, he doesn't recognize it, just as he doesn't recognize his own name, which is now being called much more loudly from beyond the room. A garment is clinging to his strange body, a cloak with a peculiar cut. When the heat becomes unbearable, he tries tearing it off his body. But he can't get it off. The more he tears at it, the tighter it envelops him. Then he feels a sharp pain in his hands. When he looks down at them, they are red with blood. Astonished, he sees that the cloak is made of blood. The candles suddenly go out and it becomes very dark in the room. The room also turns cold. Through the darkness, the voice comes creeping up to him. The voice has paws. It pants like a frightened human being. Slowly, the room begins to brighten. His aunts come wandering through the darkness. They are holding burning candles in their hands. Their faces are ghostly, and their eyes are closed. But around their bodies, they are wearing cloaks of blood. Suddenly, they are gone. Only the candles remain. In the flickering light, a big black dog comes pattering toward him. The dog is the one calling out his unrecognizable name. Once it is terrifyingly close, he hears what the name is. The name is Gun, and the voice is his father's. Even the dog's eyes are his father's. He tries to run away, but he is paralyzed. Gently, the dog lays its hot paws on his hips. Then he tries to shout out his real name. But his tongue is just a big, scorching lump. He bites and bites. When he finally bites hard enough so that it hurts, he wakes up.

He has flung his blanket on the floor. Naked, he is lying in his bed with his hands pressed against his burning hips. He is drenched in cool sweat. And he has a chewed-up handkerchief in his mouth. When he pulls it out, he remembers it. It tastes like tears and perfume. Still weighed down by the heaviness of the dream, he staggers out of bed. In the dark, he unlocks his door to the other room, and as he walks through it, he steps on something soft. When he turns on the light, he sees his mother's hat lying on the floor in front of his door. There is also a hanger on the floor. And the door to the bookcase is ajar.

But the red dress is gone. The father is gone, too. And so is the dog.

A Letter in March from Himself to Himself

Dear Bengt!

It's been a while since I last wrote to you. Some important things have happened since then. The most important thing is that I have seriously decided to stop attending lectures and seminars, though I'll still take the exam in April. I plan to study at home. That way I'll save time, and I can be home in the evenings. It's nice being at home, and in the end I think Papa will come to think so, too.

I haven't told him about my decision, and since I'm still going to take the exam, I won't have to. And whenever he asks, How was your day today? I usually always say, Fine, thanks; it went really well. There's no use saying that it wasn't good or that I missed a question since I was never there in the first place. Besides, if I were to say something like that, it wouldn't make it any less of a lie. It would just upset him, and I don't want to do that. In fact, it's the same reason why I don't tell him that I'm home all day when he thinks I'm in class. In the evenings, I sometimes tell him little details about tests or lectures.

I intentionally talk about things I know he'll appreciate. For example, that a professor came to class in a top hat and business suit because he had been at a funeral the day before and still thought he was wearing his tailcoat. He finds such stories amusing, and he still thinks professors have to be old and absentminded.

When he's in a good mood he gives me money. Of course, it annoyed me at first, but then I realized I have to take it. Otherwise, he might start to suspect something, and I don't want that to happen. And since I'm going to take the exam in April anyway, it doesn't matter whether or not I accept these little rewards. After all, it's just as much work, if not more, to study at home as it is to sit around in a lecture hall.

Besides, I like putting Papa in a good mood. It makes us both happy. On Thursday, I sat around for half a day coming up with a great story about a professor, and I told him all about it when he came home. He hasn't laughed like that in a long time. And why shouldn't I make someone happy if I can?

Yes, you might be right when you say that it's not particularly nice to lie, but I think a lie should be judged by what a person hopes to gain from it. For example, if you lie to gain any kind of personal advantage, then I consider that an immoral way to use a lie. But if you lie to make someone happy, then I can see no reason why the lie can't be justified. I also think a lot depends on the person who is lying. Isn't it a different matter altogether when a corrupt person lies from when a good person lies? An honorable person can do things that other people cannot do. If a sluggard wastes his time roaming the streets and looking for girls while his parents think he's really busy studying diligently, then it's a completely different situation when a responsible person hides a temporary postponement from his father (which, all things considered, isn't even a postponement).

And I have always been responsible. You can't deny that, Bengt! I was raised to be responsible, you know that. You also know how Mama was and that she had a bad childhood. Since her mother was gravely ill and her father was dead, she was shuffled from one poor relative to the next throughout her youth. She used to say that her childhood was a carousel, not a nice one like we have here in the cities, but a poor, run-down carousel, one that is sent out to the most impoverished and distant places. So revolved her childhood. This also explained why she didn't have a typical education. She had to learn almost everything on her own while working hard on the side. When I was little, I was always surprised by how much she knew. But when I got older, I noticed that her knowledge did have gaps. Yet I still have to admit what an achievement it was that she accomplished everything on her own. And because she had had it so hard, she wanted me to have it easier. Yet she also wanted me to learn something. Against father's wishes, she insisted that I go to high school. Throughout my schooling, she never let me forget, and rightly so, the tremendous advantage I had of being able to pick up my knowledge so effortlessly. She also constantly ingrained in me the obligations it entailed. I didn't miss a single day of school, and because of my sheer sense of duty, I even went to school with a fever at times. I, and I suppose all poor children who have been able to choose a different and more superior path than their parents, have been raised to be, above all else, responsible. Although, Bengt, you know very well that that isn't so difficult for me.

That's just it. Parents can have a different understanding from their children of what the word *responsibility* means. Unfortunately, all concepts can easily become limited for people who, whether in their work or their own curiosity, don't concern themselves with the value of words. For an uneducated person, the word *motherland,* for example, has a much simpler and more finite meaning than it does for the educated individual, who from such an ostensibly simple term immediately discerns all the components the concept comprises. Naturally, this applies to the concept of responsibility in the same way. This means that for someone like Mama, who was in some sense an uncomplicated person, to be responsible is to simply wake up early in the morning, work hard no matter what the conditions, even if that means working ad absurdum, or in other words, in circumstances that don't involve work at all. That kind of responsibility is simply identical to the word *work.*

In the same way, many complicated terms seemed to be the epitome of simplicity and unambiguity for Mama. This could often make you irritated with her, but you had to be understanding and remember the circumstances behind her education. A concept like "truth," for example, was absolutely clear-cut to her. She couldn't even accept the smallest white lie no matter how justifiable it was. Once, when I was in the fourth grade, I got a demerit, and in a moment of weakness she tried to spare me from Papa's anger and signed his signature on the form. But on the day I was to submit it to my homeroom teacher, she called during the break and explained to him that she was guilty of a treacherous forgery. In the afternoon, the teacher comically related to the class what had happened, and I was terribly ashamed of what she had done. That evening when Papa came home, I told him what had happened, and he reproached Mama for her ridiculous behavior.

I think that the more theoretical knowledge you obtain, the more multifarious and kaleidoscopic your view becomes of the reality that lurks behind concepts. This reality is so insatiably rich that a fixed determinant of a concept's position must simply be an absurdity. For me, the concept *truth* isn't summed up by a simple formula like it was for Mama. We sometimes discussed the matter, but it was impossible to get her to see how wrong we really are when we draw a fixed border around the meaning of a word. Moreover, the concept *responsibility,* for me, is so far from being identical to the concept *work* that at certain times it can even mean that we limit our performance for a time, especially when it proves necessary to do so with respect to our future goal. For weaker persons, it might be considered necessary to have an absolutely fixed value for a concept, but for a person who knows where he is going, which some say is the only important thing, a fixed definition like that can even seem obstructive at times.

One bit of news is that Papa got a dog. It's black and doesn't like me, but it likes Papa. I don't know why. When I asked him what the dog's name was, he answered, Hector. When I asked him why, he didn't know, and when I asked him if he knew who Hector was, he didn't know that either. But instead of explaining how he came up with the name, he got angry and said that he was just a simple carpenter. Anytime someone shows himself to be wiser than Papa, he always says that he's just a simple carpenter. It's his best defense, and he used it against Mama a lot. The next day, however, he told me who Hector was. So I suspected that he had looked up the name in the encyclopedia. When I checked, I rightly discovered that volume H was dusted off. But now I wonder where he got the name. I also wonder where he got the dog. He says he bought it at a pet shop on Södermannagatan, but the other day when I walked from one end of the street to the other, I couldn't find a single pet store. I think it's disgusting when he lies and when he lies so sloppily. I also think it's disgusting that he's started spying on me.

I don't know if I hate him anymore. I just think that what he has done is disgusting, sordid, and filthy. I can't stand the thought of him betraying Mama for an entire year while pretending to be so innocent the whole time. When Aunt Agnes called today, she said she knew that it was going on for a long time. I think it's despicable how they go around gossiping about it. They should at least have some consideration for my feelings.

Well, Bengt, this has become a long letter, but since Mama's death, I've had time to think things out. I miss her terribly, but I just can't express exactly how much in a letter. It's March now, and the nights are long. The other night I went out for a walk along the pier with Berit. She said she thought that spring was the most beautiful season of all. I told her I thought it was the ugliest, with all the slush and cats in heat. I shouldn't have been so harsh, because I hurt her feelings. She isn't sleeping well, she said. I know she can't help it, but she's very ugly without sleep. Mother was, too.

Good night, Bengt, and send everyone my regards.

Your friend,
Bengt

P.S. I forgot something: the other night I had a very horrible dream. I dreamt that I was standing in a large room surrounded by black candles. I was dressed very strangely, and I was sweating profusely. Suddenly, Papa came into the room and called me by the other woman's name. Then I noticed I was wearing Mama's red dress. Afterward, I realized that my dream was about my loyalty to Mama. Since then, I've been afraid, Bengt. I'm afraid that one day I'll have to meet her—the other woman. I'm afraid because I know I won't be able to control myself. I'm afraid I'm going to do something terrible.

P.P.S. Mama's red dress has disappeared. When I asked Papa about it, he told me that he sold it. To prove he was telling the truth, he offered to share the money with me. I told him I didn't want anything to do with that kind of money. I could tell he was glad to keep the money but hurt that I didn't believe him. And I don't believe him. I don't know why, but I don't.

EVENING PROMENADES

AT THE END OF MARCH, the son often goes out for walks in the evenings. The father is also out on these evenings, but he doesn't take walks. Well, he does, but they are very short. Even so, it's a long time before he comes home again. He takes the dog out for walks because dogs need exercise. And every evening when he steps out the front door, he goes in a different direction. But every evening he ends up in the same place, which makes the dog very happy.

But before he ever gets there, it just so happens that he abruptly steps off the sidewalk and steps into a pub or a café, where he immediately looks for a newspaper, the biggest one he can find. Then he sits by the window with the paper covering his face as if he were reading. But he is not reading. Every time someone passes by on the street, he is peeking over the edge of the paper. Sometimes the son walks by. He strolls by slowly, and his eyes rove around as if they are looking for something. And they probably are. To a certain degree, the father is surprised to see his son out walking about, because they were just talking about it ten minutes ago. You should go outside and get some exercise, son, the father had said. You shouldn't be indoors on such a beautiful evening. But the son told him that it would be better for him to finish the eighty pages he had to read before his lecture the next morning. Snapped at him almost.

So the father finds it somewhat strange when he suddenly passes by. But in a way he doesn't. Because he was actually sitting there and waiting for him. Though the first few times he isn't himself aware that he is waiting. But one evening, right after the son passes by, the dog starts whimpering at his feet. Then he realizes that he's sitting with his foot pressed hard against the floor and that the dog's leash is pressed between his sole and the floor. That's why the dog is whimpering. It can't lift its head off the ground. But it's not supposed to, because if its head were raised, then the dog could be seen from the street.

Since then, the father knows why he is waiting. And since then, he is never at ease until he has seen the son walk by. If, one evening, he doesn't happen to walk by, then the father waits until it's very dark out. Then he sneaks onto the street like a thief sneaks into a house. Then he runs the whole way. The dog runs, too, but it's faster. And when they arrive, they are both panting.

But one evening in March, when it is unusually warm and has just lightly rained, the father gives a start when the son walked by. Yes, walked by, because he realized—after he has let the dog sit up between the table and the window—that he didn't have to sit and wait that night. They had just walked together to the streetcar stop, where the son got on the nine to go to a lecture. This is why he gives a start. After that, he hits the dog on the nose with the palm of his hand, relieving some of his pain. Because even when you have expected it, it hurts to be deceived. To be the one deceiving doesn't hurt nearly as much. But failing to notice that you have been deceived, when you have been expecting it all along, can keep you happy.

This is why the son is happy when the father comes home early that evening. And to make the father happy, too, he makes some coffee. As they drink it, he tells him about a funny thing that happened at the lecture. The father laughs loudly at the son's story. But he isn't happy, nor does he pull out his wallet. Then the son calls the dog because the father likes it when he pets it. When the dog comes, the son notices it has a brand-new shiny silver collar. It didn't have it two hours ago. It had a leather one, brown and chewed up. He fondles the new collar for a while, and then, with a clenched fist, he hits the dog under its nose so that it yelps and scurries off to the father. The father slams his coffee cup on the table—since they always drink coffee without a saucer nowadays—and asks him what he's doing.

Hector has a new collar, the son replies.

The son raises his cup and takes a sip, even though the cup is empty. Because it's easier to really study a person when one is drinking. The father looks briefly into the son's eyes. The funeral eyes. He thinks they are ugly, and he doesn't like anything ugly. But there is something about ugliness that he fears. Therefore, it isn't his son that he fears. It's the ugliness inside him. And the ugliness inside him is so hideously similar to the dead wife that he immediately has to look at something else. So he looks at the dog. It doesn't have beautiful eyes either, but at least they don't frighten him. He also looks at the collar. The son has smudged its shiny surface. Otherwise, it's smart and cold to the touch.

I got a good deal for it, he says, squeezing it firmly like a hand. I bought it at the pet shop on Södermannagatan.

Then the son says that there is no pet shop on that street.

This is when the father forgets that he has been deceived. He probably hasn't forgotten for good, but he at least forgets in that moment. However, he who is exposed must defend himself. And to do so, the deceiver must convince the deceived that he is wrong. But if it's a fellow deceiver he must convince, then it is easier if this fellow deceiver doesn't realize that he himself is exposed. This allows him to be convinced more easily. Besides, he'll be pleased since it can be gratifying to gain false trust when he himself only has deceit to offer. And once the son has been pleased, the father is, too, because our emotions are as cunning as serpents. They are also as deceitful as serpents are said to be. Of course, the son is glad that the father tells him about his long evening promenades with the dog, but when the dog suddenly walks past him on the way to its place in the hallway, he is still skeptical about the collar. But the father—who has no collar to look at but only something he has said to believe in—is not skeptical. Instead, he is only frightened when he notices the son's suspicion. He knows that he has to keep the son's happiness alive. Or else his own happiness will die out. So he goes to fetch the liquor.

As he searches the cupboard, he asks the son to pull down the shades. Because a father shouldn't drink with his son. But if he does, then the shades have to be drawn. The son lowers them slowly. Slowly, because he's gazing out the window. It's dark outside, but the darkness is bright as it always is in March, mingled with falling rain and the soft glow of streetlights. Over the butcher shop, the bull's head glistens in the dampness. In the springtime it looks soft, almost like flesh. It's only in winter that it looks hard and cold. After the snow melted away and the spruce garlands were taken down, they started to shop there again—when they shop at all, of course. And most of it is for the dog. But it's a strange dog because it's only hungry in the mornings and never wants anything at night.

The father was making noise with the glasses and had already poured them by the time the son sits down. He has filled his own shot glass to the brim but put five drops too many in the son's, so it has spilled over. When they toast the first time, their hands are slightly tremulous. But when they toast the second time, they are much steadier. But the third time, they look each other in the eye, and their eyes are beautiful. In fact, it's not until their eyes are beautiful that they dare begin to speak about what they are too afraid to mention. They also sit closer to each other, as if they felt safer that way. The father wraps his arm around the son's shoulder. The arm is soft and warm, and the shoulder is, too.

Do you miss Mama a lot? the father asks.

Yes, the son says, I miss her.

Then the father notices that the son didn't say "a lot." So he asks again.

Doesn't it feel a little empty? he asks.

Yes, the son says, it does feel a little empty.

I want to do something for you, my boy, the father says.

Because they are drunk and quite near each other, the son

cannot say what he wants to say, so he says something else. But when he says this other thing, he realizes that it's also true.

If I didn't have you, he says, it would seem much, much emptier.

My son, the father says.

Quite suddenly, he is moved. And he sees that the son is moved, too. To keep their emotions alive, the father pours them both another shot. He doesn't want to make the son drunk. He just wants to make him beautiful. And anyone who is moved is beautiful. He is already beautiful. He has beautiful moist eyes. His cheeks are flushed, and his lips are silky. And when they toasted the fourth time, he is even gentler. And when he speaks, he speaks so beautifully.

Inside every intoxicated person is a sober will, and anything he does is not what his sober will desires but what his drunken will desires, because it's much stronger. He puts his hands on the table and studies them carefully. Then the father puts his hands next to his and they gaze at each other's hands. They both find the other's hands very beautiful, and they cannot resist squeezing them. Like two sleeping lovers, their hands fuse together on the table. Then the son says what his sober will has not allowed.

Well, whoever is dead is dead, he says.

After he says this, the kitchen becomes terribly silent and terribly still. After a long period of stillness, their hands awaken. Their bodies stretch out in their slumber, and they have dreams before they wake. Once they are fully awake, they look at each other and are surprised they are together. Then they are glad and they embrace, sinking into each other's tenderness. They part slowly, each going in the opposite direction yet longing for the other the whole time. It can be seen in their fingers. Once their hands are finally separated again, the father says, quietly:

Yes, whoever is dead is dead.

It hasn't really been true until now. Not until now does the sober person, who is sitting on a chair inside the son's inebriation and telling him what is happening in the sober world, comprehend how terribly true it is. He immediately snaps out of his drunkenness, and for a second he is struck with fear as he perceives the depth of the abyss. But his intoxication bursts like a mist and soon it is dense again. Meanwhile, the father hasn't noticed a thing, and the son has hardly noticed anything himself. With clasped hands, the father says:

Yes, Alma was sweet.

Now the son's drunken will is infinitely stronger than his other will because even though he *really* wants to say something else, he says:

Yes, Alma was sweet enough.

Now, the father is not so drunk that he fails to notice the son has said "Alma." Or that he has said "enough." At once, he moves even closer to him. He does it because he feels he has to. And because he feels he has to, he also puts his arm around the son's shoulder again. The shoulder and arm are still tender, but the father is silent, silent because he immediately realizes that one day the son will say, Yes, Knut was nice enough, exactly as he just said it about Alma. And because he realizes it so quickly, he doesn't sit quietly for long. He is a rather lonely man. He doesn't always feel it, but in the very moment he caused the son to betray his own mother with those words, a shiver of such chilling loneliness shoots through him that not even the son's heat is enough to warm him. No, for a moment the son's warmth even makes him cold. So he pours himself another shot of aquavit. He doesn't pour anything for the son. Afterward, it's almost nice and the shivers are gone. Now there is just a little snow falling through his soul, and once the snow has melted, there is nothing left, not even the cold.

Bengt, he whispers and puts his hand over the son's hand, whoever is dead is dead. So you have to move on. You have to consider the ones who are living. Sooner or later, we'll be dead, too, Bengt. And it will be good to have lived. Do you know what I mean?

Now the son knows what the father means.

This is why he remains silent. Silent for a long time. Through silence, anyone who is drunk can become a little sober. The fog disperses among the silence and darkness, and the abyss that appears is black and deep, and coldness flows throughout its depths. He frees his burning hand from the father's. Then he places it over his eyes. To be drunk is really only to see beautiful dazzling lights and soft corners where there are usually hard ones. But when you close your eyes, you only see darkness. This is why you can sober up when you close your eyes. Not completely sober but sober enough so that you can sense what is happening. Although you probably can't keep it from happening.

I know, the son says.

Then he is silent again.

But the father is not silent. What has to be done has to be done soon. Everything has to happen quickly for the one who is drunk. Otherwise, it can easily be too late, since being drunk makes silence unbearable.

She is sweet, too, the father says. She is very sweet. You'll think so, too. I think you will like her. Just as much as Alma.

After he said it, he tries to pull the son's hand away from his eyes because he knows how dangerous the darkness is. Afraid, he pulls too hard, but the son's hand doesn't budge. Now the abyss grows deeper and deeper, and the cold is even more piercing. In the end, the son's intoxication is only ice and darkness. This is when he shouts:

I never want to see her! Never! Never! Never!

Immediately, the father says:

I know you don't want to. I know you can't because of Alma. But, son, can you forgive me for seeing her sometimes? Not often, but sometimes. It's not because I've forgotten Alma. I will never forget her. She was so sweet.

Then the ice starts to melt and the darkness begins to recede. Gently, the mist surges through him again after the warmth—which his internal sober self, cold this whole time, has been longing for—emerges unexpectedly from the dark pit. Deep below was a warm well that his father's words created, his last words. No, not the father's but the son's. Because they are his words, after all. They are bright and that makes them beautiful. The son willingly lays his hand on the table.

I will never forget her, he whispers. She was so good.

Now they are both emotional. They look at each other. Then they look at each other's hands.

But I never want to see her, the son whispers.

Why not? the father asks.

Because I miss Mama too much, the son replies.

I understand, the father says.

And in a sense he does understand. In a sense the son understands the father, too. They sit there, finally understanding. Then they toast one more time, to their understanding. But before they go to bed, the father gives the son twenty *kronor.* The son takes the money and thanks him.

He is quite drunk when he enters his room. The light in the room is flashing and making him dizzy, so he leans on his desk. Then he plops down on the unmade bed and whistles as he undresses. It's his first time being drunk. Mother would have never forgiven him. But he forgives himself. Before he slips under the covers, he manages to raise himself up and open the desk drawer. Inside it, there is some money in a book. He counts it over and over again. Finally, he reaches a hundred and twenty twice in a row. It's probably right. Ten lies at ten *kronor* apiece and twenty *kronor* for an hour of understanding comes to exactly that.

The next day, he wakes up late and almost without any remorse. It isn't until he is standing half-dressed in the kitchen—where the father's wallet is lying on the firewood bin and where the shot glasses, but not the bottle, are still sitting out—that he feels a slight pain. So he sits down on the sofa and tries to remember, laying his heavy head in his hands. He remembers that he received some money. Then he remembers that they talked about his mother, and he is tremendously relieved when he recalls that they only spoke well of her. But everything is true when you are drunk and not when you are sober. Yet the things that were true during intoxication don't necessarily lose all their accuracy later. You vaguely remember what was said and you start to brood over it. Then you find that there is some truth to it and that ultimately this truth might be rather significant. He remembers that he called his mother Alma. Then he begins to feel nauseated, so he drinks the last few drops in the shot glass. Once he feels a little better, he realizes there's nothing wrong with it. Her name was Alma, after all.

He gets dressed and shaves. Then he makes some coffee. It tastes bitter, and for no reason at all he grabs the bottle from the cupboard and pours himself half a shot. Surely, it won't be noticed. Another half shot won't be noticeable either, so he pours one more. After having some coffee, he is cheerful. Then he goes into the other room. It is semi-dark because the shades are still drawn, but he doesn't open them, for he has nothing to fear. He sits in the armchair and smokes for a while. Their ashtray is broken, so they use the father's pencil holder instead. He never writes anything anyway. The son sits for a while and stares at the white door to the closet. Then he walks up to it and opens it on a whim. He really only wanted to open it, but once it's open, he steps inside just for the hell of it. He stands there for a moment, breathing in the dingy air of camphor and staleness. Then for no particular reason he opens up a brown cardboard box at the bottom of the closet. There are some old silk stockings inside it. He always thought silk stockings were beautiful. For fun, he takes out the least worn-out pair, and in the light beaming from one of the windows he lets the silk run through his fingers.

Then he sticks his hand into one of the feet of the stocking. His mother's foot had once been exactly where his hand is now, limp and hot. At one time, his mother's foot was a long, tender piece of flesh and sinew encased in a sheer, sheer stocking. He rolls up the shades a little bit and looks at the foot. It's a long, slender foot because his hand is long and slender. It's a young foot, too. He imagines it's his mother's foot when she was young.

He thinks it is a beautiful image, but after thinking about it for a while, he suddenly becomes upset. He doesn't know why. But he puts the box back, closes the closet, and rolls up the shades. He drinks a little more coffee to calm down some more. The coffee is cold and bitter. And to get rid of the pungent taste, he takes another swig of aquavit—hardly half a shot.

But afterward, he's not any less upset. Then he suddenly remembers a pair of keys that were on a shelf in the closet, and for no reason at all he takes them from the shelf. The two keys are thin and shiny, and one of them opens the desk drawer. For the hell of it, he unlocks it and cautiously looks inside. Now he is even more upset.

His hands are shaking, and when he carries the drawer from the desk to the table underneath the light, he doesn't do it for fun. In an instant, his cheeks have become hot and his heart is pounding. He takes out one sheet of paper after the other and spreads them out on the table. They flicker before his eyes as he reads them, but beneath his ruddy glaze of nervousness, he is very cool and clear-headed. Otherwise he wouldn't be able to sort the papers so precisely as he does, exactly as he found them in the drawer.

Some old bills are at the very top. The latest are from January and already paid. Underneath are old scraps of paper, the kind you keep in your pockets for a while and later think a shame to throw away: a restaurant bill saved as a memento of an exceptional celebration; a flier someone got on the street and found interesting; an article that someone clipped from a newspaper, why and which paper was quickly forgotten; or an advertisement, because someone wanted to buy something that was never bought.

Underneath these are letters. He flips through them like a deck of cards. There are three kinds of handwriting because there are three kinds of letters. Some begin with "Dear Knut and Son!" and end with "Mama Alma." Some start with "Dear Alma," and close with "Truly yours, Knut." Finally, there are some that start with "Dear Mama" and far down the page is always "Bengt." He reads through the letters meticulously, and he is no longer trembling. Because it can't be wrong to read your own letters.

With the other key, he unlocks the bookcase. His index finger glides slowly from book spine to book spine and abruptly stops at three books that he knows very well. They are his own textbooks. They were probably sitting out in the room at one time, and the father put them away without saying anything. They are very dusty, so he wipes off the dust and switches them with three other books.

After all the excitement he is very tired, so he lies in bed for a while and smokes. When the sun starts shining in his eyes, he pulls the shades down halfway. He falls asleep at once. And he has a dream as he sleeps. It's a very strange dream. He dreams about a foot. He is holding the foot in his hands, and it is very hot. It is also very beautiful and bare, too. He slowly raises it to his mouth and kisses it. It isn't until then that he notices the foot is dead, dead yet burning. Then someone screams from another room.

But no one has screamed. He was merely awakened by the ringing telephone. With it still sounding like a scream, he unlocks his door and rushes to answer it. He is tremendously relieved to have been woken up and relieved that it was a woman calling. It's his fiancée. She is worried and asks him how he is doing. He asks why she is upset. She admits that she has been worried about him for a long time but that she doesn't really know why. One time she dreamed that something happened to him. Then he asks what, but she doesn't know. Or she doesn't want to say. Then she says something that surprises him.

Bengt, she says, I care so much for you.

She has never said that over the telephone before. He asks her why she is saying it now, but she cannot answer. Then he suddenly notices how warm his body is and how hot his cheeks are. A soft, warm wave of desire is now surging through him.

I have to see you, he says; I have to see you tonight. I have to see you at your place.

And it's true. He has to. Then she surprises him again.

Yes, she whispers, come!

He has never been allowed to come before, and she has never wanted to go to him when he was alone. She said she didn't want to, because of his mother. And now that his mother is dead she says she doesn't want to, because his mother is dead. When he asked if he could come to her, she said that she's a roomer and that it's never quiet there. Someone will be knocking on the wall if you so much as move, so you're never really alone there either. When he then suggested they get a hotel room, she started crying. She didn't tell him why. But after speculating about it, he never suggested it again. There were a few times when they lay next to each other in the grass at Djurgården or Gärdet. But then after a while they always started to get cold and they got up again. And somebody always comes along, even when they think they have the place to themselves. Besides, grass is always wet for people in love. So he had to wash his own handkerchiefs, like Hemingway's sick bullfighter. But since his mother's death, he just throws them away.

After all of that, he is tremendously surprised when she says yes. When he hangs up, he has already forgotten about the dream. He has also forgotten to take the keys out of the desk and bookcase locks. He is simply happy and aroused. Since it's almost five o'clock and the father will be home soon, the son puts a pan on the stove to warm up yesterday's peas. Then he washes two soup plates and two spoons under the faucet. As he's about to put the bottle away, he finds the father's wallet on the table. He immediately grabs it and starts rummaging through the compartments. It happens so fast that his emotions can't keep up. There's nothing unusual in the wallet except for a yellow ticket stub that has a phone number on the back of it. It's clearly a number from Södermalm since it starts with four-zero. Then he hears the black dog barking on the stairs. Sometimes the father takes the dog to work with him in the mornings. Because the barking startles him, he drops the wallet on the table. He thought about writing the number down. Instead, he stuffs the stub inside his pocket.

Over soup, the father asks him how his classes went. The son tells him they went well, but he doesn't tell him any stories. Instead, he tells him that he'll be at Berit's tonight. The father is very happy to hear this, almost as happy as when he hears a funny story. He doesn't really understand why he is so happy. But since the shot glasses are still on the table, he pours them both a shot. As he pours, he notices that the bottle has gotten lighter. Because fathers with grown sons always know how much is in a bottle when they put it away.

When the son reaches the street, he is giddy and in high spirits. He's also a little drunk and doesn't feel the wind. And he thinks it's brighter than it really is. When he turns the corner, he buys a newspaper. There's no streetcar in sight, and as impatient as he is, he cannot stand still. So he crosses the street and continues walking a bit in the opposite direction. When he still doesn't see a streetcar, he goes into a café. He sits by the window and orders a coffee. The streetcar finally comes after he's been sitting for a while. Suddenly, he feels like he's in no hurry at all. This surprises him, but he accepts it because he is used to trusting his instinct. He smokes a few cigarettes and begins to read the paper. After reading for a little while, he sees the father and the dog walking on the other side of the street. They walk right past a beerhouse, but after walking a few yards, the father seems to change his mind, turns around, and goes inside.

The son moves his table toward the wall because the father has also sat in front of a window. He is sitting there and reading, but the dog is not visible.

Then the son gets up and goes over to the telephone at the counter to call his fiancée and tell her that it will be a while before he can come. But when he lifts the receiver, something strange happens: he hears the scrap of paper rustling inside his breast pocket. He takes it out and, on a whim, dials the mysterious number. He listens for a while, but nobody answers. Then it occurs to him that somewhere in some room somebody knows it's he calling. That's why no one is picking up. When he sits down again, he sees the father is still sitting, too. So he sits for a little while longer—actually, for a long time. The father leaves at nine.

At that time, it isn't dark yet but still twilight. A few cars have turned on their headlights. Some streetcars, too. A long streetcar, so long that it doesn't look like it will end, comes clanging by. After it passes, he sees the father running down the street as if it were raining. And it isn't raining when the son leaves the café, but he still marches briskly down the street. When the father and the dog disappear behind a corner, the son moves faster, even though it still isn't raining. When he turns the corner, the father and the dog are gone. Directly on the corner is a tall entrance of a building. He hastily opens the gate and listens, but the building is completely silent. Then he suddenly hears the barking of a dog, not from inside the building but still very close.

A small movie theater called the Lantern is next to the building. And above the entrance there are three lights—white, red, and green—enclosed within a blue lantern. At night there are always a lot of young men smoking outside as well as bareheaded young girls who are eager to laugh. Whenever the picture is over, the attendant with a limp turns off the three lights in the lantern. Then he comes out to lock the double doors and the emergency exit, and then he fastens three large padlocks around the closures of the display case. Lastly, he closes the wrought-iron gate on the street and locks it. Long after the film has ended, the boys and girls are still there. They are loudest and laugh the most right before they leave. In the mornings the display window has been found broken three times already, but no one has ever stolen a photograph. And every morning the ground behind the gate is littered with cigarette butts.

The son goes inside this cinema. The floor slants down toward the box office. A worn red carpet stretches from the box office to the wide doors of the auditorium. He stands still on the carpet and looks around, but the father has disappeared. And no dog is barking. Because he thinks the cashier is looking at him, he buys a ticket to avoid looking silly. He is nervous and forgets a *krona* on the green rubber mat at the register. When she calls him back, he can scarcely resist looking at her. She smiles at him, and as he picks up the *krona,* he smiles back at her. Ever since his mother's death, he thinks all women who smile at him look like her. All assistants, waitresses, and women on stairs. And almost all of them have the same dress as she did. The cashier's dress is red. And there is a large telephone next to her.

The auditorium smells like a cellar. In fact, it used to be one a long time ago, and the smell has never left. He sits at the very back, even though the usher tells him he can sit wherever he wants. And whenever someone comes in, he covers his face with his hands. But by the time the newsreel begins, the father still hasn't come. There are eight of them in the theater, excluding him, and they are all sitting in front of him. There is a draft along the floor, and it's terribly cold. What is more, this is a theater where it always rains in the newsreels, and he has already seen the main feature.

When he leaves the auditorium, he immediately looks back at the cashier to see whether she notices that he is leaving just as the film is starting. But the booth is empty and the light is out. Then he finds the small panel door to the lavatory. He opens it very quietly and looks inside. It's also empty.

As he hurries up the slanted aisle that smells like a cellar and paint, he realizes that he's in a hurry. His anxiety has subsided and his desire has returned. In the taxi he thinks about his fiancée's smooth arms, and when he places his hands on his hips, it is her hips he feels. As the cab drives through an intersection, he sees a girl in a red billowing dress waiting for a streetcar. He has been with a girl before. She had a red coat, but underneath it she had a blue dress and underneath that a white slip. It was in September during his military service. They went into the woods after just one dance and had to search a long time before they found a dry place. Afterward, his knees still got wet, and he ended up with a bad cold. A month later, he saw the girl on the main road in the rain. He saluted her, but she didn't recognize him.

When he reaches the front of the fiancée's building, she is already holding the door open for him. She has been waiting by the window for a long time. At first, she is surprised when he arrives in a taxi. Then she starts imagining things. But she almost always imagines things. She has warmed up some tea on the Meta cooker three times, and three times it has turned cold. They sit down in separate chairs in her chilly room. On one side of the room, someone is learning to play the banjo. On the other side, some men are playing cards, and their bids can be heard clearly through the wall. He suddenly falls to his knees before the fiancée's chair and starts rubbing his brow against her knees. He notices they are harder than he imagined. The fiancée puts her arms around his neck. Then he feels that her arms are hard, too. He has never noticed this before.

After tea, he pulls her over to the sofa with him. It's an old rented sofa with a tall, carved wooden frame. Hanging over the frame is a blue tapestry with white writing: "A woman is a flower. Pick her gently." But when he sits on the sofa, the frame falls down on him, hitting his back.

We can't sit on the sofa, the fiancée whispers, because the back always falls down, and I can't fix it.

Then he lifts up the frame.

If we can't be on the sofa, then we can just lie on the floor, he whispers as he pulls his fiancée's black dress up high above the knee.

He is very aroused and he is breathing very heavily. They knock a chair down as they tumble to the floor. The linoleum creaks beneath the fiancée's body. He is on his knees and when he shifts his gaze from her breasts to her face, he can see she is afraid. But even though she's afraid, she still wants it. She has never wanted it before. She is ugly when she is afraid, but this makes her eyes very beautiful. And her fear doesn't frighten him but it makes him cold—strong and cold. He picks up the fallen chair and sits down on it. When the fiancée gets up, she grabs on to the sofa. Then the frame falls down again. All of a sudden he bursts into laughter. He can't help it, nor can he check his laughter. He thinks he's laughing about the sofa, and when he stops laughing, he thinks the fiancée is crying. But she isn't crying. She is standing in front of his chair and breathing very heavily, as if she had been running. And he is astonished, almost shocked, when she screams.

You can't! she screams and clenches her fists.

I can't what? he says calmly. He thinks he isn't supposed to laugh.

Go, the fiancée whispers.

Then the banjo player stops playing and bangs against the wall. The card players knock, too. Then one of them bids three hearts. And although she is pale, she still walks him out. She tries to kiss him through the crack of the door but only manages to grab his hand, which is cold. Hers is cold, too. Through the window, she watches him as he waits on the street for a taxi. She hopes that a taxi won't come, but one does. She doesn't close the window until much later. Then it occurs to her that she could have made up the bed on the sofa.

As the car starts to slow down in front of the gate, he asks the driver to keep going. He doesn't want the father to see him coming home in a taxi. Whoever is poor is always ashamed to be seen in a taxi. And should he be alone, he will sit in the middle, so that no one will see him. When he finally gets out of the taxi, it is stopped very close to the cinema. Since it's hardly out of the way, he walks up to it and looks at the posters—just as the lights go out. The red light goes out first, then the green and white lights at the same time.

The attendant appears with his padlock. After the gate is closed, he stands around smoking for a while. And since it's so late, some girls are smoking, too. One of the remaining girls is looking at him. Her coat is unbuttoned, and underneath it she is wearing a red dress. But she's too young to look like his mother. When she pulls up her sleeve to look at the time, he sees that she has very spindly arms. He flicks his cigarette through the bars of the gate and leaves.

As soon as he enters the apartment, the telephone rings. And because the light isn't on, he is afraid. So he turns it on before he answers. It's his fiancée. She is crying yet manages to speak every now and then. She says that she's so worried about him that she can't sleep. He is listening, but he doesn't feel anything. Nevertheless, he promises her they will go for a walk the following evening. Behind her crying, he can hear the banjo player strumming his evening entertainment.

When he hangs up, he suddenly finds the ticket stub between his fingers. And for the hell of it, he dials the number. When nobody answers, he feels both relieved and disappointed. Then, while stuffing it back in his pocket, he suddenly remembers with terrifying clarity that he has forgotten the keys in the locks. So he dashes into the other room and turns on the light, but the keyholes are empty. And the shelf in the closet is empty, too. When he steps into the closet, the door suddenly slams shut behind him and he is filled with maddening terror. Then, with clenched fists, he beats the door open. It was only the wind, since one of the windows is open and swinging to and fro. He closes it, but he doesn't pull down the shades. Instead, he draws the ones in the kitchen. The bottle is still on the table. There are just a few drops left at the bottom, but when he empties it, he feels a little warm.

In bed, he lays his pillow against his chest. Pillows are great for the lonely. From a pillow, he can make two soft thighs. He can also make a soft arm that wraps around his body. No one has as soft an arm as a pillow. Nor such a warm arm, since he can make it as warm as he wants. The arm makes him warm. It also makes him less lonesome. He sleeps dreamlessly throughout the night.

At six the following evening he meets his fiancée on the Räntmästare steps. She wants to go to Djurgården, where they can dance at Nöjesfältet and then go home from there. She mentions that she has fixed the sofa.

Which sofa? he asks.

Then he takes her arm and they walk up to Södermalm. They walk up Götgatan and do some window-shopping. The fiancée is so upset that she hardly sees a single display. At the top of the hill, she is out of breath and says they should turn around. Then he tells her that he doesn't have enough money to go to Djurgården, but if she wants, they can go to the cinema. When they reach the Lantern, she says it's a bad theater. They have been to it once before, and it was cold then. Besides, the films are always so worn out. Moreover, they only play bad films. They look at the posters for a bit. He thinks she is taking too long. When they go inside, she mentions that they have already seen the film. He gets upset and says that she has a bad memory.

She buys the tickets because he doesn't have any money with him. But he stands next to her at the box office. When the cashier tears the tickets from the block, she looks at him and smiles. She recognizes him. He smiles back at her because she looks like his mother. She's old enough. Yet she isn't that old. She has a red dress with short sleeves and a little blue spot above her elbow, as though someone has pinched her. Even though it's too early to go inside, he takes the fiancée's arm and they proceed to the entrance. As the attendant tears their tickets, he looks back at the box office to see if the cashier thinks they're silly for going in so early. But she is merely sitting there, gazing out at the street. He is relieved yet disappointed at the same time.

They sit at the very back of the theater. His fiancée wants to sit closer to the screen because she has poor eyesight, but her fiancé says the auditorium is so small that it doesn't matter—and to a certain extent, he's right. Then he tells her that this is where Greta Garbo saw her first film. It isn't true, but his fiancée comes from Härjedalen and doesn't know any better. But as he tells her, he isn't so sure he is wrong.

When the six white half-globes on the naked green walls start to dim, he starts counting the people. Including himself and his fiancée, they are twelve. During the newsreel, he counts them two more times. During the break, he hears the telephone ring, and when the film starts, the fiancée whispers that they have in fact seen it. This doesn't make him upset but cruel. Because she whispered this, he pinches her arm very hard and tells her to be quiet. So she is. And to keep her from crying, he acts as if the pinch was only an affectionate squeeze. So he ends up sitting in the dark and stroking the sore area. He tries to watch the film, but he can't make any sense of it, even though he has already seen it before. And when the ten other people laugh, he laughs with them. His fiancée is not laughing.

They are the first ones to exit the auditorium, and even though he is blinded by the only light in the hall, he immediately tries looking at the cashier to see whether she is looking at him. But she is merely sitting in her booth, looking out at the street. Then he leaves his fiancée by herself and goes to the lavatory. Since it's empty, he stands in front of the mirror and smokes a cigarette. As he smokes, he examines his face. He is bright red and his cheeks are burning. When he comes out, his fiancée is standing underneath the bright light. She is also very red, particularly her lips. When he comes closer, he notices for the first time that she's wearing make-up. She has never worn any before. And when this occurs to him, he merely feels indifferent. Then, on the short walk to the gate, he turns around twice and looks back at the box office. The cashier is looking in his direction—but not at him, exactly. When the fiancée asks what he's looking at, he asks her whether she thinks the cashier looks like his mother. She says she doesn't think so but she does have a nearly identical red dress. Because she said this, he pinches her again. But this time he doesn't caress her.

It is raining hesitantly, and the oil left behind by cars glistens underneath the streetlights. Church bells strike thirteen times, nine strikes of bronze and four of crystal. When they turn the corner, the fiancée wants to look at some baby items in a display window. But she doesn't even get to do that, because he pulls her across the street with him. Soon after they reach the sidewalk, the father comes out of a café farther down on the other side of the street. Then, in the twilight rain, the dog and the father run down the same corner

Bengt and Berit had just turned. As they run past the display window, the fiancée says:

I think that was your dad and his dog.

The fiancé snaps at her and says there are obviously a lot of black dogs in Stockholm. Then they walk back to the display window, but when the fiancée faces it, she can't see a thing. Everything is just a haze of rain and tears. But after drying her eyes, she is finally able to see a little. There is a baby in blue clothing sitting in a high stroller, and a light is shining directly into its rosy face. She doesn't notice when her fiancé lets go of her arm, nor does she notice when he takes two steps back. But he notices. Standing two steps away, he looks at his fiancée as though she were someone he didn't know. He has never done this before and is surprised he's doing it now. But the longer he looks at her, the less surprised he is and the less he recognizes her. The display window is big and bright, and standing in front of it, under the rain, is a skinny girl in black; someone you would normally walk by without noticing; someone you could stand next to in front of a display window or sit with at the cinema and afterward feel as though you've been alone the entire time.

Aren't his clothes adorable? the fiancée asks.

Then the fiancé responds:

I'm not your son.

He never imagined saying something like that before. But he says it all the same. And now that he has said it, he doesn't regret it. They walk straight to his apartment building from the display window. He walks quickly, and when he pays attention, he hears that her shoes have high heels. She is wearing them especially for him. She is also wearing a red dress, although he thinks it's black. When he tries saying good-bye to her in front of the building, she tries to come up with him.

I have to, she whispers.

You have to what? he says rather impatiently, because he suddenly feels he's in a hurry, a terrible hurry.

But when she tries to tell him that she needs to come up with him, someone walks out of the building. It's an old blind woman rapping with her cane. The cane frightens her. Then the knocking frightens her. In fact, almost everything frightens her. But the old woman doesn't see poorly; it's only Berit's fear that has made the old woman blind. Then Berit whispers:

Go!

He kisses her fleetingly on the cheek and leaves. And before the rain has the chance to dry on his lips, he is already four flights up after running the whole way. He is in that much of a hurry. After unlocking the door, he realizes why he's in such a hurry. It's because it is well past nine. He dials a five instead of a four on his first try. Then he dials correctly. It's almost completely dark in the hallway, but he doesn't turn on the light. Now he is afraid of the light.

But he is not afraid of what will happen. For within us, we all carry an image of something dreadful that will happen to us one day when it's very dark; an image of someone we will meet one night when it's very rainy and stormy; an image of someone waiting behind a door for us when we enter a dark room someday. We all carry an image of a ghost within us. And this is why we are never truly afraid at that dreadful encounter, because every time it gets dark, we are already expecting it. A sensation of confirmation mingled with terror is all that we feel.

This is why—when the woman answers in his ear, The Lantern Theater—he can very calmly say into the receiver:

Are there any tickets left for the nine o'clock show?

Yes, the soft voice answers impatiently, but the film has already started.

Sorry, he is able to say and still remain quite calm.

Now Bengt can hang up.

Gun has already done so.

A Letter in April from Himself to Himself

Dear Bengt!

Today at three o'clock it was exactly three months since Mama died. Tonight, while we were eating our soup, Papa suddenly pulled out his watch. After looking at it for a while, he looked at me and asked whether I knew what day it was. I said it was Friday. Then he told me that Mama had died three months ago today. Of course, I knew that, but it wasn't so critical that I had to stand by the window at precisely three o'clock today and think, It's exactly three months to the second since my mother fell off a chair and onto the ground of David Englund's butcher shop. After all, such a thought didn't do any good. It's three o'clock every day. Therefore, you could, strictly speaking, be justified in thinking the same thought every day in front of the window at three o'clock. Besides, three months is a rather arbitrary amount of time, especially in this case. And because February only has twenty-eight days, these three months don't even make up ninety days anyway.

I told all of this to him, not because I wanted to hurt him in any way or to show any lack of respect for Mama's memory, but because of my genuine belief that you can't bind your remembrance of a dead person to a specific time and date. The loss of Mother is constantly alive for me, which is why a fixed date doesn't mean the same to me as it does for someone grieving less. However, I noticed that he was hurt, so in order to soften my words (not because I thought I was wrong in any way, but because I knew that he, with his undeveloped sense of the value of words and of the sincerity of intonation, misunderstood what I had meant), I said, Hasn't it been longer since Mama died? My words didn't express what I was really feeling, didn't express anything at all; it was just a placating phrase purposely meant to reassure him. Since you know him as well as I do, you know how easy it really is to reassure him, if you're clever enough to hit on the right word. But the words I uttered didn't seem to be the right ones, because instead of reassuring him, I made him more upset. Have you already forgotten your mother, Bengt? he asked.

I have to admit that I was genuinely shocked by the question. This was truly the last thing I expected him to ask me. It came so abruptly and seemed so cruel and unfair that I couldn't get a single word out. I was on the verge of asking him what right he had to say something so brutal and untrue to me, but out of consideration for his feelings, I held back my words. You see, everyone who knows him knows just how wrongly, in the truest sense of the word, he treated Mama. And I'm positive that he knows what others think about him, too, so I didn't have to remind him. But I can personally swear to you that I didn't let him off so easily. I personally condemned him a long time ago, and if I could have, I would have abandoned him a long time ago, too.

For the time being, I'm unfortunately dependent on him and his goodwill that allows me to continue my studies. If I had wanted to tonight, I could have pinned him to the wall with one word, one intimation, and forced him to realize how

horribly he wronged me with his suspicion. I remember, for
example, a little episode that occurred the day after Mama died.
It was a Sunday. We were sitting at the table in the other room
and both reading the paper. We hadn't said a word to each other
all day. Then the clock struck three. As I walked to the window,
I said to him: it's exactly twenty-four hours since Mama died.
He didn't respond. When I repeated it, he crumpled up his
paper and left the room. That evening, he didn't wind up the
clock like he usually did on Sundays, so it stopped that night.
And when I asked him why he didn't wind it up, he said that he
had lost the key. It wasn't true then, but it's true enough now, I
suppose.

I could have reminded him of this if I wanted to. But I
don't want to hurt him too much, even though he deserves to
be hurt badly. He is still my father, and I suppose you have to
forgive your father things that you wouldn't be able to forgive
anyone else.

Of course, I'm aware enough of my own feelings about
Mama not to let them be contaminated by insidious questions
from someone who doesn't even have the right to ask them.
The three months since her death haven't meant anything to me
but continuous martyrdom. Now, I know from my own bitter
experience how a dead person is so far from being obliterated
from existence that she instead continues to live on in the acts
and dreams of the one who really loved her. No one can deny
that she hasn't left my side even once this whole time. She is
constantly in my thoughts all day and constantly in my dreams
at night. I once told you that I had a dream about her red dress.
Since then, the dream has recurred in different forms. I'm just
as frightened every time I wake up, but at the same time I get a
feeling almost of happiness at the thought of someone I loved
being so alive in me. I could almost say delight instead of joy,
because in the dream it's truly delight I feel. It's so beautiful yet
frightening at the same time. Twice I have dreamt that I was
holding her foot in my hands. I kissed it both times because
it was so beautiful. I still consider this martyrdom because my

aching for Mama and the forms it has taken against my will have made it impossible for me to work.

For example, yesterday it was my intention to take the exam, but since I couldn't study as I wanted to, I had to pass on it. I had tried by all means to devote myself to studying, but thinking about Mama—perhaps mostly about the pain Papa had inflicted on her—made it truly impossible for me to concentrate. Everything in the apartment is impregnated with her. Every chair you sit on, every spoon you put into your mouth, every stocking you trip over when opening the closet, every handkerchief, every brooch, and every letter that catches your eye as soon as you open a drawer. Sometimes, especially lately, it's even been impossible for me to stay indoors. So I've had to go out for walks, but as soon as I'm outside, I feel absolutely weak. I cannot go very far, so I just roam around the block and come back home. But to avoid going home, sometimes I go to the cinema. And quite often lately. The theater is nice, better than books. And whether you want to or not, you are forced to focus all your thoughts on one thing, on whatever is happening on the white screen.

Papa has been acting quite strangely lately. Sometimes I think he's starting to suffer from a persecution complex. No matter where I go, I run into him and his black dog. I think he's hunting me with that dog, having him track my scent. I can't describe it any other way but that he is constantly on my heels as soon as I leave the house. And the other day, I noticed that he had put a rubber band around the bottle of aquavit, as though he imagines me drinking in secret while he's away at work. His dirty suspicion irritated me and to get back at him I poured myself a pretty large glass and pulled the rubber band down. Besides, it's very stupid to use a rubber band if you want to see whether there's less alcohol in the bottle. All you have to do is move the rubber band.

He's also strange in another way. The other night the dog came into my room, and this was quite unusual. It jumped up on my bed so it could sleep there. I didn't throw it out, because

I've gradually come to like it a little. But instead of sleeping,
it started digging under my pillow with its paws. Soon, it
jumped off and disappeared. After a while, Papa came in with
a handkerchief in his hand. It was a little yellow handkerchief
that the dog had had in its mouth when it left my room. Papa
asked me where I got the handkerchief. I wasn't able to tell
him. Then he tossed it to me and left. It seemed like he actually
thought I went around stealing handkerchiefs. One morning, I
found a pair of Mama's stockings on my bed. I don't know why
he put them there.

He might be acting strangely because, despite everything,
he is grieving. But I did manage to make him happy yesterday.
I was supposed to take the exam yesterday, but because of
everything that has happened to me regarding Mama's death, I
had to postpone it until the fall. In this way, I'll have the whole
summer to study, and I plan to study intensively. So I don't
think I'll get a job this summer as I usually do every year. Of
course, I'll be more dependent on Papa than ever before, but
on the other hand, I really want to finish my studies with a
degree. Otherwise, it would feel like defeat. It just so happens
that I've been talking to Papa this whole time about the exam,
so that he'll see that I really have been working toward an
immediate goal. Immediate goals have a stimulating effect on
him, probably because he thinks they are the cheapest. Without
a doubt, he has high expectations for the exam. That isn't my
fault, but once I finally realized what a great disappointment it
would be for him if I didn't do well on it, I had to pretend as
though I had already succeeded.

When he got home last night, he asked me how it went
as soon as he walked in the door. I never meant to exaggerate,
but when I saw how full of hope he was, I told him that I had
passed with *laudatur.* Since he didn't know what that meant,
I told him it was the best grade you could get. Then I showed
him the exam book. I hadn't actually intended to, but I did it
to see him genuinely happy for once. That day, I had sat around
leafing through the empty book. I had a pen with me, and just

for the hell of it, I wrote *Cum laudatur* and then the professor's name. Since I didn't have anything special to do, I put a little stamp together and placed it below his name. Just for the hell of it. My joke made Papa very happy, and I didn't have the heart to tell him that it was just a joke. Besides, it amused me a little to see how believable I could make the forgery. After all, if a single confession would upset him, and if you don't hurt someone with a little gag but instead make him happy, then there's no reason at all to expose the joke as a joke. And there is just as little reason to be sorry about it.

It's midnight.

He just got home and walked straight into my room. I had a bad feeling. I don't really know why. He said it as soon as he came in. I've been expecting it for a while now, but it was still a shock to hear it. He said that his fiancée is coming to visit us tomorrow evening around nine. She worked till nine, which is why she couldn't come earlier. I didn't say anything. Then he asked whether I had a problem with it. I said that I did. But once I said it, I was sorry I did, and he must have noticed because he said, Invite Berit, too. But he didn't know why I suddenly regretted it. Only I know why. I've known for a long time now that it's necessary for her to come. She has to find out the truth, and I'll be the one to tell it to her. Once she has learned the truth, she will never come back. Nor will she want to see Papa anymore. So she has to come for Mama's sake.

The other night when Berit and I were at the cinema, I jokingly said as we were leaving, I'm the Avenger. We had just watched a film by that name. I didn't mean to frighten Berit, but she got very scared. She was so scared that she told me why she has been so worried about me lately. She's afraid I'm going to hurt the other woman as soon as I find out who she is.

But I know who she is! She's a little cashier at a dirty little theater a few blocks from here. I've seen her a few times. She looks very plain, at least compared to Mama. She has to be very old, though she likes dressing as if she were very young. She has a hoarse voice, probably from smoking. I've heard her voice a

few times over the phone. You see, I once found a scrap of paper
on the table with a phone number on it. Just for the hell of it,
I dialed it and she was the one who answered. Since then, I've
called her a few times at a quarter past nine. That's when she
closes the register. That's also when Papa usually arrives with the
dog to pick her up. She always gets impatient when I call so late,
and it amuses me to keep her from leaving. I also like to hear
her calling out "Hello" without saying anything back to her.
Her name is Gun Berg. That name is much too young for such
an old woman.

So I know very well who she is, and I have even called her.
But otherwise I haven't caused her any harm. But tomorrow I
will tell her the truth, and I'm looking forward to her visit. For
Mama's sake, I've wanted it for a long time now. That's why I
told Papa he could bring her here. But there will be five at the
table, I said. Five? he asked. I'm bringing Mama with me, I
responded. Then he told me that I should be sensible. I retorted
that I would be as sensible as I could. Then he said I was capable
of being very sensible.

Now I'm alone again. Tonight I'll stay awake and think
about what I'm going to say. I've been thinking about it for
several nights now. I bought a candle, too, which is why I've
been waiting for her to come.

But it's late now, Bengt, so . . . good night.

Your Friend

TEA FOR FOUR OR FIVE

SOMETIMES WE DO SOMETHING without knowing why. And once it is done, we are surprised that we did it. Or sometimes we are even afraid. But from the surprise, as well as the fear, comes an explanation. It has to come. Because the unexplained fills us with a dread that we cannot tolerate for long. But by the time the explanation is thought of or uttered, we have already forgotten that it came after—that the deed came first. If we're never reminded of it, because the act corresponds with the explanation, then everything is fine. But sometimes everything is not fine. This is when it suddenly occurs to us that the explanation given to us is mendacious, and that after the consequences of our action become clear to us in light of all that has happened, the explanation reveals itself as a distortion of our true intentions. This is when we experience real dread, because real dread is being unable to rely on your thoughts on their own. Real dread is knowing that your thoughts lie to you, even when you think you are being honest.

It's nine o'clock when the son becomes afraid, nine o'clock at night. They are otherwise ready. The table is set in the other room. Because he is the one who set it, there are five teacups and five saucers and five spoons and five small plates for the cake, which the father has brought home with him. It's also set with five wine glasses because the father has also bought some port wine from the liquor store. The table also has a candle, which is in front of the place setting without a chair. The son didn't put a chair there on purpose. He wants to make it clear that no one should sit there—but that someone should only be present. Otherwise someone else might sit there. And he knows what he's doing because he has spent the entire day planning how everything should be. This is why he hasn't been able to study.

His fiancée has done everything else. She has swept all the floors, including her fiancé's room—even though he didn't want her to. When she asked him why he didn't want her to, he said that his floor was clean. Nevertheless, she went into his room and when she came back out, the dustpan was full of dirt. Amid the dirt was a little yellow handkerchief, rolled into a ball. He let her throw it away, but when she did, he took her by the arm and told her that she shouldn't go snooping around in his room. She didn't understand what he meant, so she started imagining things. But after he said it, he felt sorry. Sorry because he wasn't sure himself what he had meant and because he had hurt her. He regrets almost everything he says to her nowadays. But in spite of this, he still says it.

Other things are done, too. The books are dusted and so are all the picture frames. All the dishes are washed, too. She had to do that on her own because the father just stood by and watched. Well, he did do one thing at least. He brushed the dog. Now its fur glistens black like a woman's fur coat. Then he caresses it as one caresses a woman. At one time, he wanted to buy Alma a fur, but he changed his mind and bought her a big black coat instead. It makes me so ugly, she had said. He replied that it suited her. He was the one who picked it out; he picked it because it made her ugly. He wasn't aware of it then, but he realized it when her clothes came back from the morgue. And because he didn't want anyone else to notice, he hung it up in the attic. He thinks about this as he strokes the dog.

He doesn't do anything else but comb and pet. Well, he does walk back and forth in the apartment, here then there. It might seem aimless, but he's actually following a plan the whole time. He doesn't want to leave the son alone. In fact, since he came home he hasn't left him alone for a single moment. If the son is in his room, he knocks and claims to be looking for something that might be in there. And once he's inside, he doesn't leave. He stands around chatting about this and that and doesn't even notice the son isn't listening until he asks him a question. But it doesn't matter. The most important thing is that the son is not alone.

Berit arrives at eight. She is anxious because she can't find any coffee. She is always anxious, even in ordinary situations, and she breaks a plate in her nervousness. There is no coffee, yet at nine o'clock there is to be coffee for five, or at least four. So the father goes to borrow some from a neighbor. And he takes the son with him. Standing in front of his neighbor's door, the father realizes that this is the first time since the funeral that he's had to deal with a neighbor. A woman opens the door. It's one of the women who came to the funeral. But when she sees the widower something peculiar happens. She doesn't open her door the way neighbors do for other neighbors but peeks through a small slit, which she doesn't open any wider. She doesn't say anything, either. Then the widower asks her if he can borrow a little coffee because they are going to have company at nine o'clock. The woman tells him that she's out of coffee, but perhaps someone else has some. But they do not ask anyone else.

Instead, Berit makes tea. They wait in the other room as the water boils and Berit carries on slamming doors to cupboards in the kitchen. It's very quiet in the other room. The father seems to be looking for a book in the bookcase. And in a way he is. He notices that the son's textbooks have been moved, and when he notices, he looks immediately at the son. The son is standing by the desk, which has a pen without a penholder and a dried-out inkwell on it. There's also a little glass jar with green beads in it that you're supposed to dab your pen into when you're done writing. This makes the beads rather dirty but the pen very clean. For fun, he picks up some beads and starts rolling them back and forth across the desk. Five beads don't make a lot of noise, so he grabs some more. Yet not even ten beads make enough noise to drown out what he doesn't want to hear. So he puts the beads back and starts banging on the desk with an ink-stained ruler. But he can still hear it. The father hears it, too. It's because of this that the father is looking at the son. And it's because of this that the son is not looking at the father.

What they hear is the noise from the kitchen. In the silence of the room they realize it hasn't been noisy like this for three months. And suddenly it's like a grave has been opened. At once, they remember her with a terrible, crystal-clear clarity. Does he remember Alma? Does he remember Mama? Maybe. Yet in a sense it isn't she they remember. It's the racket she made whenever she was in the kitchen and they were in the other room. A twenty-year-old noise. The rattling of spoons pulled from a drawer, the slamming of drawers, the sharp clinking of china against china, the scraping of chairs across the floor. Now she is back after being away for three months.

This is when the ghastly certainty strikes the son. It strikes the father, too, but it can't frighten him the same way; it can only arouse a few minutes of uneasiness. But it hits the son with such force that he intentionally knocks over the glass jar with the green beads in it, so that he can lie on the floor without being suspicious. The linoleum is nice and cool. And to see the beads better, he lays his face on it, making his face nice and cool, too. Then he slowly begins refilling the glass. Before it's filled, the father cries out to the kitchen:

Berit, he yells, sing!

Then she starts to sing because he yelled at her to sing. She will do anything if you yell at her. She will even do anything if you simply ask her. This is why some people like to ask her to do impossible things. "Pull down the moon, Berit," you want to shout, or "Put out the sun!" And if you do, Berit will cry. Not because you are being mean but because she can't do it.

In any event, it's good that she is singing. Not because they can really hear what she's singing, but because what they do hear is enough. They hear that it's not Alma in the kitchen. They hear that it's someone completely different. Yet they don't hear Berit. Because that's not what they want to hear. And as she sings, the father straightens out the chairs at the table. They are fine where they are, but the son is the one who put them where they are. So it's good to move them around. Meanwhile, the son thinks there aren't many beads left to find, but when he's done picking them up, he sees there aren't as many in the glass as there were before. There never is. They've upset the jar of green beads several times and some were always missing. There was only one time when none was missing. That time, Alma knocked it over while dusting, and they had to help her move the daybed because several of them had rolled underneath it.

Now the son doesn't have to move the daybed, because Berit is singing. Had she been singing the whole time, he wouldn't have needed to knock over the jar. And he wouldn't have needed to know what he now knows—incidentally knows. We get to find out a lot of things. But much of what we learn, we forget. Even though it's often said that we don't forget anything. And by the time he puts the jar of green beads back on the desk behind the inkwell, he has already forgotten what the sensation of certainty meant. It was horrible, and horrible things are the easiest to forget. But they are also the easiest to remember. Before Berit started singing, he was standing by the desk and thinking that it isn't his mother he's been missing for the past three months. It's the noise that came from her being alive.

Berit comes singing into the room, but when they realize it's she, they ask her to stop. Then she tells them it's nine o'clock. The clock hasn't chimed, because it has stopped. And it has stopped because the key is gone. One evening, almost all the keys were gone. But out of habit the father still looks at the clock. For a month now, the father has been used to it showing half past eleven when he wakes up in the daybed in the mornings, and the same time when he turns out the lights at night.

Now it is showing three o'clock.

It's impossible, but when he looks at the dial again, it still shows three. Then he looks from the dial to the son, who is standing by the window. And it's by the window where the son will become so dreadfully afraid. In fact, he didn't even realize he had gone up to it. But standing there, all of a sudden he knows he is there because he wants to look down at the glistening bull's head, look at it and remember—because it's three o'clock. Now it is always three. So he should stand by the window forever.

It's three o'clock, or a few minutes past nine, and everything is ready. Berit, however, can't seem to accept that everything is ready. She moves the cups and plates around, arranges the heap of cookies so that they look beautiful, moves the glasses from their places, and puts the wine bottle in a new spot. Not even the cake may stay where it is. She suddenly takes the cake tray and puts it on top of the plate at the fifth place setting. Since this causes one cup to be left over, she turns it over and hides it in the shadow of the large cake. But this also leaves a candle, so she puts it at the place setting where it was never meant to be. She puts everything in place. Berit always puts everything in place. She does this because she means well. When she is finished, it is still three o'clock but several minutes past nine, and instead of a table for five, it has suddenly become for four. The father sees this and keeps it to himself. But Berit doesn't notice.

The son hasn't noticed anything either. He has been standing with his back to everything and only heard that something had happened but not what had happened. Finally, the commotion at the table stops. Then the father coughs and says:

What are you doing at the window, Bengt?

He did ask gently and friendly, but the crushing answer is still painfully clear. There is only one answer, and Bengt already has it on the tip of his tongue: Because it's three o'clock, he wants to say. Really, the father would say, is it three? I thought it was ten past nine. He would say this, too, very warmly because he is being nice tonight. He is afraid and when he's afraid, he is always nice. But even though he is being nice, there is also only one answer to his other question, and even this answer is crushing: Look at the clock yourself. Don't you see it's three? Since Mother died, your clock is always three.

All of this should have been said, but it isn't said. He only gives the first answer and not the others. This is partly because the father says something he isn't supposed to say. And partly because the son becomes afraid.

Because it's three o'clock, the son answers. And you know very well why I'm at the window at three o'clock.

This is true. The father does know. But because he knows, he doesn't ask why the clock has been changed. In fact, he knows that he shouldn't ask. Besides, he knows that he wouldn't be able to prove it. So he says:

To think that they took the head down.

By *head* he means the gilded bull's head above the doors of the butcher shop. It's been gone for a few days now, probably so that it can be freshly gilded or because someone suddenly noticed that it wasn't exactly pretty. Nevertheless, one might consider this a rather harmless statement about a harmless fact. But it terrifies the son immensely. Standing there at the window, the son looks out and notices something absolutely dreadful: he has failed to see that the head is gone. At once, he realizes his thoughts are deceiving him. He didn't go to the window to see the butcher shop straight across from him. He wasn't standing there because it was three in the afternoon, but because it's almost a quarter past nine in the evening. He is standing there so he can see her coming.

When he realizes that this is the reason, the son feels genuine dread. Then he starts to hate not himself or his thoughts but her, the one who is coming, because she is the one who duped him with his own thoughts. And anyone who does such a thing to us deserves our hate.

For a few minutes it's absolutely silent in the room. And amid the silence, the father starts feeling bad. And he feels bad because he's afraid of what might happen because of his own carelessness. But he only regrets his carelessness. And nothing else. At one point in the evening, the son put his coat out so that his fiancée could brush it outside in the hallway. The father stood there feeling the pockets, explaining that he was looking for matches. When he felt nothing hard in them, nothing that felt like a weapon, he started laughing. Berit thought he was laughing at her and started imagining things. But he was laughing at his own fear, which had allowed him to believe that his son was armed. He wasn't laughing before this. Nor was he laughing after. Because now he was imagining all the things one could hide in the pockets of a pair of pants.

As for Berit, she is merely afraid in the silence. She has nothing to be sorry about. She only has to put things in place, and she has already arranged a few things. And now that it's so quiet, she notices for herself that there will only be four at the table, four people for tea, some who love each other and because of that love, there is someone who hates one of them and maybe more. She is afraid of hate, and she herself has never hated anyone. She has only ever liked people, because she's also a little afraid of love. The only thing she isn't afraid of is to like. Quietly, she moves the cups and glasses around a bit so everything will be just right. It's a quarter past nine when she lays the matches next to the candle.

Then the son sees her coming. Alone in the bright night, which has its own natural lamps, she turns around the corner. Then she crosses the street. She is walking quickly in a short unbuttoned fur coat that glistens as it catches a ray of the twilight sun. In one hand she is holding a bouquet of flowers wrapped in tissue paper. She holds the bouquet with the flowers pointed down because it's easier to carry it that way. With her other hand, she is clutching her coat so that it won't blow open. However, a tiny slit remains and through it he can see she is wearing a red dress. The dress is as short as the fur coat. His mother's red dress was long, partly because she was tall, partly because she didn't like short dresses. She steps onto the curb, where a red bicycle is. She doesn't have particularly long legs, but they are quite fair underneath the dark fur coat. And when she looks up at the apartment, he notices that she is blonder than he imagined. He also sees that she's wearing a black hat over her blonde hair. Furthermore, he notices that she must have already known where they live because she looks straight at their window. He takes two steps back into the room and stands with his back to it.

Then the father knows she is coming, and Berit does, too. So she arranges the cookies so they will look even nicer. The widower looks at her and when they look at each other, he nods to her and walks away. She nods back, but her face has turned bright red. The son stays where he is. And when the doorbell rings, he continues to stay where he is. But only for a second. Because when it occurs to him that no one has rung their doorbell for three months, he walks over to the desk. A white sheet of paper is on it, the back of an unpaid bill. He puts the jar of green beads on top of it so that it won't blow away. Then he fills it with meaningless scribbling with his pen. As he is scribbling, the door opens and the entrance is filled with an even greater silence than before. At first, only the dog can be heard, then a subdued voice. Berit quickly moves behind her fiancé so that she won't be so dreadfully alone. But because what he wants to do calls for a moment of quiet solitude, he grows irritated with her and leaves the desk. He also leaves the sheet of paper he was writing on. When the fiancée looks at the note, she sees that the scribbles he made aren't entirely meaningless. In fact, they make a name, and when she deciphers it, she grows even more afraid than she already was. She crumples up the scrap of paper and stuffs it into the jar of beads.

The son is standing by the bookcase, but he isn't looking for a book. He is not even looking through the glass. He is looking in the direction of the door. It is open, so everything being said in the hallway can be overheard, as well as everything not being said. In front of the doorway, there is a curtain that his mother once put up to make it look nicer. When she put it up, she thought it was beautiful, but they thought it was ugly. And this is why it hasn't been used for three months. They hardly even noticed it was there. But earlier when he was alone, he pulled it across and it stayed that way the whole evening. Now Berit is squeezing his hand so that she won't have to be lonesome. Irritated—nearly disgusted, really—he feels that it's clammy.

Because the curtain is there, he doesn't see them at first. He only hears their footsteps approaching, one set is gentle, light, and brisk, and the other is heavy, deep, and squeaky. The footsteps stop behind the curtain for a moment. Then the curtain rings rattle as the father sharply slides it open. Because the son was listening to their footsteps, it is their feet he sees first. Or shoes, to be precise. The woman slowly entering the room has black shoes, and they are very beautiful. There was only one other time, he thinks, when he had seen such beautiful shoes. But he can't remember when.

Now she comes so close to him that he has to look up so it won't seem like he's bowing. And when he does look up, he sees flowers. They were not for the father since they are still wrapped in white paper. The footsteps stop again, and the flowers are raised up to him, as far as they can go, right up to his chest, making him go cold inside.

How do you do, Bengt? Gun says.

Bengt looks at Gun. Coolly, like he imagined he would, maybe not exactly, but it isn't warm either. If anything, it's a look of confusion, as he is also confused. When you intend to be harsh, the person you want to be harsh to must behave the way you expect her to. Otherwise, you won't be harsh at all, but instead how you're normally supposed to be.

He didn't expect flowers. If he had expected them, then he would have planned it so that he would have taken the flowers and plopped them on the daybed, letting them just lie there. But now he takes them and stands in the middle of the room as everyone quietly watches him unwrap the tissue paper. It's a lot of paper, which is why there's much silence. When the paper is unwrapped, he has five roses, five red roses, in his hand. He doesn't know what to do with them, but he knows what he ought to do with them. He knows that he should give them back, that he should be firm, with a piercing glare, a stern voice, and that he should say harsh words: Thanks, he should say, but keep your roses. Roses are inappropriate for mourning. Especially red roses.

That's when Gun first notices Berit. It's often the case with Berit that even when you know she will be there, you don't see her. She must be somewhere else, you think. But then you hear that she's in the room, after all. Even furniture can let you know it exists, because it creaks. And when you do see her, you find her standing with her back to you. It's not until later that you realize she isn't standing that way at all. It's just that her face and the front of her body can sometimes convey a solitude and silence that only a back can convey.

Hello, Berit, Gun says.

Then Berit extends her hand to Gun as if she's handing her a gift. Behind them, the father is watching the two women. Berit is a bit taller and therefore thinner, too. Berit has straight black hair and straight legs. He doesn't like women with straight legs. And he doesn't think Berit is pretty. What he does find attractive is that Gun is looking at Berit like a mother. He finds mothers very attractive, especially beautiful mothers. But because they were looking at her for so long, Berit turns red and dashes off to the kitchen to look for a vase.

Then the father says:

Let's sit down then.

As soon as he says it, he remembers he had said it once before, but he can't remember where. Then he looks at the son to see if he remembers, but he doesn't seem to recall either. He is merely standing there with the flowers. The roses are very red, but Bengt is very white. After standing for some time, he goes to sit down, holding the flowers in his hands the whole time. With both hands, though he only needs one. When he sits down, he notices there are five roses. Then, when he looks up, he notices the table is only set for four. So that they will be five again, he stuffs the flowers in the vase that Berit brought him and lights the candle. As soon as he lights the candle, he notices that Gun is watching him. The father is also watching him. Berit, too.

What are you looking at me for?! he wants to shout. But he only shouts with his eyes. It's the only yell he can get out. Deep down inside him, the other cry, the real cry, is buried. It's an egg buried underneath the baking sand, and it has to get much hotter before it will hatch. Then, once it has hatched, it will come out, but no one will know what it's going to look like until the shell cracks. Not even he will know.

But even the roaring of his eyes can be heard. At least the father hears it. This might be why he is scratching his ear and keeping quiet. But Berit is holding one hand to her mouth as if she were the one who wanted to scream. And she probably does. Because she has suddenly discovered something that frightens her more than all the other things she has recently seen. What she noticed is that the candle, which is just starting to blaze, is in front of Gun. She is the one who put it there, but she wasn't exactly sure she did it since she often does things that later surprise her. She is usually afraid of what she has done, and lately she is almost always afraid. Her sofa also broke again, and she doesn't dare sleep at night. She is afraid of her own fear. But now she is afraid of the candle.

But she doesn't really have to be afraid. Because nothing ever happens with the candle, nothing else but that a flame flares up searchingly high, like flames usually do. But after that, the candle burns like an ordinary candle. After lighting it, Bengt sits down between his mother and his fiancée. Yes, his mother. Because even though it's true that a white cake is on her plate and that her cup is turned over in the shadow that the tall cake is casting over a small portion of the table, he still knows she is there. And he knows that they know she is there. Even she who is sitting behind the candle knows it because she can't possibly think someone would light it for her. She can't believe that a son in mourning would light a candle for the one who has hurt the deceased. Therefore, he purposely leaves the candle there. In the end, the candle will burn her and whoever is burnt suffers greatly. Whoever is burnt will also remember why she is burnt. Every time she looks at her hands, she will remember.

For the time being, however, she doesn't burn herself. Probably thanks to the father. Because he takes the candlestick by the base and slowly moves it to the center of the table. Bengt watches his hand as he moves it. It isn't burned but it's afraid, because it grips it harder than a candle needs to be gripped. The father's hand grips it so tightly that Bengt can see that it knows what candle it's really moving. So that she will know, too, Bengt moves the candle back with one hand and offers her a cookie with the other. As she takes it, she says with an air of surprise:

What happened to your hand, Bengt?

Suddenly, he lets go of the candle and nearly drops the plate. Then he puts both of his hands on his lap.

I burnt myself, he answers without looking at anyone. I burnt myself on a candle.

It must have been quite recent, Gun says.

She looks at him when she says it. Then the father looks at her and wants to say something, wants to tell her what's really going on, partly to correct a mistake, partly to say anything, because he knows that silence is dangerous. Just as he's about to tell her, he realizes that he can't. Because then he would have to talk about a time that burnt, so he talks about something else. He talks about the weather.

But Gun was right. Bengt has burnt himself quite recently. At three o'clock he burnt himself on the candle. On a whim, he put it on the table to see how it would look. For fun, he lit it. But just for a little while so that it wouldn't be too short at nine o'clock. When he decided to put it out, he tried doing it with his hands by squeezing the flame, as people sometimes do to flames. Then he burnt his hands. He had forgotten to spit in them first.

Candles can be dangerous, Gun says after the father stopped talking.

Yes, Bengt responds. Just *yes.*

It isn't much. He had wanted to say more, and he even knew what he should have said. Especially some candles—he should have said—the ones that burn at funeral meals. But it's hard to say something like that. Much harder than he imagined. In fact, it's difficult to do anything at all, except for looking down at his hands and grabbing a cookie now and then. After all, there is little we can do when we're sitting at the same table and drinking tea with someone we hate. Judas himself could be sitting at our table, and we wouldn't ask him about Jesus. We would talk to him about the weather.

Although, there's actually a lot you can say about the weather. And only a moment after the father stops talking about it, he begins talking about it all over again. He says the weather is good, damn good, you could even say. Gun says it's wonderful walking weather, but terrible for the cinema. Berit has nothing to say about the weather because she hasn't noticed it. She has had a lot more to notice. Besides, she usually only notices it when it rains, because she likes the rain a lot. But Bengt says:

Yes, it's nice now, but it wasn't so great in January. There was a lot of snow. And it was so windy that you always had watery eyes.

Then the father notices that it's burning up in the room. Bengt notices, too. What he also notices is that he hasn't noticed it from the beginning, and this bewilders him. As for Berit, she drops a spoon, and it's good to drop spoons when you sense it heating up. Maybe even Gun senses it. Then all of a sudden, she looks at Bengt, silently and for a long time. The father notices before the son does. The father thinks she looks at him beautifully, beautifully like a beautiful mother. But when Bengt notices, he is quite mystified again. He doesn't like that she is looking at him, but he does notice that she has rather lovely eyes. Then he likes it even less. Because the one you despise cannot have beautiful eyes. Not because you really think they're ugly, but because you don't want them looking at you. So he lowers his eyes.

Don't you come to the theater sometimes, Bengt? Gun asks.

No, pretty rarely, he answers rather sullenly. I haven't been there for quite a while. I don't like going to the cinema.

But I think I've seen you at the Lantern, Gun says.

Then Bengt replies that he almost never goes to the Lantern. It's silly to say this and stupid to lie because he knows she must recognize him. Still, he can't keep from lying. Then it's even stupider to have lied, because Berit says:

But Bengt! We've been to the Lantern several times lately. Of course, you remember.

It's absurd for her to say this. Quite meaningless, too. Strictly speaking, it doesn't matter whether Bengt goes to the cinema or not. Or to which theater he goes, either. But she says it all the same. Because the one you love isn't supposed to lie. At least not so that anyone will notice it. This is why she thinks she says it. But after she said it, it occurs to her that maybe no one noticed that Bengt lied. This frightens her and to distract them from what she had said, she sweeps it under a haze of words.

But she also rambles because she knows that silence is bad. For she has suddenly become terrified of the silence, just as much as the father was. And whenever she speaks quickly and frantically, her accent comes out without her noticing it. Only the others notice it. And suddenly the son realizes that her dialect is vulgar. Sitting there, listening, he is surprised that he hasn't noticed it before. The father thinks her accent is ugly. He usually likes accents—but beautiful accents, the accents of beautiful women. Gun smiles.

Berit talks about a sofa, the sofa in her room, the kind of back it has, and how it falls off whenever you sit on it. This makes Gun smile. The father does not smile. Nor does Bengt smile. Soon they are just uncomfortable. They think it's so embarrassing that Berit is so odd right off the bat that they can't bring themselves to smile. A person should never show herself to be stranger than she's presumed to be. Otherwise, the audience, which everyone has at her performance, becomes disappointed. Not because the new show is bad, but because it's new. Someone who has just appealed to our compassion, to our melancholy, or to our fear cannot suddenly start experimenting with our joy as she has just experimented with our earnestness! Too much cannot be contained in one and the same person. Otherwise we become skeptical, and we don't like anyone we're unsure of. And the person who seems to boast everything— we hate her, because it's against the rules of the performance to have it all. The truly popular people are actually the monotonous ones, the ones who are always themselves, that is, the ones we believe them to be.

Therefore, it's a relief for both of them when Berit finally stops talking. The father wipes his brow, which is now sweaty. Maybe it's the candle that's too warm. Bengt takes the cake from his mother's plate and holds it in front of Gun. Then his hands start to tremble, because if Judas were to sit at our table, we would talk to him about the weather, of course, but if we were to offer him a pastry, our hands would tremble. He thinks they are shaking with hatred, so the son is pleased with his hands. But as soon as he is pleased, they no longer shake.

As Gun slices the cake, he studies her face. He looks at it through his mother's candle. Gun is looking at the cake, which is why he dares to look at her. The candle is burning very brightly, and through the flame he sees her face as it is when it's alone; how it looks when it thinks no one is watching it; how it looks when it sleeps. Now it has dark shadows under the eyes and lines around the mouth, fine, like needle marks. Now her face is forty years old and he wants the father to see it, too. So he says to the father:

Would you mind holding the cake for a moment?

But it's already too late. His triumph has died out. Gun looks at him and smiles, smiles and says:

Are you tired, Bengt?

He doesn't manage to avert his eyes, so he's able to see that when she looks at him her face is younger—not young but somewhat younger. Because of this, his hands tremble some more when he hands the cake to his father. And when he tries to hide the shaking, it only makes it worse.

As they eat the cake, drink the last of the tea, and sip the wine, the candle continues to burn. It burns all alone because nobody is looking at it. And because nobody acknowledges it, it's no longer the mother's candle. It's just an ordinary candle, purchased one day at a department store. But to transform the candle and to break the silence, which is deep and dangerous, Berit bangs her cup on her saucer and says:

What a nice candle. I haven't seen such a nice candle since the funeral.

She didn't mean any harm by what she said. She never means any harm. She only meant well, only wanted to get Bengt to see how much she cares for him, how much she is on his side, for she was suddenly struck with a curiously emetic certainty of what the most important thing is: to make sure, above all else, that he is not alone. Even so, it's as if he didn't understand what she said, because as soon as she says it, he glares at her. And the horrifying thing is that his eyes are not grateful. The horrifying thing is that they don't understand a thing. The horrifying thing is when his mouth sharply asks:

Berit, what kind of accent is that?

But for him it's horrifying because he knows she didn't say it with an accent. So he hopes she won't answer. And she doesn't. She doesn't say anything for a very long time, not until everything they have to drink is drunk and everything they have to eat is eaten. She gets up quickly and says with a lonely, high-pitched voice:

I suppose I'll clear the table.

Then the son blows out the candle because he doesn't want to burn himself again. In silence, Berit gathers up the cups and the plates. But the silence seems to be too deep for the father, too. He gets up quickly and the moment he stands up, all three of them know that he is now the Comedian who will entertain them, the one we see at every party, the one who would travel the world to be funny at all costs.

He pushes Berit back in her chair because the Comedian is here and he is going to clear the table in the world's funniest away. He rattles some spoons and makes a racket with cups and clinks the glasses because the point for the entertainer and the ones who are watching in fear is that it should never get quiet. The thing that makes the loudest noise, however, is in his pocket. He had anticipated it would get so quiet that he would have to entertain, so he asked a coworker named Fritz, who entertains all the time, what the funniest thing to do is. Then Fritz gave him something that would really please his company. It's nothing special, just a piece of metal, in fact. You have to drop it for it to be interesting, and when you drop it, it sounds like someone spilling a load of porcelain from a tray.

So he puts it on the tray. To make them laugh even more, he then puts only three cups on it and walks into the kitchen. He purposely stumbles on the threshold as he drops the piece of metal. They find it very funny, and when he comes back with the empty tray, he drops that, too. They think it's very amusing the first three times, but by the tenth time they are slightly bored. By then, Berit is the only one who laughs.

Bengt does not laugh. Because when the father goes into the kitchen with the last of the wine glasses and, as usual, trips on the threshold, he suddenly notices something strange about the father's back: he doesn't recognize it. That's the peculiar thing, and since he doesn't recognize it, he thinks, Is this man really my father? Is my father a clown?

As soon as he thinks it he is sorry, because it hurts to think about his father that way. Feeling guilty, he happens to look at Gun—not intentionally but inadvertently. Just then, the piece of metal falls on the hallway floor again and he sees what she is thinking. She is smiling with that strained smile one has when the one you love is making a fool of himself, smiling and thinking, Can that man be my future husband? Then she senses someone is watching her, and when she sees that it's Bengt, she smiles at him. But in his confusion, he sees that this smile is different. Confused, he smiles back. He knows that he shouldn't, knows what he ought to do instead. Be stern and harsh and don't smile. But even if Judas were to drink tea and port wine with us, we would smile back at him, too, if he smiled at us. But then we would leave the room.

Therefore, when the father comes back, the son says that he and Berit have to leave. The father is happier than he lets on because if they didn't leave, he would have to continue entertaining them. In which case, he would put the candlestick on the tray and be forced to let it fall. He is happy to be absolved.

I suppose you won't be out long, he says as he stuffs the piece of metal in his pocket.

The son hears the joy in his voice and replies:

Well, I'm just taking Berit home. And we'll probably walk, at least to Katarina Elevator.

Before they leave, Gun breaks off a rose and sticks it in Bengt's buttonhole. She stands close to him and her perfume fills his nose and mouth. The father is standing with the tray under his arm and thinks it's a lovely gesture. That's how a mother should behave. He wants the two of them to like each other, like a mother cares for a son and a son his mother. So he's irritated when Gun extends her hand and Bengt doesn't take it. To avoid shaking her hand, he pretends to be looking for some matches. But the father still forgives him because he is leaving.

Once Berit and Bengt reach the street, Bengt has a headache, so he wants Berit to take the streetcar. Nowadays, he always lets her take the streetcar, but he always gives her money for it. Bengt thinks the streetcar stop is too far, but Berit thinks it isn't far enough.

You should have shaken her hand, Berit says.

Then Bengt lets go of her arm, but Berit takes it again because she's afraid of leaving him alone right now.

I don't want to shake *her* hand, he says. I never will.

Then, Bengt, she asks, curiously relieved, why did you take the flower?

At once, Bengt rips the flower from his buttonhole and chucks it into the gutter. He also tears his arm away.

On his way back, he checks to see whether the flower is still there. It is, but someone has stepped on it in the dark. His headache has subsided, but now he feels a strange wave of heat in his body that he usually only feels after certain dreams, a heat wrapped in a thin layer of fear. Earlier, he experienced something strange. He tried to forget it immediately, but since it wouldn't let itself be forgotten, it was part of the reason why he left the apartment. They were still sitting at the table. Gun suddenly tells his father that she must have a rock in her shoe, so he kneels down at her feet—clumsily yet well meaning. At once, the son notices that the curtain is no longer drawn, so he gets up and pulls it across. He stays by the door for a while, straightening some of the rings that had gotten tangled up together. When he turns around, the father has just taken off Gun's shoe. Now he is holding her foot in his hands. Then the son is suddenly shocked when he realizes that he recognizes the foot, that he has seen exactly the same foot once before in his life. Even though it's a preposterous thought and a preposterous feeling, shivers run down his spine.

Now when he tries entering the dark building, another strange thing happens. He is already standing with his keys in his hand when he suddenly puts them back in his pocket. For he feels he can't go inside. The feeling is so overwhelming that he starts shivering again. Instead, he walks across the street and stands in the doorway next to the butcher shop. A thin veil of rain separates him and the building they live in. The night's dark clouds spill over the roof, thick as pitch. I have to wait until she's gone, he thinks and looks up at the window. The candle is burning in the other room, and the windows are closed. He creeps farther into the darkness of the doorway and prepares to wait a while. But, standing in the doorway, he is struck by something else that had just happened, something extraordinary.

When they were on the way to the streetcar, he suddenly grew irritated with Berit, partly because he was forced to walk in the rain with her—it had just started to rain then—and partly because she was holding his hand and squeezing it so hard. Then all of a sudden he snaps, Do you always have to wear that damn black dress? Then she stops in front of a display window and unbuttons her coat. Underneath her coat is a red dress. But it's dark red, so he can be forgiven. But then she asks, Did you see what dress she was wearing? A red one, he must say since he did in fact see it. It was your Mama's dress, Bengt, she says. Then he becomes terribly upset that she's lying, because he had seen for himself that it wasn't her dress but a different one altogether. And a son should know his own mother's dress. And your Mama's shoes, too, she added. Then he becomes so upset that as soon as the streetcar is visible around the curb, he storms away from her. Bengt! she yells after him so that people stop and stare. Bengt! Bengt! But it's raining, so he's in a hurry to get home. That's why he didn't even turn around.

Now there's only a small lamp on in the other room. And when the curtains are drawn, he slowly leaves the doorway. Now he knows she is leaving. He lights a cigarette as she proceeds down the stairs, but it's raining harder now and the rain puts it out. Somebody is coming out the door. The rain is dreary. All he can see is a shadow and an umbrella that quickly dissolves into the rain. Then he runs across the street. He runs up the stairs, too. Although the pouring rain was cold, his body is burning. But his head is cool. Quietly, he rushes up to the fourth floor, but even though his head is cool, he doesn't know why he is so quiet. Nor does he understand why he sticks the key into the keyhole so gently, as one sticks a finger in his lover's mouth. He just does. He doesn't turn on the light as he stands in the dark entrance. He feels inside the dog's basket; it's warm but the dog isn't there. Then he walks silently through the hallway and up to the door of the other room. He doesn't hear a sound from inside. The father must be writing. Cautiously, he opens the door, and it doesn't creak because the father has greased all the hinges, so they wouldn't creak when he was alone.

As soon as Bengt sees it, he slams the door and runs to the entrance. Like a whip, the scream stings the back of his neck. He opens the front door, slams it shut again, but stays inside. Gasping, he thrusts his burning brow against the cool doorpost. Suddenly, the tension fades and he feels himself turning completely soft inside, not a hard bone is left in his body, not a single taut muscle. Just a floating, hot mass that burns against the walls of his body. A minute later, when the mass has cooled off and his body has gotten its bones back, he realizes that what he had seen—a naked woman's body on his mother's daybed—is not the worst part. The worst part is that he knew he was going to see it but that his mind concealed it from him.

He hears voices from the room, one calm, low, and deep and the other light, rather high-pitched, and very worried. Eventually, both voices are calm and subdued. They think he ran out. And they know how it is with young people; they run away, thinking they'll never come back. But the older ones left waiting in the room know very well they'll come back very soon. Then quiet footsteps approach their door. A streak of light flashes in the hallway but goes out the same instant. Afterward, someone comes pattering out toward the entrance.

It sounds like a frightened human being, but it's a dog. It finds him in the darkness with its soft nose and is friendly to him. Then he quietly opens the door and entices the dog out. It isn't difficult. He has the leash and thinks about walking the dog around a couple of the dark blocks.

But when he reaches the end of the stairs, he goes out to the yard instead. He doesn't turn on the yard light. And even though the yard is dark, he still seeks out the darkest spot behind a tall carpet-beating rack. There, he takes the dog by the nose and grips it tightly so that it won't bark. Then he starts beating it with the leash. As he flogs it, the dog twists around, trying to free its nose from his grip, but he is too strong and unyielding. Sometimes it falls on its back, but it still can't break free. And every blow causes Bengt pain because he's actually beating himself, and it's his own mouth he has to clench shut so that he won't scream out in agony. Or with joy because he is hitting her, too. Instantly, he realizes it's her dog.

Then a patch of the yard is suddenly bathed in light. Someone has turned on the light, so he stops thrashing and falls to his knees over the dog's body. It's writhing around like a snake but cannot break free. Window after window, he glimpses a flash of her distinct silhouette gliding down the stairs. After the last window, he hears her footsteps echoing from the front entrance. Then the door reverberates as it shuts again. When the light goes out, he notices for the first time that it's raining. He is drenched in a brew of sweat and rain, and his shoulders are throbbing. At the same time, he is listless and wrung out like a wet rag. He puts the leash back on the dog. As he leads it across the yard, he holds it on a very short leash so it won't bite him.

After he turned on the light, he falls to his knees before the animal in a vestibule and is affectionate. He gently wipes the gravel and rain from the dog's back. He rubs its upper neck and embraces its hind legs. Finally, he looks it in the eye. In that moment, he knows that the dog can never have the kind of eyes he wants to see. Cold with shame, he drags it upstairs with him.

The worst thing about hitting animals is that you can never ask them for forgiveness. And you can never get forgiveness. Though, in the end, forgiveness is the only thing you need.

A Letter in May from Himself to Himself

Bengt!

I'm all alone as I write this, alone in my room. And he's alone
in his. The other night he asked, Shall we play a game of chess
like we used to, or a little poker? Come on, let's go to the other
room. He went first and evidently thought I would follow him.
When he noticed that I wasn't coming, he asked if I didn't like
playing chess. Now, he knows very well how much I like to
play chess. He also knows that I like playing with him—in the
kitchen or in my room. However, he also knows that I've been
refusing to go into the other room lately. He hasn't asked why,
because he knows all too well. Night after night, he's tried to
beguile me by any means necessary into breaking my promise to
myself. As for me, I'm always trying to make him ask me, Won't
you tell me why you're avoiding the other room? I'd be very
glad if he asked because I have a crushing answer on hand. My
answer: Because you and she have made the room so filthy that
only the two of you can go into it without feeling ashamed. If

I were to go in, I would not only defile myself but also my pure memory of Mama.

It's possible that he might not understand this at all, because I think parents always have a different understanding of purity from what their children do. For them, at least as far as my own experience goes, the quality of purity has lost every semblance of practical meaning. It may be possible for them to consider it something worth aspiring to for teenagers going through their "awkward years," but in their own actions, parents constantly deny that such a concept even exists. Parents always live a more sordid life than their children because parents have always condoned all the things they do themselves. That is, to be able to excuse everything for themselves, yet practically nothing for their children, is the reward that "experience" affords adults. What parents call experience is really nothing but their attempts—successful to the point of sheer cynicism— to deny everything they once considered pure, true, and right when they were young. They themselves don't realize the terrible cynicism behind all the incessant talk of "experience" as life's highest goal. They only notice the "inexperience" in their children; that is, the kind of inexperience called purity and honesty, and then they become irritated. And when they're irritated, they take their irritation out on their children. They call this "raising children" because what else is raising children but the attempt of frustrated parents to stifle in the child what they recognize as the stifled goodness in themselves? And if they aren't vexed, they act superior, superior because they erroneously pride themselves in their great life experience, as if it were particularly respectable and remarkable to destroy the best within us.

Papa is arrogant. I think he's far too aware of the wrong he's doing and has done to want to "raise" me to accept it as simply something every experienced adult can do without remorse or feelings of shame or guilt. Instead, he acts as if I'll see that he, at least, isn't bothered by it. And nowadays he doesn't even make the slightest attempt to hide it when he visits her. He often goes so far as to extend her regards to me and facetiously says that she's looking forward to seeing me again. So she thinks I'm sweet. Very sweet. And it's just like her to use such a word, as if there weren't any less vulgar words to flatter someone. Now, I know very well that it's only flattery because not even Berit has ever told me that I'm especially handsome.

They also have other ways of trying to win me over. For instance, she apparently promised me free tickets to her theater, according to Papa, as if it's really so great to go to such a tiny, dirty, and sordid place as the Lantern with its old, dreadful films. I do go there sometimes to look at the posters in order to see what they're showing, but it would never occur to me to go in. In a way, that would be to admit that she and Papa, when all is said and done, probably aren't so wrong for what they're doing.

I'll never admit that, no matter how much they try to tempt me. And I know the temptations can be both overpowering and multifarious, but I think that anyone who knows himself and constantly analyzes his own situation as well as his own actions cannot be coaxed into doing something that he doesn't want to do. Analysis—that is, awareness—is a person's most noble weapon against both the bad examples of others and the passions within himself. I've recently come to see what a particularly excellent tool analysis really is for someone who wants to keep himself pure and untainted—or, in other words, young. More than anything, my aim is to avoid the kind of "experience" described so fervently by the ones who have already lost their youth. It won't change me no matter how many times Papa comes home humming at night or late in the evening after being with her, carrying on—while practically smacking his lips—about what an exquisite woman she is. I can see in his red, self-satisfied face *why* he finds her so enchanting, and I could tell him why if I wanted to: it's because he sees in her the very irresponsibility and lack of sense of duty that he wished Mama had had.

I could also tell him what she's really like, the woman he thinks brought "happiness" to him. Based on her only visit here or the few times I've coincidentally seen her leaving the cinema alone or walking with Papa down Ringvägen, where she apparently lives, I have a very distinct and reliable impression of her. With the help of these experiences, I've analyzed both her and her temperament, and I've come to the conclusion that she has to be utterly cold and truly indifferent to the suffering of others by nature. Otherwise, she could hardly harden herself to the point of disturbing my father on the day of my mother's funeral.

In a sense, I can strangely understand why she'd make a certain impression on a man like Papa. After all, she's exactly the kind of "experienced" woman he considers to be the highest conceivable form of human being. I really think she's seen a little of everything. She isn't exactly ugly, and even though her type doesn't exercise the least bit of attraction on me, you could even go so far as to say that she's rather pretty, or at least she used to be. Her real age can be detected behind the mask of youth she dons in her conscious moments. She has to be at least forty, and I'm positive she'll start to look her age the day someone tells her that she looks as old as she really is. I don't think anyone would ever notice how old she really is if she didn't go to so much trouble to keep her face so young. And in the same way she tries to exaggerate any residue of beauty, she exhausts any likable features that, despite everything, she might have. For example, she has a very beautiful smile, but she ruins it by smiling too much; maybe it's an occupational hazard, I don't know. Her eyes aren't ugly either, but she makes them ugly by the provocative way she likes to look at people. She has very nice legs, but, of course, she has to show the whole world by wearing short skirts that would better suit a young girl. Her voice is pretty soft, but when she talks, she tries at all costs to make it softer. As a result, she only sounds ingratiating and insincere. To take another example: she wears a perfume that smells very pleasant indeed, but by applying it excessively she only repels people with the overpowering fragrance as soon as they get near her.

Incidentally, something happened the other night that says more about her than any lengthy description. I was lying in Papa's daybed and reading a very good novel by Stefan Zweig when the telephone rang. (Parenthetically, I can say that it's naturally only when Papa's home that I refuse to go into the other room. He's the one I want to punish—not myself!) When I answered, it was Papa. He didn't say where he was calling from, but I heard from the background noise that he must have been calling from a restaurant. By the way, it wouldn't have surprised me if it was the same restaurant where we had Mama's memorial dinner. With his first word, I could tell he was drunk. I generally detest drunken people because they instantly lose any bit of innocence they may have had. Nowadays, I especially loathe Papa when he's drunk because he refers to Mama as "Alma" in such an unbearably vulgar way, as if she were something we had lost on a walk or while moving. Then he said to me, There's someone here who wants to talk to you, Bengt. I suspected who this person might be, but I was still inexplicably upset when I heard it was she. I was even more upset when I heard that she was drunk, too, not very drunk but enough to notice.

Still, I hadn't expected this from her. That's why what she said, which would have normally left me rather disinterested, made me furious. In fact, the words were probably pretty innocent. When will I get to see you again, Bengt? she asked. It was the tone she used and the way she pronounced the words that especially made me react so harshly. Apparently, it took everything within her to sound as kind and well meaning as possible, but since she was in no condition to control her voice, it turned out entirely mawkish and unnatural.

I don't know what I said, and I was so upset that I didn't even notice until later that she had addressed me so cheekily. But as soon as I hung up, I darted from the hall to the other room. Suddenly, the disgraceful image that I'd been trying for weeks to suppress from my consciousness thrust itself on me with such a terrible force that I simply knew I couldn't go on without unleashing my rage. In that moment, I can assure you, she was lying in the daybed as she was that night I happened to walk in on them. So I pulled the cover off the daybed, and with a pillow in each hand I attacked her so violently that I tore one of the pillowcases. Afterward, I was completely worn out yet simultaneously satisfied that I had finally avenged the harm inflicted on me. Afterward, while resting in the daybed, I was still filled with the kind of joy that only purity can offer a person. I think that the greatest happiness in the world is to get revenge on the ones who are filthy. Purity is a terrible master, Bengt, but you'll end up happy if you submit to it. Therefore, you must listen to it, obeying it always, even if your loyalty leaves you unbearably conflicted.

Bengt! This is what my purity has done. I must finally confess to you that something horrible has happened, something I can only endure by analyzing it to death, until I'm able to understand something of its nature. The same night of the phone call, though a bit later, something downright terrifying happened. I was still lying in the daybed. I wasn't asleep, but I wasn't really awake either—I think I was on the verge of falling asleep. I heard a whisper waft through the room, a whisper that I immediately recognized as my mother's. "No, no, not now," the whisper said, "Bengt can hear." That was all. But in reality it was a lot. You see, in the same moment the whisper faded, I remembered that I had heard my mother whisper these very words once before. And I suddenly remembered when. I must have been about twelve then. I was home sick with the measles, the shade was drawn, and I was terribly bored. The doorbell rang the first day I stayed home, and I heard Mama greeting someone I didn't recognize at the entrance. It was a man, and she called him Erik. They were talking in the kitchen, but then they went into the other room together. The daybed was where it is now, against the wall on the other side of my room, and I could tell they were sitting on it. They were talking quietly, and even though my door was ajar I couldn't hear what it was about. Then the whisper came out of nowhere. There was something I was absolutely not allowed to hear, but Mama must have gauged incorrectly because it was actually her whispering that was clearer than anything else she had said before. "No, no, not now," she whispered, "Bengt can hear." At once, this Erik character left and didn't come back again. The whole time I lay sick in bed I pondered over what it was I wasn't supposed to hear. I could have simply asked Mama about it, but I instinctively suspected that she wouldn't care to answer or that she would tell me something that wasn't true. Then school and friends came along, and I forgot about the whole thing. It had never reappeared from out of the blue until this night. I have to confess that my forgotten memory stunned me, of course, now since I fully understand the significance of what really happened. What I wasn't supposed to find out was, quite simply, that this stranger Erik was my mother's lover. It was horrible to catch such an unexpected glimpse of a relationship that I was completely unaware of my whole life. To make sure that my memory wasn't deceiving me, I very cautiously asked Papa the following day if our family had ever known someone named Erik. He immediately answered that he used to have a coworker named Erik. He had since moved to Södertälje and disappeared. He was incidentally quite fond of Alma, he said after a while, but she always kept a tight rein on him. Later still, he added, Though, you never know.

Though, you never know. I knew this last part was merely the bait he wanted me to bite—a weak, shameless attempt on his part to justify himself and his actions. In reality, I could tell that he was firmly convinced that Mama never betrayed him with Erik. Still, I have to admit that he's right. *You never know.* Isn't it terrible, Bengt, that no one ever knows? You can't trust anyone. The one you trust most, the one you have loved the most, even she can betray you. Your own mother can say to you, I'm going out shopping now, Bengt, when she's really going out to catch a cab to her lover. Your own fiancée can say, I have a headache tonight, Bengt, and can't go out, while another man is in her room, lying on a made-up sofa. There's only one person in the whole world you can trust, and that person is you. It's a horrible thought, but once you've thought about it for a while, you realize that it's also a soothing thought. As long as you can trust yourself, then you have nothing to lose. It's only when you discover that you can't trust yourself that all is lost. Therefore, it's necessary to be trustworthy to yourself at every moment, to not let you trick yourself. That's why it's so important to be aware of your own actions, and the only way you can do that is to analyze every last ounce of your emotions and your deeds.

This is what I have done, and of course I've realized that what happened cannot in any way minimize the shamefulness of my father's and his fiancée's relationship. It is and remains a disgraceful act that betrays another person, even if that person has also betrayed. On the other hand, it obviously can't help changing my feelings about Mama to some degree. Of course, I miss her all the time, but a tinge of doubt has crept in, dulling the intensity of my mourning and diminishing its permanence. It's clear that I can no longer miss her with the same sadness now that I know that even her purity, the quality I loved most about her, was not untainted.

The important thing is that I'm no longer obligated to mourn my mother. Having suddenly discovered that she committed the same act that I've been despising Papa for, it's obvious that my innocent grief has been tainted. I don't enjoy mourning for the sake of mourning. I'm no self-tormentor, after all. Now I understand that the revenge I've felt obligated to carry out against Papa and his fiancée on behalf of Mama is really for myself, because the virtue I cherish most, purity, has been so ruthlessly violated.

Furthermore, what has happened has made me suspicious of everything and everyone. I don't even trust Berit anymore. The other night I told her that no one could trust anyone, not even your own mother. We were sitting on a bench in Djurgården. Instead of starting to cry, as I had expected, she became surprisingly angry. She said, Why do you constantly defend her? She meant I was defending Papa's fiancée. It was so absurd that I could've laughed. Lately, I've noticed that Berit criticizes her all the time, as if she were trying to divert attention from herself. I'm keen enough of an observer to be able to separate embellishment from the truth. After recently seeing Berit to her door one evening, I noticed that she lingered in the window, as if checking to see if I had really left. A little later, I called her for no particular reason and told her, also for no reason at all, that I saw how painstakingly she had checked to see if the coast was really clear. She started crying, and it relieved me a little.

Later.

Papa just got home. He's been walking back and forth in the other room all night, so I knew he had something to say, but he couldn't come out with it. Finally, he said it. His fiancée wants us to spend Midsummer in a cottage she's borrowing in the archipelago. I surprised Papa by answering yes. My answer didn't surprise me at all. I know now that if I'm ever going to have the chance to take revenge on her, it has to happen when we're together because then she won't be able to be evasive or hang up the phone—which could happen if I were to write her or tell her what I think over the phone. Besides, the cottage is supposedly on a small island, which makes my job much easier. I could tell Papa was happy I said yes. Based on the things he's been saying lately, he still seems to hope that I'll come to think of her as a mother one day. He is so naïve. I hoped you would be sensible, he said afterward. We'll see how sensible I am, I answered. Then he stroked my hair. Then I heard him leave and call someone. Evidently, she must have a telephone at home, even though I couldn't find her number in the phone book. And I wouldn't be surprised if she were divorced, perhaps several times. So the number is probably in her husband's name. I can't describe how happy I am that my revenge is finally within reach. On Midsummer, I won't leave a single word I'm going to say to her and Papa to chance. There's still a month to go, but I'll use it wisely!

Now I can hear that Papa's asleep. I'm going to sleep, too. See you soon.

Your friend, Bengt

P.S. Papa gave the dog back. He claimed that I wasn't nice to it, which is a lie, so he sold it to his fiancée. I saw through his trick, but I let him keep thinking he's an exceptionally shrewd person. It won't hurt him to believe that. Besides, his sisters think the same thing about themselves. They haven't visited us since they raided the closet, although they have called us a few times. The last time, after they found out that she had visited us, they said, Forgetting Alma already!

As if I was the one who invited her! As if I could ever forget Alma!

UNDERWATER FOOTPRINTS

THEY ARE AT SEA FOR THREE DAYS. At sea, they say playfully. That sounds like living on a boat. In reality, however, they are not on a boat but an island or, more precisely, two small islands connected by a funny little wooden arch, which they jokingly call a bridge. The open sea encircles them, and the coast disappears into the dark water, which blackens as the night approaches. To the west, the sun has just set behind a glimmering strip of land. Looking at it, they think, Look how dark the sea is out there, far back, by the lighthouse. The lighthouse, of course, is a church tower during the day. And when they hear sounds from the mainland at night, a honking car or a roaring train, it's only natural for them to say, Did you hear that big ship? Now, that was a torrent! Therefore, at night they really are *on* the sea, not in it and definitely not by it. They are in a boat, in a little boat on a very large sea.

Something strange happens when people are in a small boat, something that rarely happens with people in a car or an elevator, on a train or even a boat large enough to say that you are on it instead of in it. What they experience is the sense of solitude. There are only a few thin boards keeping them from being totally engulfed by the surrounding deep sea. They are lonely, but it's not an isolated loneliness, because they feel lonesome together, together with the others in the boat. This is why a temporary bond forms between people in a small boat. They only have each other, the deep sea is frightening, and small boats are very fragile. Therefore, each one of them becomes the other's lifebuoy. If you're not afraid, then neither am I, so we shouldn't scare each other, and we ought to be nice to each other as long as the water surrounds us.

It's a Saturday evening when they row away from the large pier, which they had reached by bus. Almost silently, because they aren't in the boat yet, they put their baskets, bags, and small pieces of luggage on board. The father wants to row first. Bengt and Berit sit in the stern, but Gun sits in the prow behind the father. Berit is gazing at the sea, which glistens black under the drifting clouds. At first, she is afraid because it is so still. She is always afraid of water and even small boats. And the black water makes her think of death. But, then, when the swell comes and gently rocks them, she becomes even more terrified and immediately thinks the boat is going to capsize. So she grabs Bengt's hand, which is lying wet and cold between them, and places it on her coat, a black coat that Bengt didn't like. That's why, when they were still in the bus, he said, Are you going to a funeral? She also owns a blue coat that is lighter and better suited for Midsummer, but she didn't want to wear it. Nor did she want to come along, but Bengt had practically forced her, saying that she ought to come—if for nothing else than for the sake of his mother. So she gave in, and this is also why she's wearing the black coat.

Bengt likes the sea, especially when it's vast and dark. He likes thunderstorms the same way, which explains why he is curiously exhilarated when lightning suddenly blazes forth in the north sky. Out of nowhere, it suddenly leaps to life over the luminous horizon and slithers down into the sea like a fiery snake, almost hissing before dying out. Bengt is sitting on the ledge and smoking. And the tobacco tastes acrid because his fingers are wet. Earlier, they had to bail out the boat, which had been half-submerged in the water for a long time. He has been morose and defiant the whole day, has hardly responded to anyone, and has refused to do what anyone asked him. In fact, he did the opposite. As soon as they boarded the bus and Bengt pretended to drop the case of alcohol, the father yelled, If you don't want to come, then just stay home! Yes, let's just stay, Berit wanted to say, but Gun beat her to it. Everything will be fine once we get off, she had said and smiled. So Bengt stayed. But he didn't smile back at her.

Now he is sitting and watching the father, who is rowing and who has unbuttoned his jacket. So he can see how his chest heaves underneath his red silk shirt with every movement. But the oars are splashing against the sea very choppily, and no matter how much he strains himself, it is sloppy rowing. Sometimes water splashes up and spatters inside the boat, so he makes excuses: If it weren't so damn windy! In reality, however, it's perfectly calm. The swell is mere child's play and a sailboat is adrift. The flag is not even moving. The three who are not rowing simply smile.

Bengt isn't smiling at the rowing. Nor is he merely smiling at the silk shirt. Nowadays the father only buys silk—silk underwear and silk sweaters and silk shirts. He never did before; he never bought anything, for that matter. Before it was always Alma, and she bought Doctor Lahman's tricot. But the son isn't smiling at this alone. He is smiling because he is happy. He has been happy the whole day—he just didn't want to show it. It's part of his plan to show displeasure at first, to pretend to join them reluctantly. He won't be happy until they arrive, and then they will be pleased with him. For two and a half days they will be nothing but pleased with him. After that, the attack will come, just like lightning from a joyous sky. But during the attack he will continue to be happy, for what can arouse more pleasure than taking revenge for the sake of purity?

There's a can of drinking water between Bengt's legs. It's a 50-liter milk can that was difficult to get into the boat. Without a thought, he suddenly lets go of the fiancée's hand and starts drumming lightheartedly on the tin. They are already far out now, almost halfway. He spits his cigarette into the sea and starts whistling, quietly and softly. Then the father raises the oars into the boat. One of the blades ends up on Berit's lap, so she gets cold but doesn't dare move it away. Berit is almost like a small lake. For every cloud that drifts over her, she becomes dark, not just on the surface but at the bottom, too. Now she is dark because of the oar and Bengt's whistling. She doesn't like that he is happy. She doesn't like it right now, anyway. Now it only makes her want to cry.

But the father likes it. He thinks the son whistles beautifully, and he likes beautiful whistling. The drumming is beautiful, too. Otherwise the evening is perfectly serene and the sea is perfectly silent, only the seashore can be heard sighing as it slowly dims. They have rowed so far out that they are nearly alone. The sailboat is now lying askew at the end of the curving disk, and when its sails are taken in for the night, it resembles a tiny skerry with a solitary tree on it. The coastline sinks lower and lower, and eventually the water is up to the gunwales. And from their tranquil, drifting boat they also see two islands. The one to the left is a narrow and high cliff, blanketed with low trees. A bird is squawking above it. The one to the right is a long and low island with luminous white rocks along the water's edge. But straight ahead, only a half-hour's row away, is their island, so small and low that it nearly disappears when the swell comes. The water surrounding them is getting imperceptibly murky even though the sky is still shining above. Is it strange that the rower is happy?

When the bird stops squawking, Berit is also a little happy, but then Gun starts to sing. She sings softly as Bengt whistles softly and drums softly, too. He doesn't notice it until a while later, and then, almost ashamed, he stops. He wipes some water off the can and lights a wet cigarette. He looks over his father's shoulder and glances at Gun. She glances back at him and suddenly stops singing, but the song isn't over yet. Then the father turns around and drops his heavy hand on her shoulder. She is wearing a white, luminous blouse.

Sing, he says.

But she doesn't sing. She forgets the melody and the words, too. She just wants them to keep rowing. When Bengt looks at Berit, she is sitting with the wet oar on her lap and crying a little. She's probably crying because the song was so beautiful—at least he thought it was. But he, too, thought Gun should have stopped singing, although he doesn't know why. The father's hand is still on Gun's shoulder, causing her to gradually sink down, and it's probably making her dirty, too.

Let's go now, she says.

Just then, Bengt suddenly has the urge to row. Men in small boats are only too happy to row in the company of women, and Bengt wants to row for Berit. He takes her by the shoulder, not rough or violently, though he can feel through the rough material of her coat that her shoulder is trembling. She herself is not afraid, but her shoulder is. It quivers like a small animal.

Don't be cold, he says consolingly. Stand up. We're almost there.

But this is precisely when her chills begin. When Bengt takes a step toward the father, the boat cants, a basket starts sliding across the floor, Gun cries out, though subdued and mildly, and the father lets go of her shoulder to grab the oars.

I want to row, Bengt says and looks into his eyes.

But the father doesn't want to let go of the oars. The boat is aslant, and a small suitcase is tipping over. Bengt lifts one of the oars over the gunwale, which frees Berit's lap and she can put her hands there now. The bird starts shrieking again over the tall island. Then the oar sinks, sinks until it's almost hanging straight down from the gunwale. On one side, the water is rising over the planks. It seems like a lot, and the case of liquor gets wet.

Are you crazy? the father asks. Do you want us to tip over?

Bengt looks down at the oar. It sparkles as the blade turns. Then he looks at Gun and sees her hand, more than anything else, stroking the red collar. He has never seen her touch his father before, so he raises the oar again.

Let Bengt row, Gun whispers; you shouldn't row the whole way.

So the father makes his way aft, and Bengt sits down to row. When the oars touch the water, he feels how heavy the boat is. The shore isn't as far as he presumed either. In fact, he can still see the bus with its bright headlights pulling away from the large concrete jetty. But the long island has spun around and the glinting of its white rocks has gone out. The father puts his arm around Berit's shoulder. Her shoulder is tremulous, but she doesn't dare break free. Only Bengt notices this. The father's arm is still there.

Slowly, the boat takes off. A little water still splashes inside every time the oars plunge into the sea, so much that Berit and the father are completely wet, but they don't say anything. The father merely squeezes the son's fiancée a little, just a little closer to him. He never noticed before how nice her shoulders feel. Bengt doesn't really care and only reacts to it in fun. So to get back at the father, he mischievously leans back a little. This allows him to make more powerful strokes with the oars. But it also allows him to feel Gun's knees digging into his back. She doesn't move them away, even though she ought to know that he needs more room to row as fast as he is going. He becomes a little irritated by this, so he takes up even more space. The wake is getting rough and deep, and the depressions left by the oars are filled with sparkling foam. Above them, the sky is getting even brighter, but over the water's black surface and a few feet above that it's twilight. Now even the sailboat stops shining, and the mast is long gone. But underneath her black hair, Berit's face is completely white.

Bengt turns around to see how much farther they have to go. At first, he's unable to see it. At first, he can only see Gun's shoulder. A shadow from the father's hand lingers on her white blouse. After the shadow, he sees the island. He also sees the cottage. It's by the narrow inlet, whose sand is dazzling through the dusk.

Are you tired, Bengt? Gun asks. Not reproachfully, but very gently. Now he needs to show her that he isn't tired. Needs to show her that he is just as strong as his father. Needs her to see that he has enough strength to do what he has to do. She needs to know. Then she needs to be afraid. Soon, they will both be afraid, perhaps all three of them. He's the only one who won't be afraid, because he knows what he's going to do. He whips the water with the oars, sending the ivory foam flying into the boat.

It's just a little windy, he says while panting.

But it's still calm, warm, and serene—and motionless. When he says it, however, no one smiles. Then Gun starts singing again but stops as soon as they approach the shore. She takes off her shoes, splashes into the water with her bare white legs, and pulls the boat up as far as she can, while chatting a little about this and that.

They are exhausted after carrying everything into the house. Bengt, for that reason, is sweaty, although Berit is cold. They unlatch the shutters and open the windows up to the night. They have put everything on the floor in the main room. Now they are sitting around the open fireplace and the charred fire for a while. They grab some beer and sandwiches and sit down to eat. Berit doesn't want any beer, so the father is nice and goes on his own to get her some water from the can. Then he thinks it would be nice to have a nip. He opens a bottle and mixes his beer pretty strongly with some aquavit. Then Gun holds out her glass and gets a dash, too. But Bengt suddenly changes his mind and doesn't want any at all. He is suddenly down, and he can't help it.

You two can drink, he says.

After he says it, he realizes he said it very loudly. However, no one drinks anymore. Then the father catches something in his throat and spits it into the extinguished fire, causing Bengt to cringe. Now it's time to make up their beds. There are two alcoves at opposite sides of the main room, one with a sliding door separating them. Both alcoves have bunks fixed to the walls. Bengt and Berit will sleep in the outermost alcove. Berit wants the upper bunk, says that sleeping too close to the ground gives her a headache. Then Bengt gives her the lower one. As they spread the sheets over the cold mattresses, he hears Gun laughing from the inner alcove. He thinks it's an ugly laugh. He walks out of his alcove, but he still can't hear what she's laughing at.

They wash up in the little inlet directly in front of the cottage. Berit is the only one who goes straight to bed without washing. She isn't feeling well. And to avoid freezing, she spreads her black coat over herself. The other three wade into the water. Gun goes out the farthest. The father is standing closest to her and splashes water on her legs. He has rolled his pant legs up to his knees, but Bengt has hardly rolled his up at all. He has absolutely no desire to go too far out into the water. The father and Gun have the soap. After the father rinses his face, he blows his nose into the water. Bengt cringes once again. Soon there are white rings of foam around them. The rings are resting perfectly still on top of the water and twinkle a little before they dissolve. After Gun pulls up her hair, she abruptly takes off her blouse and tosses it to the father. Bengt goes back inside.

It's an infinitely long time before they come back. And so that it won't get too stuffy in the room, Bengt has opened the window. He is lying very close to the brown wooden ceiling and listening to their voices from the inlet. His underwear was wet with sweat and he couldn't find his pajamas, so he's naked underneath the blanket. Lying there, he suddenly gives a start. Something strange has happened to their voices. They have changed all of a sudden: one is much deeper than before; the other is much lighter. Then he notices that the voices are coming from behind the closed sliding door. Hearing it makes him so blistering hot that he flings the blanket off. After he has cooled off again, he hears a loud splash from the inlet and after a short moment of silence, he hears another splash. Then he climbs down from his bunk and leans out the window. Nothing is visible in the inlet. But there are two piles of clothes in the sand, one that is dazzlingly white and one so dark that he can hardly see it. Soon, he can see their two heads, like two dark balls bobbing up and down in the water. But before the swimmers wade back to shore, he slowly pulls the curtain from his fiancée's bed. It occurs to him that he never said good night to her. When he came back from the beach, she had drawn the curtain that separated the hallway from their alcove as well as the curtain to her bed. Now he is leaning soundlessly over her. She's breathing like she's sleeping. But her eyes are open.

Are you cold? he asks. Is that why you have your coat over you?

No, she whispers.

But she doesn't touch him, even though she sees he is naked. Her hands are on her chest and clasped like a sick old woman.

Are you ill? he whispers.

She turns her head to the wall and closes her eyes. Playfully, he pulls some hairpins from her hair and covers her face with five locks of her own black hair.

No, she whispers. Just afraid.

Now he's afraid, too.

Of what? he asks while listening for sounds outside.

So afraid of being alone, she whispers, wiping her hair away from her face. And afraid of your dad.

Now they are coming. He hears their soft pattering up the steps. He quickly hides himself behind the curtain of the fiancée's bunk. Then, when the father and Gun are inside the other room, they close the sliding door again. He can't hear them anymore.

Don't be afraid, he whispers sharply, I will . . .

But she never gets to find out what he would do. He leaves her all alone, and he closes the window. Then he goes out to the hallway, where he burns his feet on their wet footprints. He slowly opens the sliding door again and peeks through the small opening. No one's in the other room and the curtain to their alcove is drawn. Then he creeps back to his alcove and climbs into his bed. But he leaves the sliding door slightly ajar, so that the room won't get too stuffy.

Beneath him, he hears his fiancée tossing and turning now and then, not for long stretches of time, but often. Then the walls of the wooden cottage start to creak. Otherwise, the cottage is completely silent. Beyond the silence, the sea murmurs impatiently, like the audience at a theater. But it isn't the noise that keeps him from sleeping—it's the silence. Or, more precisely, what he can't hear. And for a long time he waits for sounds that never come. He waits, for instance, to hear the clinking of glasses. He does hear it in the end, but only because he wanted to so badly. At almost the same time, he hears the father snoring. Now he can roll over to the wall. Now he's able to fall asleep, almost instantly.

In the morning, he is the first one to wake up. He forgot to close the shutter, so it's very bright very early in the alcove. Behind the curtain, the fiancée is sleeping on her back. Her coat has slipped off, so he spreads it over her again. At his touch, she gives a start as though she were being punched and flings her hand over her face to protect herself. This upsets him, and he quickly leaves her. He opens the window and quietly climbs out. The rock is still cold underneath the coolness of the shade. He walks around the cottage just to see what it looks like in daylight. All but one of the green shutters are open. He stops in front of the closed shutter and lights a cigarette. He uses three matches for a single one. When he finishes it, no one has woken up yet. But he has a bad taste in his mouth.

Then he goes down to the shore, whistling quietly and carrying a flat stone in his right hand. Except for the inlet, the island is a single cliff, bordered by deadly, steep edges. He walks around the slippery edge and gazes absentmindedly into the naked sea. Faint smoke from invisible boats drifts against the horizon. Silent gulls are poised between the sun and the sea. Three sailboats have anchored by the low island. A quiet blue motorboat sweeps past the one on the right, its noise scarcely reaching him. A narrow, deep cleft runs through their own island, and the water can only surge through it when it's really windy. It must not have been very windy for quite a while. The cleft is entirely arid and filled with dried-up seaweed and round little rocks. He tosses his flat stone away and meticulously selects a new one, one perfectly round and entirely shiny. For fun, it seems, someone has built a little smooth arch out of brown-painted wood over the cleft. And for fun, he walks over it. This side of the island is utterly barren; the rocks are as smooth as a person's back. In the middle is a large, level depression where someone has laid soil and sowed grass and flowers. Now the flowers are wild and the grass is sparse. Despite this, he lies here on his back fiddling with the rock and looks up at the clear Sunday morning sky. After resting a while, he feels like a swim. Still lying there, he chucks the stone diagonally and hears it hit the bridge. He undresses and hides his clothes in the crevice, putting rocks over them. Since he still doesn't remember where he left his swimming trunks, he doesn't go back to the cottage to get them but instead goes out to the sea naked. He thought about diving from the cliff and straight into the green bottom, but since he is never brave when he's on his own, he goes to the inlet instead—slowly. Partly because it's cold and partly because he has the absurd feeling he has lost something.

Finally, he finds it. At the bottom where he is wading, he thinks he sees some dark shadows between his own steps. Suddenly, he realizes the shadows are footprints. This discovery makes him curiously anxious. He is no longer cold, and he follows the shadows farther and farther out, blocking the sun with his hands to see them better. There are two rows; first, far apart from each other, then, parallel and close, but where the bottom descended abruptly and steeply, they merge into a single large shadow. He treads into it with his foot, digging into it with his toes, deeper and deeper until it becomes a pit. He stands in it and cautiously looks around as if he were doing something dangerous. The water in the hole is warm. To avoid thinking about why he's still there, he begins studying the coastline. It's a few inches high and strikingly blue. He thinks he can see white spots amid all the blue—a bridge, a white house. He sees a black church tower, too. It protrudes from the edging like the point of a knife.

Then a shutter slams from the back of the cottage. His feet jerk from the pit. Fleeing almost in a panic, he thrusts himself into the deep part of the water. He swims with short, nervous strokes as he always does when no one is watching. When he hears someone coming down the stairs, he is already out in the inlet. Freezing, he creeps back to shore and hides behind some sparse bushes. Between the branches, he sees Gun standing on the steps. She is alone and wearing a red bathing suit. He hopes that she'll wait until the commotion in the water has managed to subside. She walks slowly down to the shore and stands for a while with her hands on her hips, playing in the sand with her toes. Then she goes quietly, almost soundlessly, out into the water. He suddenly recalls his mother so vividly that he freezes up. Alma didn't swim often; she was rather afraid of the water. Whenever she went in it, she had the habit of frightening the water, splashing it with her fat legs and screaming at it. She always embarrassed them at beaches, that is, when other people were there.

When his mother was gone again, he sees that Gun has stopped. The water is up to her knees now, and with cupped hands she pours water over her thighs so that she won't be cold. Believing she is alone, she pulls down the strap of her bathing suit and vigorously rubs her back. Almost immediately, she pulls the strap back up. Even so, her shoulder was naked for just a brief moment. But in that moment, he was able to figure out what it was about her that he hates. It is her body.

He also learned why he hates it. He hates it because it's so unlike his mother's, because it's so beautiful, and because it's so relaxed. The entire time she wades into the water—and that time is infinite—he keeps on hating her. He sees her body under the water, green like glass. But when she starts to swim, it is white. And when she floats on her back, her body shimmers through the water like a white stone. Then he picks up a black rock off the ground and throws it in her direction. He didn't mean for it to hit her, and it doesn't. He just wants to startle her. She whirls around in the water and looks in the rock's direction. Then, when she sees a wide ring on the surface, she swims very calmly to shore, most likely thinking it was a fish. As she swims, he realizes why he threw the rock. He also realizes why he has to get revenge. It's because her body has shimmered so in the water. It's because her body is tainted. It's because it is so beautiful. Furthermore, he realizes that he has been waiting for her all morning. The rock has waited, too.

When he goes back inside, the sliding door has just been shut. It's warm inside, and her footprints have already dried. When he opens the sliding door, he hears the father snoring, so he closes it again. He darts to his alcove and yanks the curtain from his fiancée's bed. He pulled the other curtain, too. When he lies down on her coat he sees that she's awake. Then he becomes aroused and excited, caressing her and then kissing her. She says that she is ill. She said the word *ill* in that telltale way women do when men ought to know why they are ill without having to ask. With those words, his lips dry up, he releases her shoulder, is irritated, and lies silently next to her.

Draw the curtain, she whispers, someone might come.

He doesn't draw the curtain but instead hopes that someone will actually come and see him lying there. When some footsteps approach the door, he kisses her again and rather violently. But when the footsteps turn in the opposite direction, he sees that her lip is bleeding. Then he lies silently on her coat for a long time, pondering whether she is really sick. The first time he knew her, he always tried to remember the date, so that in the future he would be able to know whether it was true or not. He can't remember anymore. So he is upset with her.

Breakfast is late because the father has slept in. They eat it on the porch outside the kitchen. There, they have a view of the long island, just a small portion of the mainland, but a large portion of the sea. While Berit sets the table and Gun clatters about in the kitchen, Bengt and the father are sitting on the red folding chairs at the green wooden table. The father is looking at the sea, which he hasn't seen in a long time. But Bengt is smoking and looking at the clothesline that stretches from the porch railing to a little pine tree. Gun's white blouse is hanging out to dry, and the father's silk shirt is flapping next to it, almost dry. For the first time, except for in his thoughts and dreams, he realizes that his father has another woman. So it's difficult for him to tear his eyes away from the line.

The father is pleased and content, and for the first time in a long time, he is happy to eat. When he is happy, he likes to touch women, so he grabs Berit by the hips—as a joke, of course. She stiffens up and starts dropping the glasses, but the father doesn't notice. The one who notices is Bengt, but when Berit looks at him, he still refuses to make eye contact with her. Just then, Gun emerges from the kitchen with fried eggs, but the father still doesn't let Berit go. Laughing, he says to the son:

Take over!

Gun leans over the table. She is wearing her bathing suit and a yellow silk robe over it. For just a brief, brief moment, Bengt actually wants to touch her, just to get back at his father, of course. But he doesn't, after all. A gust of wind thrashes the clothes on the line, so he looks at that instead.

When they eat they are all silent, except for the father, of course. The father can't help but talk. He often speaks with his mouth full, so they can almost never understand what he's saying. Bengt cringes. He doesn't want his father embarrassing himself in front of Gun, because it will make her stronger. So he glances at her to see what she is thinking about his father. Gun glances back at Bengt and laughs. She is still laughing when the father offers her some liquor, but as she laughs, she holds her hand over her shot glass. Though it's none of his business, Bengt is somehow pleased. Maybe not because she's laughing, but because she doesn't want to drink. His own glass is filled. And as the father screws the cork back on, Bengt gets a strange idea.

He personally finds it absurd, but he doesn't do anything to stop it. He takes Gun's shot glass and puts it in front of Berit, who is sitting next to him, poking at her food with a fork. She has her coat on, but he knows she is still cold, and therefore she should have a drink. The father also thinks it's funny and pours a few drops— or several, really. When Berit refuses to drink, Bengt forces her by grabbing her harshly by the neck and raising the shot glass. Then she drinks voluntarily, so that he won't cause her any real harm. After she drinks it, he is glad she did.

In the middle of the meal something beautiful happens. Gun suddenly points to the sea and they all look. A gray destroyer is coming in from the sea, clearing an ivory path through the water. Like a tiny rat, it scuttles rapidly into its hole between the high island and the mainland. Then it disappears. The ship isn't what is beautiful. It's what happens after the ship has disappeared. It is then that the swell comes gushing toward the island, no, toward the cottage, toward their porch—blistering, glass-green, and shimmering edges. This is when they instantly, and so beautifully, feel like they're sitting together, all four of them, in a little boat. They are frightened by the vast size of the wave, but knowing that nothing could happen, nothing other than a little splashing, they become euphoric. There's not a joy in the world that can bond people as strongly as fear does. Even Berit screams a little, out of enchantment, fear, and perhaps a little alcohol. Gun's shoulders are soaked from sitting closest to the sea. So she pulls her robe down, and the father dries her off with his hands. When Bengt sees her shoulders, he thinks they are shamelessly naked, even though the swimsuit straps are covering them.

Now he is no longer happy. He has already started craving his revenge, and he will get it through a memory. Suddenly he says to his father:

Do you remember that time in Tjärholmen?

Bengt remembers it well. They had once taken a trip to an island in Lake Mälar. With a little white motorboat that belonged to a coworker. It was the year before the war, just a Midsummer's Eve. The father and his colleague, who was steering, were sitting in the stern, eating sandwiches and drinking beer and hard liquor. Bengt was lying in the prow and reading a book by Marryat. The mother was sitting next to the motor and mending socks. The boat was moving quite slowly, so they were already very drunk by the time they got to Stora Essingen. Then the boat started wobbling, and when they got to Tjärholmen, the father fell in the water. He had wanted to jump ashore and moor the boat. But it wasn't very deep, so no harm was done. But the mother still started crying.

Yes, the father says, I remember Tjärholmen.

When he says it, he looks at the son and grins. It isn't until Bengt sees his smirk that he perceives his own stupidity. Because for anyone who wants revenge, Tjärholmen is a dangerous memory. He mentioned Tjärholmen because they had once been on that island with Mama on a Midsummer afternoon. Now he remembers that they both hated his mother at the time because she had ruined their Midsummer. Every minute of that Midsummer was filled with her complaints. When they set up the tent, she complained that they were pitching it in the worst possible place, even though there was no other place to put it. When they ate, she complained that they didn't appreciate the trouble she took with the food but that they ate voraciously like animals. At night, she kept them from sleeping by complaining with incessant stubbornness that the mosquitoes were keeping her awake. Of course, it was their fault there were mosquitoes since they were the ones who chose the spot for the tent. She complained about the island all Midsummer Day because everything on it was wrong: the rocky and dirty swimming spots; the ugly and brushy woods; the muddy ground. Bengt had wanted to get back at her, but he couldn't. But on the way back home, the men got their revenge by drinking the rest of the alcohol together, and they most certainly would have been taken in by the police at Bergsund Beach if Bengt hadn't managed to catch a taxi in time.

With his question, Bengt only intended to arouse the father's memory of his mother and not all the embarrassing things that accompanied it. Or did he? In any case, he's remorseful and tries to forget it, but he simply can't. Though he doesn't want to, he can't help comparing this new, peaceful Midsummer with the old, forgotten one. And to his burning shame, he notices that he feels better now, and to escape his shame he drinks a little more, and his eyes become beautiful. He looks at Gun with these eyes. But you eventually long to touch the one you have been staring at, so when he gets up from the table, he notices that Gun has some salt on her shoulders. He wipes the salt off with his fingers because it needs to be wiped off. Then he ventures to ask why the dog isn't there. Gun says that dogs are simply bothersome on trips. Besides, they don't like small islands like this one. Bengt agrees.

From then on, that Sunday passes by rather peacefully. They lie on blankets and beach towels at the inlet's shore. When they are warm and dry after a swim, they go for another, immersing themselves, splashing around boisterously, swimming to the bottom and snorting as they emerge in almost the same place, even though they thought they had swum several feet under the water. And when the speedy boats make swells, all three of them leap into them, laughing at whoever gets knocked down. Bengt laughs most of all. After all, it is Gun's body that he hates, so he enjoys seeing it roughed up, if only by a wave of water.

Berit isn't laughing. Every time they come in from the water, shouting and wet, she pretends to be asleep as she lies in her black dress with a thin blanket over her lap. To be sure, she does look up whenever they splash water in her face, but she doesn't like it. Bengt is irritated with her because she isn't having fun. For he knows they'll be having fun for only so long. Being happy is just the beginning of his revenge. As they drink their afternoon coffee, made on an open fire in the cleft, he tries getting her to drink a shot of vodka. He just wants to arouse some pleasure in her. She drinks it because she's still afraid, but even after she drinks it, she still isn't happy. So when the father pushes out the boat to row them around the island, she doesn't join them—she doesn't want to. When Bengt climbs into the boat, Gun says to him very kindly:

You can't leave Berit alone.

So he climbs out again, leaving Gun and his father alone in the boat, and flings himself furiously into the sand next to his sleeping fiancée. He watches the boat as it quickly glides away from the inlet and around the point, leaving only a streak of darkness in the water. He is furious with himself for letting himself be outwitted. He is furious at Gun because she has outwitted him and stopped him from taking out his revenge, the part that's to make certain they aren't alone for a single second. But when the fiancée pretends to wake up, he is most furious at her for pretending to be asleep and not joining them on the boat. However, Berit is glad when she wakes up and finds they are alone. She joyfully wipes the water from his hair, but, annoyed, he jerks away and starts digging a hole in the ground. He is digging out a footprint, digging deeply and laying wet sand over it.

Meanwhile, Berit is staring at the sea and the distant coastline. Because she is in good spirits, she thinks the ocean is beautiful. It is quiet and pristine and the sails are becalmed.

The sea isn't cold today, she says, almost whispering. When the water is cold, it quakes and makes breakers, and children are told that the sea is wicked. But the sea isn't wicked—it's just cold.

Bengt flattens the sand over the buried footprint. He makes the mound hard, very hard, and he's also hard on her. Harshly, he says:

I don't want to be your child.

What do you want to be, then? she whispers, still very happy.

Your lover, he says. He is still harsh.

Then she lies down, spreading the blanket over her face. He looks at the blanket to see if it will start quivering, but it doesn't.

After a moment, he quietly gets up and begins exploring the island. A long time has passed, but the boat hasn't returned. Not a cry was heard, not a splash of the oar, not even a whistle. He is walking very fast, and he is very upset. Maybe they rowed out far. It's dangerous to row out so far when the boat is so small. But when he reaches the cliff facing the sea, the boat is there and very close to the shore. It is anchored and rocking in the swell. He cannot see them, so they are probably lying at the bottom. To scare them, he throws a rock pretty close to the boat, but only playfully. They don't seem to hear the splash. In any case, neither of them looks over the gunwale, so he wants to scare them even more. He manages to slip silently into the water even though it's even colder on this side. After about thirty long and quiet strokes, he glides underneath the boat's thin shadow. Then he actually thinks about shouting, a high and playful yell, full of laughter and recklessness. But after swimming, he is now too strained to do anything but pant, so he's content with only grabbing the edge and rocking the boat harder than the waves are able to do. As he rocks it, he doesn't hear a single sound from the boat. And it feels suspiciously light. So when he heaves himself over the edge, it's naturally empty.

Furiously, he swims back. He can't help it, and he knows it's absurd, but he feels betrayed. He is panting and thirsty when he reaches the shore. His mouth is full of saltwater and it burns. His rage subsides a little, but his thirst is unbearable. To get to the drinking water faster, he decides to climb over the porch and go straight to the kitchen, where the can is. One of the shutters is closed. When he climbs over the rail, the floor of the porch is damp from wet footprints. When he tugs at the kitchen door, it is locked. And when he runs around the cottage and tries to open the front door, it is locked, too. So he shakes it, pounds on it with clenched fists, and kicks it—what he wouldn't do to quench his thirst. When the father comes and opens the door, he looks scared and pretends he was asleep.

Why have you locked all the doors? Bengt yells.

What do you want? the father asks.

A drink of water, the son answers.

When he walks into the room with the open fireplace, he notices that the curtain covering the alcove is trembling as if someone is standing behind it, someone who is panting. He drinks some water in the kitchen, and when he's done, he drinks some more. But he never quenches his thirst.

They eat dinner late. Bengt has no appetite. Berit hardly eats anything either. And Bengt doesn't give her anything to drink, because he has no desire to make her happy. The father picks at his food and tries to come up with something to say that will make them all laugh, but they finish before he can think of anything. As Gun gathers up the dishes, she asks whether they want to go out rowing. Nobody wants to.

But a little while after they have all gone to bed, Bengt slowly and silently escapes through the window. He pushes the boat out into the deep water, rows around the island and then straight into the ocean. A little ways out, the swell is rougher, beating against the plank, like whips. The wind is more acrid, scratching his face with its nails. It gets harder and harder to row. But the harder it gets, the more he enjoys it. And the deeper the island sinks into the sea, the more he likes that, too. He wants to row until the island completely disappears, as far into the sea as the boat can take him. He wants to row straight into the night. Until the last of the darkness ultimately swallows him up. After a while, the waves develop white crests and shower the boat with dazzling water. It is still fairly light, but darkness is beginning to descend over the coast. Finally, he is completely surrounded by water, nothing but water. But when he rows past a skerry, which is nearly black except for where it is mottled with white specks of birds, he notices how terribly slow he is going. So he lunges with the oars so powerfully that they start to bend. What gives him so much power is a vision, a vision that has compelled him to take the boat out in the middle of the night. In the vision, it is morning and bright. Gun steps onto the stairs in her red bathing suit. Just as she's about to head into the water, she notices that the boat is gone. Terrified, she runs up to the house. Where's Bengt?! she shouts to Berit. Then they feel around for him in his bed, but it's cold and empty. She runs to the father's room. Knut! she screams, Bengt is gone and so is the boat! So they run around the island, peer into the sea, and look back at the land. The most they can hope for is that he only rowed to the mainland and that he'll come back as soon as he has calmed down. That is when Berit suddenly discovers the boat, the rowboat, floating bottom up and coming toward them—black, like a coffin. Finally, they realize he is dead, that he has avenged himself for all the pain they have caused him.

The vision is so vivid and so real that he suddenly starts crying. There were many times before in his life when he contemplated suicide, but he has never enjoyed it like he does now. In reality, he is so thoroughly riveted by his vision that he doesn't know what he's doing at all, where he is, or into what danger he is drifting. He could row all the way to Finland without realizing it. Not until he hit Finnish soil would he know that he was sitting in a boat and that he had rowed it across the ocean.

However, for anyone who could row to Finland, something always manages to wake him from his dream. For Bengt, it's that his boat abruptly hits a rock. The impact makes him fall flat on his face, almost breaking one of the oars, but he barely manages to let go of it. As he struggles to get up, he sees that he's on top of a modest yet sharp submerged rock. A ghostly green shines underneath the black water. That is when he, to his horror, realizes where he is. The faint darkness floats like a black and ominous fog between the sea and the sky. Invisible birds are squawking. They must be horribly massive since they can't be seen. And the water surges high and gloomy all around him, threatening to flip his boat over at any moment. He is freezing down to the marrow, and with a fear that's absurd for someone who is going to die, he breaks an oar loose and repeatedly beats the rock until the boat is free. With violent exertion, he gets the boat around it. The sea is high. Every wave that approaches seems ready to leap into the boat and fill it to the brim. With eyes wide open, he looks the sea in the eye. Then he rows the way people row when they're terrified and utterly alone: short, wild strokes of the oar and oarlocks screeching. Canted and jerky, the boat drifts slowly onward. He doesn't dare turn around until much later. Then the island is lopsided in the sea's right-hand corner, lopsided but very near. It's his vision that has tricked him into thinking he was gone so infinitely long. And it's his fear that fed the lie.

It isn't until he is standing and panting in the alcove that he realizes how dead tired he is. Soaked, limp, and heavy as lead, he is barely able to climb up into bed. He is even too exhausted to open the sliding door to the room and the alcove with the closed shutter. Nevertheless, beneath his extreme exhaustion is a lump of happiness. Because he is glad to have been saved. So he doesn't need anything else to make him happy. And when the fiancée leans out of her bed, and up to his, and says in a whisper, I'll be better tomorrow, he can only manage to sigh an incomprehensible word, a single little word. Then he falls asleep. Berit does not sleep.

They are quite happy on Midsummer Eve. People are almost always happy on Midsummer Eve, even they who have no reason to be. They eat and go swimming. Even Berit swims to show Bengt that she is well. Otherwise, she is afraid of swimming, she doesn't swim well, and she freezes in the water. But she swims all the same. They row into the tall, brazen waves, away from the boats that rattle or glide past them by motor or wind. They row so close to the mainland that they can see all the flags waving in the yards. The four of them are together the whole day, for each one of them knows that it's dangerous not to be together. At night, each one of them has felt it, whether consciously or in their dreams.

They put the record player on the table outside on the porch. There's also wine, glasses, and flowers that the women picked from a skerry. It is late and beautiful, and they hang a kerosene lamp by a nail to illuminate all the beauty. Then they dance underneath the light. That is, only three of them dance—Bengt does not. He can't dance. Well, maybe a little foxtrot. Besides, he doesn't even want to, at least not with Gun. Because then he would be forced to touch her, but after last night he knows that isn't possible. Besides, they are only playing hambo and old-time waltzes. Bengt doesn't watch when the father dances with Gun. He just drinks. But he does look when the father dances with Berit, and he drinks some more. After so much wine he becomes rather tipsy. Gun has been drinking, too, but only enough to make her carefree. They are all drinking wine, but none so much as he.

The stack of records gets smaller and smaller. Gun is glowing and happy. She is wearing her bathing suit and a black skirt over it. The father dances mostly with her and is therefore able to dance faster. He has to dance slowly with Berit or else she gets a headache. And maybe she already has one, because she is pallid under the light of the lamp. At last, the bottles are empty. Bengt grips the table as Berit strokes his arm. Excited, Gun and the father are standing by the rail and watching the sea. Boats with lights and music onboard glide by in the distance. Suddenly, a rocket shoots up from the low island. They cheer in awe as a dazzling shower of blue and green sparks flutters down. They wait for another one, but nothing comes. Then they get cold and want to go to bed. But Berit, who is standing next to Bengt, is flipping through the records. She finally finds a foxtrot and puts it on. She wants to dance with Bengt. He knows he's a clumsy dancer, but when he dances with Berit, he only does it to show the two others he can, but that he didn't want to before. Because Berit also dances pretty badly, they are already dissatisfied with each other before the song is over. When they finish, the father says:

Bengt! Now you have to have a dance with Gun.

Gun puts on the same record again, goes up to him, closer than she really should.

Otherwise I'll be hurt, she says to Bengt.

So he takes her by the shoulder, reluctantly, almost as if touching her is revolting to him. He does want to punish her and what better way to do that than to dance with her and show her how much he despises holding her body. But the dance seems to last forever. It's the first time he's ever touched her for so long, and by the end his hands are completely wet. When they finally do stop, he notices he was holding her tight; maybe he even hurt her, because afterward she grabs her shoulder as if feeling for the pain. He no longer regrets the dance.

He notices something else when the dance is over: Berit is gone. When he goes to bed, he hears her quiet sobs behind the curtain. He doesn't feel like asking her why she's crying. He has no desire to speak with her, to touch her even. The wine has made him too tired. The father and Gun have also gone to bed. He waits to hear the father snoring through the half-open sliding door. But he never hears it, and while falling asleep, an unexpected noise jolts him wide-awake. It's a doorknob that turned with a creak, the kitchen doorknob. He jumps noiselessly to the ground and puts on his pants and a shirt. Just as quietly, he opens the window and lands on the rocks outside. On tiptoe, though he wouldn't have been heard anyway, he sneaks around the island. The boat is still in its place. No voices can be heard. They must be somewhere in the silence. It's just before sunrise. Above the sea, the red-hot sky is about to burst. As he tiptoes across the little arch, it creaks but not too loudly. He quickly hides himself behind some bushes. For a short yet danger-ous moment, he peers down at the little square patch of grass and flowers. Gun is sitting there. Her body is wrapped in her yellow robe—only her shoulders are bare. Her shoulders are white and na-ked, and when the father, who is sprawled out next to her, suddenly puts his hand on one of them, it doesn't become whiter. But it does become more naked, excruciatingly naked.

When he goes back to the cottage, he leaves the door ajar and opens the sliding door a little more. He draws the curtains and plops down heavily beside the fiancée. He is aroused and full of hate, and when he kisses her awake, he does it out of hate. But she thinks it's out of love and since he has never kissed her like that before, she becomes warmer than she has ever been before. She is so warm that she's finally able to be happy. Afterward, he is warm and limp, and his hate is limp, too, but also very deep. He gets up and closes both of the doors. He also draws the curtains and closes the shutter. He hopes to sleep in for as long as possible the next morning. It's the morning of their last day at sea, the day he will get revenge. From the darkness, the fiancée stretches her pale arms up to him.

You have made me so happy, she whispers.

Then he leans over and kisses her rather coldly on her lips. They are too open, and one of them has a sore. When the father and Gun do come back, he only hears it in the form of a dream, a short and insignificant dream.

On the day of his revenge, they all sleep in very late. Berit is particularly happy that day. When they swim, she laughs louder than the others and thrusts herself more boldly against the waves. Her body is slender and white, whereas Gun already has a nice tan. Berit is wearing a black bathing suit that is pretty old-fashioned. In the water she acts almost like his mother, which irritates Bengt. Apparently, the father is also irritated. When she voluntarily asks for some liquor at breakfast, they're taken aback—as if they had

heard an unusually crude swear word. And she isn't upset when
Bengt moves her glass away. She only said it because she wanted
to be loved, not because she really wanted to drink. She isn't upset.
She just doesn't understand. There is a lot she won't be able to understand as the day goes on.

It's very hot in the afternoon. They grow tired and weak and
lie out on the beach, half-sleeping till evening. The men are lying
on the outer sides. Gun is wearing sunglasses with red frames and
opaque lenses. So it's difficult to see whether her eyes are closed. Despite this, however, Bengt takes a chance and slowly props himself
on his elbow and gazes at her, starting from the top and working his
way down. Then he flings himself into the burning sand, his hatred
burning so hot that he has to find some shade. So he leaves the sand
and goes alone to the square patch, where he lies down in the cool
grass. As soon as he lies down, he realizes that it's a very bad spot if
he wants to cool off. Because now he is even hotter. But instead of
leaving, he throws himself on his stomach, rips up the grass, bites
into it like an animal, digs his body into it, and attacks it. Berit, who
suddenly catches him, doesn't understand a thing. She merely runs
away in fear.

Worn out, he stays in the hollow until somebody calls him.
They eat dinner on the porch as usual. It is hot and airless, and the
drinking water is almost gone. Down at the mainland, vacation-
ers' boats are flowing toward the city in a steady stream. They are
very quiet: Berit, because she doesn't really understand; the father,
because he's very hungry and because the hard liquor is gone; and
Gun, because she is suddenly afraid of Bengt, who is looking at
her as if she's supposed to be afraid. Bengt isn't saying anything either, even though he knows he should. And whenever he opens his
mouth to say what he ought to say, his heart shrinks and he always
says something else: "Can I have another beer?" or "Could you pass
some more herring?"

However, he is able to look at her without difficulty. And when
he realizes he can frighten her with just one glance, he feels proud.
But that night as he lies next to the fiancée, he feels disappointed in
himself. Disheartened, he is like a cold stone next to her, and despite

this, she tries to fondle him. He is disappointed because he didn't really get revenge. After they had finished eating, they packed up and then something always got in the way. They all went to bed after they packed, everyone except for Gun, who wasn't fully ready. Through the sliding door, Bengt can hear that his father is sleeping. Gun isn't asleep yet. She's busy with their suitcases in the kitchen. Then he mysteriously senses that the right moment has arrived. Entirely clear-headed and with every word burning on the tip of his tongue, he climbs out of bed. At the same time he has an insatiable thirst. So when the fiancée anxiously asks him where he is going, he answers:

To the kitchen for a drink of water. I'm so damn thirsty.

But there must have been something that frightened her, something in his voice or in his face, because then she tries clinging to him with her hands. He impatiently jerks away. When he entered the main room, he closes the sliding door behind him, stands with a pounding heart and burning feet, and looks straight into the kitchen. Aware of what he is going to do, he is not afraid. A sense of freedom warms him, a certainty that what he is about to do is something that needs to be done, if he didn't choke, and that everything will be much better afterward. Then he thinks he sees shadows on the floor, shadows of wet footprints. It frightens him a little.

He grows even more afraid as he comes silently closer and finds Gun standing with his mother's dress in her hands, about to pack it up. In the same moment, it occurs to him that he ought to warn her before he comes in. But when he tries to call her name, his mouth is completely empty—empty of words, anyway. Nevertheless, she must have heard him coming because she shoves the dress into the bottom of a suitcase and sharply turns around and faces him. She looks at him and her eyes are very afraid, bright and afraid. Then she says something very strange.

How old are you, Bengt? She whispers without really knowing why.

Only twenty, he mumbles.

Then he notices he said "only." Suddenly, he presses himself up against her body, as close as he can, throws his arms around her and kisses her.

Afterward, they part, leaving each other without a word. Gun goes out to the porch and stands motionless by the rail for a long time. Bengt dashes down to the sea, where he undresses on a rock and plunges into the water, sinking lower and lower. It's the terrible ecstasy inside him that weighs him down. When he floats back up to the surface, he climbs back to shore, slings his clothes over his arm, and runs wet and naked into the cottage. He shuts the door and draws the curtain. Berit is leaning out of her bed. She dries the water off him with her hot hands. She can see he is overjoyed.

Why are you so happy? she whispers, herself happy.

Then, while beaming at her, beaming into her eyes with his delight, he says:

Because it feels so good to swim at night.

But he knows better why he's so happy.

It isn't because he has finally exacted his sworn revenge.

It's because he has been freed from a long-standing jealousy.

A Letter to a Girl in Summer

Dear Berit!

Thanks for your lovely letter. I'm glad to hear that you arrived safely and that your father and mother are doing well. It's also good to know that I'm welcome up to Härjedalen. But, as you know, there's unfortunately no way I can come. For one thing, I have to spend the summer studying. Yes, I did do very well on the exam in April, but it's best if I'm not too confident in the future—besides, you've said the same thing yourself. There's also the question of money. As you know, I have no income of my own, and Papa seems to understand as little as ever that I need money, even though I don't have time to devote myself to a fruitful job. The other day I even had to sell some of my books at a secondhand shop to get money for some basic necessities. It was a little annoying, since the books have been in the bookcase for a long time and he considers everything in there his personal property, although some of them actually are mine. I got them so long ago that he's forgotten they don't belong to him. But you don't have to worry about my giving him any chances to make a scene. He usually doesn't notice anything you don't tell him directly. And why should I trouble someone with things they don't care about, especially when they don't even notice them?

In your letter you sounded a little worried about how I'd manage being alone when you're not in town to look after me. My dear, of course, I feel miserable that you're gone, sadder than you could imagine! After the wonderful thing that happened to us at Midsummer, you know that you mean everything to me. But once you have a person who means everything to you, you're never alone again, as you can surely understand. I'm actually doing quite well here. And to study better, sometimes I take my bicycle out and go for a swim. I lie by the water and read, since anyone who's spent a lot of time studying knows that you are most mentally efficient when you're able to release your physical energy at the same time. This is quite true for every student—which I'm sure you know from your own experience at school. Yet it's anything but obvious to Papa. One evening, he made quite a scene when he found out I was out swimming all day. He asked me if that was how I've been applying myself. I didn't answer him, of course, but now I simply let him think I stay home every day. As you know, it's not particularly nice to lie, but unfortunately, sometimes we're forced to even when we are personally against it. But the whole thing is quite harmless. Because when all is said and done, it doesn't really matter where he thinks I spend my days. So I don't feel the least bit guilty.

When you wrote about how I had threatened to commit suicide, you must have misunderstood me somehow. It's possible that I do get very depressed now and then, which is a very natural response to Mama's death and to the pain Papa has caused me. But what I mentioned on that last night on the island, that life is only a postponed suicide, or whatever my exact words were, I don't want you to take it too seriously, as you have obviously done. I didn't mean to frighten you at all. As far as I recall, my point was only to get you to understand how depressing our stay on the island was for me in spite of everything, especially since I had to feign pleasure and indifference toward all of Papa's tactlessness the entire time. Otherwise, I still stand by my theory that, strictly speaking, to live means nothing more than to postpone your own suicide day by day. Surely, you have experienced this as well, even if you can't bring yourself to put it into words, but you know it subconsciously.

You also wrote that you would prefer to come back as soon as possible. My dear, you shouldn't cut your vacation short for me! There's nothing going on here in the city, but even if I could visit you, you know very well that I can't keep taking your money as you have suggested, especially not since you spoke to your parents about it. It would be too humiliating. So I'll just stay here in the heat. But I'm with you the whole time in my thoughts. You also asked whether I go to the cinema a lot. No, I don't. Most of them are closed, especially the ones that usually have interesting pictures. Besides, you know that I really don't care for films.

You don't have to be worried about me. As far as I'm concerned, there's nothing to be worried about. I'm over the most painful part of my grieving for Mama, although I'm still sad and I do still miss her, but these feelings are manageable. My relationship with Papa hasn't improved, of course, at least not as far as any emotional or mental connection. However, I'm trying as hard as I can to refrain from judging him too harshly. What he did is inexcusable in many ways, but I also have to be capable of some magnanimity, and I think I've punished him enough after six months of silence. Therefore, I'm trying to show some kindness in my outward conduct with him, not without some obvious reservations, of course.

Now I've written too much about myself and my world. I look forward to hearing from you soon. I'm very lonesome without you, as you probably know.

Yours lovingly,
Bengt

P.S. Just remembered that you asked how Gun is doing. I really don't know, and I really don't care, as you can probably understand. In fact, I haven't seen her since Midsummer. Papa never brings her up either. So I can't complain. I never did like it when he used to constantly talk about what they were up to. So it's just as well that he doesn't mention her anymore.

A TWILIGHT MEETING

HELLO, BENGT, she says when he opens the door.

He does not say a word. Thirty seconds go by, maybe more. In her red dress, Gun is standing completely still on the cold, gray doorstep. Bengt doesn't look at her but past her, looks out at the stairs that slowly lead up to the silent and empty attic. But when he finally does look at her, he notices that she isn't looking at him either. She was looking past him, through the dark entrance as if she were searching for someone. He turns around and looks for himself. He can see farther than she can. He can see the broken sewing machine underneath the dusty cover all the way at the end of the hallway.

Papa isn't home, he mumbles.

It isn't until then that they look at each other, uncertain of what to say, afraid of what might be said.

Oh, Gun whispers, but he should be home tonight.

Then she turns not only her gaze from him but her head, too, and looks up at the same staircase. There is a smooth gray wall beyond the staircase window, the wall of a newly built building, where she lets her gaze hang for a while, like a window washer hanging

from his ropes. Bengt pulls the door toward him. He eventually decides to close it, but she holds her hand on the doorknob. So he lets
the door stay where it is.

Papa's at a fiftieth birthday party, he says. He'll probably come
home late. Very late.

Gun notices that he said "very late." Or more precisely, she notices how he said it. Suddenly Bengt notices, too, and, confused,
he wants to take it back since it's none of her business. But instead
of taking it back, he opens the door a little wider, and she lets go
of the doorknob. Downstairs, the front door slams. Someone whistling is approaching, coming up quickly. Then it occurs to him that
she can't keep standing where she is, not when someone is coming.

Please come in for a bit, he says, I was just making coffee.

Of course, it isn't true. She realizes this once she's in the kitch-
en, and Bengt does, too. He sits down on the kitchen bench and
stares down at his hands. He doesn't look up until Gun turns on the
gas. She is standing with her back to him, a slender, straight back in
a red dress. It's a dress he recognizes, but he isn't sure he has ever seen
this particular back before. She opens the jars on the shelf and finds
the coffee in the last one. She is busy for a while washing spoons,
drying cups, and slicing bread. She dries more cups than they need
and slices more bread than they will be able to eat. He is glad that
it's taking so long, but he's afraid it will suddenly be silent in the
kitchen, and then he won't know what to say. As she sets the table
for him, he feels ashamed. It occurs to him that he's sitting in his
mother's kitchen and that a stranger is using it as if it were her own.
What will he say if his mother asks him about it? But when they sit
on opposite sides of the table, they talk about something else.

They talk about Berit. And Bengt is the one who initiates the
conversation. He has just written a letter to her, a still unsent letter.

I sent her your regards, he says and looks at her, in a separate P.S.

Then he realizes how stupid it is that he said "P.S." It doesn't
matter whether he did it in a postscript or in the body of the letter.

I think Berit is sweet, Gun says.

Papa thinks she's ugly, Bengt replies.

Then he quickly adds:

But I don't think so.

I don't think so either, Gun says. I think she is very sweet.

So they both think she is sweet. They sit for a while thinking of what else they can say about Berit besides that she is sweet. But then Bengt realizes there's nothing more to say, so he comes up with something else. He talks about Härjedalen and about her parents who live there. Gun mentions that she has also been to Härjedalen.

It was beautiful there, she says as she finishes her coffee, especially at night. We used to walk barefoot in the forest, and the cows roamed around with bells on.

It's nice to walk barefoot, Bengt says; it's almost the best thing there is.

He has also finished his coffee, but he knows they have to keep on drinking, so he gets up to get the pot. When he leaves the stove, he notices that the strap of her black shoe has come undone. Then he remembers that they were just talking about walking barefoot. He isn't barefoot himself; he is wearing slippers, brown leather slippers that he got from his mother for Christmas. He didn't like them then and neither did his father. They're for hermits and oldsters, his dad had said. So it wasn't until after his mother's death that Bengt started wearing them. And he didn't mean for Gun to see them, but she does anyway.

Nice slippers, Bengt, she says as he pours the coffee.

His hand is so tremulous that five drops fall on her plate.

Got them for Christmas, he says, from Mama.

After that, she doesn't say anything else, nearly nothing the entire time it takes them to drink the next cup. Nor does Bengt say anything. He is looking down at his coffee, which is capped by a skin of cream. When his cup is empty, he stares down into the bottom of it, the whole time thinking of his mother. Then a ridiculous thought occurs to him. He thinks Gun might be wearing his mother's shoes, but he isn't sure, and he doesn't really want to be, either. So he sits there thinking about the time his father came home with the black shoes. It must have been a Saturday, since he got home very early and was very drunk. He had a box under his arm, and he dropped it as he stepped over the kitchen threshold. His mother picked it up and put it on the table. She knew it was for her, but she didn't bother to open it, because she was annoyed. So the father tore the strings and ripped off the paper himself and held up the shoes under the light. Do you think I'm seventeen? he now remembers her saying. Not particularly loud but she said it, although she was no longer annoyed. It sounded more as though she was sad that she wasn't seventeen anymore.

But when the memory is over, there is nothing left to distract him. He slowly puts his cup aside as he leans over the edge of the table and looks down at Gun's shoes. He can't help it. No one can help it. He recognizes them all too well. But he doesn't let her know.

The strap has come undone, is all he says.

To fasten the strap, he kneels down next to her, very gently and very quickly.

Bengt, I have to go, she says. But she knows it's already too late.

Wait, I have to fasten the strap, he whispers, whispers quite helplessly and puts his hand around her ankle.

But he does not fasten the strap. Instead, he takes off her shoe and sets it down by the leg of the table. She is not surprised. She doesn't say anything, though she knows that she should. Instead, she places her other foot into his hands. Then he unfastens the strap of the other shoe, and carefully, as though it were made of glass, he places it next to the other one. Then he gazes up at her, not afraid but trembling, like someone on the edge of a diving board being forced to jump. She leans over and looks down at him as one looks down a well, uneasy yet very enchanted. She can't help herself. But it isn't his eyes at the bottom of the well. It is his lips. Slowly, they part as if somebody dropped a rock down the well.

After the kiss, he fumbles after her hands as if he can't see a thing. Nor can he see anything, nothing but her blonde hair with the curved white comb in it. When he finds her hands, one on each hip, he pulls her down to him. She sinks silently to the floor. They sit for a long time between the chair and the table, like two children in the sand. Even though they know the situation is absurd, they are sincere and do not dare say a word. It's completely silent in the kitchen. The evening casts nothing but shadows through the closed window, and the only thing they hear is each other, though no one is saying a word. Silent and afraid, they hold each other's hands, each seeking the other's help against their own bodies. They know that if they let each other go, they will be lost, but if they hold on any longer, they will be just as lost.

I've dreamt about your foot, Bengt whispers.

And it's probably true. As she bends her nyloned foot, he realizes it's the same foot he has already held in his dream. Then he frees his hands—though Gun tries to hold on to them—takes her foot, and raises it slightly off the ground. It is warm and dry, like a stone that has been basking in the sun. When he puts her foot back down, he says:

You have beautiful shoes.

He knows that he shouldn't have said it. He just can't help it. Nor can she help answering.

I got them from Knut, she says, almost inaudibly.

At once, they notice she said "Knut." She could have said "your father." But now he is glad she didn't, because Knut is not his father. Knut is a stranger. And this stranger has given Gun a pair of shoes. This doesn't really matter to him, but the way she says it makes it clear that she doesn't know whose shoes they had been. This makes him happy, and it makes her pure. And the one you love has to be pure. Otherwise, you cannot love her.

But to love someone is also to make her pure. So he shoves the shoes into the darkness under the table and asks with burning cheeks:

You have a beautiful dress, too.

A question, indeed, but perhaps a question unnoticed. In any case, she does not answer. He takes her gently by the shoulders and feels how naked the material is. But it's only so naked before he finds out what he needs to know. And to get the answer, he looks directly into her eyes, afraid yet hopeful at the same time, and of course he sees what he wants to see: she has never found out who the dress was meant for. Then he starts to unbutton the red dress. One by one, he takes the soft, tiny buttons and slips them through the holes. Gun watches in silence, watches how his hand sinks lower and watches how calm and beautiful it is.

She knows she shouldn't. She knows there's still time to get up and leave. She is very discerning and knows very well what would happen if she left now. They would suddenly hear all the noises from the street again. All the noises in the house, too. For a brief moment they would stand and face each other in shame. Then he would bend down to get her shoes, and as he put them on her feet, she would button up her dress again. How simple everything could be. In spite of knowing this, she doesn't leave.

She doesn't leave, because she is paralyzed. Not paralyzed with fear, or desire either. What binds her and what binds him, too, is the beauty of the moment. Nothing is ever as beautiful as the first isolated minutes with someone who might be able to love you— with someone you yourself might be able to love. There is nothing as silent as these minutes, nothing so saturated with sweet anticipation. It is for these few minutes that we love, not for the many that follow. Never again, they realize, would anything so beautiful ever happen to them. They might be happier, more impassioned, too, and infinitely satiated with their own bodies and with each other's. But never again would it be so beautiful.

This is why she doesn't leave, and why he continues to hesitantly unbutton the red dress, trying to get it to last as long as possible. But when there are no more buttons, she slowly pulls the dress over her head. Carefully, she pulls the white comb from her hair and places it between them without making a sound.

But the moment before it happens, they look into each other's eyes. Her eyes are bright and soothing; they hypnotize him into tranquility. It's because of her calmness that he loves her. And the one we love has to be calm because nothing is as loathsome as anxiety. Never before has anyone he loved been so calm. Never before has he himself been so still. When they come together, they come together in a great moment of peace and stillness. They are not afraid of the unimaginable thing that is happening. All they can feel is that one calm is joining another calm, like a great calm wave washing over a warm calm rock. They do not even pant, but they breathe rapidly yet without difficulty. Their bodies are hot but not sweaty, their lips are not bleeding, just slightly moist, and when they look into each other's eyes, their pupils do not gleam with the hysteria of desire but with a tender and unexpected serenity.

Afterward, he places the white comb in her hair, delicately, like a flower. They go into his room and lie quietly next to each other for a long time. He doesn't cleave to her, because he knows he doesn't have to. She's not like someone else who you could never let go of, someone who, through her fear of being quickly forgotten, tensely clutches you and forces you to think, think the entire time it lasts, Now I'm lying with her. Now I'm stroking her. Now I'm moving my hands up higher.

They aren't surprised even after it happened. They speak peacefully with each other, lying on their backs and letting the words fly up to the ceiling as if they were talking to themselves. Because they are so calm, they can tell each other everything without shame and without it sounding like a confession. Nor are they surprised by what they learn about each other. Quite openly, she tells him how she has longed for him every night since that evening when Knut invited her over for tea. Quite openly, she lets him know that she always expected it would happen if only he wanted it to. She also admits to him that she knew Knut wasn't going to be home tonight.

Just as candidly, he talks about his solitary promenades—always in her direction—about his cold nights outside patrolling the cinema, about his dreams, and that whenever he kissed Berit, he always closed his eyes and imagined it was Gun he was kissing.

Everything is natural and free of shame. A bit later, when they are at Bengt's desk and leafing through his books like lovers do, Gun finds his letter to Berit. He has already sealed the envelope, but she doesn't ask him to open it, just as he doesn't reproach her for the time she locked herself in the cottage with his father. All she says about the letter is that he should send it and that he should write more letters more often. And they aren't cynical when they tell each other, once again, that Berit is sweet and that they can't hurt her. They are only considerate because their tenderness toward each other also makes them compassionate to others. As for Knut, they say that everything should go on as usual. Gun will continue to see him, will continue to let him love her, because it's the only possible way if they are to go on loving each other. They speak calmly and without bitterness about Berit and Knut, two poor strangers who are not allowed to be hurt.

Later still, when the light is off and when the roar of the city sounds like the humming of a gigantic shell, they carry on whispering in the darkness about the future. They will meet seldom and in secret, but one time they will meet for a long time. In this future, there is nothing threatening, nothing that could not be dealt with, because through their calmness they have disarmed all dangers.

Perhaps all but one, and it's her fault that they notice it. She suddenly lays her hand over his eyes as if there were something he wasn't allowed to see in the dark and then whispers over his face:

I'm so afraid.

Of what? he whispers back.

That I'm too old for you.

Then her hand cools but only for a moment. He spreads the blanket over them along with all the thoughts he had during the loneliness of spring. Then he folds his hands around her back, as if protecting them both from all threats, and whispers:

I'll make you young, just as young as I am. Now you're just as young as I. Don't you feel it?

She does feel it and then takes her hand away from his eyes. For a long time, she is just as young as he, and there is nothing silly about it. Only something beautiful.

But much later, no magic can help. They are not asleep, nor are they fully awake. Peaceful and relaxed with all desire dormant within them, and happy as one is when there isn't anything more to ask for, they rest in each other's arms—he on her right and she on his left. Then, suddenly, a car door slams on the street below. At first, they don't grasp what it is, because they've forgotten all reality. This causes their fright to descend all the more rapidly, tearing them violently apart. And when he slightly opens the window shade, the magic is gone.

For the one leaning quite drunkenly on a taxi and searching his pockets for money with one of his tired hands is not a stranger named Knut. It is Bengt's father, and this is why he shivers by the window. Not because he is naked, but because he has instantly discovered the truth. For a moment this discovery is so horrible that he wishes something dangerous would happen to the man down there. That he would fall flat on his face under the car just as it takes off. Then Bengt feels Gun's nails digging into his chest. She was leaning over his shoulder, and he can tell from her nails that she also recognizes the man staggering on the sidewalk and waving his hand at a moving car. It's not someone named Knut whom they hardly know. It's a terrible man who is Bengt's father as well as the lover of the woman Bengt loves, too.

This man bends down to pick up a coin on the sidewalk. Then he falls, of course, but he doesn't stay down. As he slowly heads up to them, Gun swiftly gets dressed under the light of the lamp. And before Bengt turns the lamp off, they look at each other for a brief, shameful moment. Neither of them is particularly beautiful then because they are both flustered. He turns off the lamp just as the key begins fumbling after the lock. With her shoes in her hands, Gun crawls into his bed. He hides her securely underneath the blanket, pressing her as close to him as he can so that she will take up less space; he crumples the red dress in the same way. But the darkness and intimacy provide them some comfort, which allows them to endure it to some degree.

Otherwise what is happening is quite horrible and unbearable. They hear him fumbling about the entrance, trying to find the light, and almost in unison they whisper:

We haven't forgotten anything, have we?

It's a dreadful thought that they could have forgotten something, but they soon realize he's too drunk to be able to notice anything anyway. As the father makes his way through the darkness with dragging steps and sudden outbursts of rage against everything he bumps into, they both try to remember that the doors to Bengt's room are locked. Finally, they hear him find the daybed and thud into it, as if falling from a blow. After that, it's silent for a while. Gun is no longer afraid, but she is crying. Nor is Bengt afraid, but he isn't proud either. And he's not at all pleased that his father has made her cry. If Knut had been a stranger, he could have been amused by it, but now he can only hate. He recognizes the hatred at once. It's an old, familiar hatred, as firmly attached to him as his own ears. It's the hatred he's known almost his entire life—every time his mother cried on account of his father.

Once they hear him snoring, they jump up and turn on the light. Bengt slips Gun's shoes back onto her feet and fastens the straps around her ankles. This time, when they look at each other they are genuinely beautiful again, and they kiss each other even more beautifully. When they are done, everything is almost as natural as before. He gives her Berit's letter to put in the mailbox so that she will get it sooner. He unlocks the door, and they sneak hand in hand across the dark hallway. At the entrance, they kiss each other again, childishly long. Gun will call him. In the future she will always call, but they will only meet occasionally.

When he opens the shade, he sees her standing in the moonlight and waving to him from the other side of the street. He sees her lean far over the gutter, as if trying to reach him. Then she starts to walk away, going slowly past the butcher shop and all the other shops up the corner. Turning the corner is difficult when you are in love, but once she has done it, she isn't truly gone. The light itself has taken on a reddish tinge from her dress. And when he pulls down the shade and turns around, the entire room is saturated with her. He flings himself on his bed and buries his face in his pillow. The pillow is saturated with her, too. His pillow will never be lonesome again.

After some time, he opens the door to the father's room and goes inside. He turns on the ceiling light and tiptoes to the daybed. Then he kneels over the sleeping man and takes off his shoes. Without a sound, he sets them down on the floor and then loosens his collar. As he watches the slumbering face, he is struck by a tenderness so unexpected and so overwhelming that he puts his hands over the father's face and caresses it. While caressing him, he is filled with an irrational joy. He gently peels off his father's jacket and unbuttons his vest. He hangs the jacket on a hanger in the hallway and pulls out an overcoat. As he spreads the overcoat over his father, his eyes begin to cloud with tears. Then he sits on the floor next to the daybed, and with his father's hand in his, he gazes up at the ceiling as he cries and cries with joy. Joy, because the room is filled with her and because the room is devoid of his mother. He doesn't go back to his room until all of his tears are drained.

There, he immediately falls asleep and sleeps so deeply, dreamlessly, and peacefully, as one can only sleep when the unimaginable has happened. The night after discovering America, Columbus must have slept as he never slept before.

A Letter to an Island in Autumn

Beloved!

I've done what we've agreed upon, and I'll be coming to the island soon. I didn't enjoy doing it, but I knew I had no other choice. It was harder to forge the draft papers than I thought. In fact, making your telegram was much easier. Of course, I just took an old one and found a new envelope and stamp; the hardest part was changing the date. I didn't need to go to so much trouble, after all, because Knut hardly looked at it. He just found it a bit strange that I was being called up for military service now, but he was convinced when I reminded him of the four weeks that I got off last year for my studies. I can assure you that it's quite painful to have to deceive him like this. It's the first time in my life that I've ever forged anything, and I'll never become a great forger—this much is certain. My conscience is much too delicate for that. And as soon as the draft papers served their purpose, I burned them up and blew the ashes out the window. It wasn't until then that I started to feel a little better.

But I won't truly be at peace until I'm with you again. If I only had the words to convey to you the indescribable peace you give me, what you mean to me, and the infinite significance you have added to my life!! For the first time in my life, I understand what it means to really love someone. This means that I can never be truly alone because you are constantly in my thoughts. Whatever I do and wherever I am, you are always there. If you only knew how happy this makes me, and how happy I can make others because of it.

As you know, Berit has returned. As we agreed, I see her fairly often—much more than before. Our relationship is much better now than it has ever been. I no longer get annoyed with her bad habits, and since I no longer need to feel myself bound to her, I don't feel the need to hurt her like I did before. This has been quite good for her, in fact. She doesn't constantly burst into tears, and she seldom has headaches. Of course, she thinks I love her like never before, and why shouldn't I let her believe it? If you can make someone glad and happy by simply refraining from confessing every single thing you think or do, then I don't see any reason why you shouldn't. To downright lie is an entirely different matter. But it won't hurt her in the least if she doesn't know. If anyone should be hurt, it should be me, but I'm intelligent enough to be able to differentiate between real duplicity, which aims to harm people, and a smart moderation of the so-called truth, whose only goal is to make life easier for everyone involved.

You will forgive me if this becomes a longer, and as you will probably notice, more philosophical letter than the ones you're otherwise used to, but the fact is that I feel the steps I'm taking are important enough to me that I really have to analyze my situation thoroughly, so that we can both spend the time we have together in peace and quiet. You see, there's nothing more dangerous than not knowing what you are doing. Most people don't, and that's why it's often a dreadful shock for them when they are one day forced to define their actions. In their subsequent fear from this shock, they lose any chance of seeing reality as it really is, and instead they see a grotesque distortion. This is precisely why it's so important to be clearly aware, at every moment of your life, of what your actions imply and the consequences they can have. This is why I also devote myself with almost scientific fervor to analyzing our mutual actions. To deceive others isn't pretty, but to deceive yourself is dangerous.

I've thought a lot about what you said since the last time we saw each other, especially when you asked whether I know what I am doing. Of course, I know; otherwise, I couldn't do it. You can only do such a thing when you know exactly what you're getting into. In reality, there's nothing better than being aware of your own actions because, then, there's almost nothing that you can't do—I mean without regretting it afterward and becoming miserable. What we are doing is something everyone does, but most do it without really knowing it because they cannot face it. Alma did it, and Knut has done it several times. Berit probably hasn't done it yet, but she will eventually, of course. I'm sure that most people regret it afterward and become afraid. But I will never regret it. Besides, I love you too much, and I'm much too aware of what I am doing. We who know what we're doing are like chess players. We don't ask the pawns where we should move them. We don't even have respect for the queens.

You also said that you're ashamed sometimes. I don't understand why. We two have nothing to be ashamed of. Anyone who loves as we do is pure, and, until now, I didn't know what purity was. It is to be so absorbed in a feeling that it burns away all doubts, all cowardice, and all cares within you. You become whole and strong, and you go straight to the goal without hesitation. You become brave, too. To be pure is to be able to sacrifice everything but the one thing you're living for. I'm prepared to do that, so there's no need to be ashamed. People like Knut, on the other hand, do need to feel ashamed. What do you think he would sacrifice for his love for you? Nothing! Not one workday, not a single wholehearted act of ruthlessness. And do you think Alma was any less small-minded, or purer? She didn't even dare to love enough to let her lover come back, not even enough to lie to me.

I don't want to be petty like them, so petty that everything I touch turns just as small and paltry. I've detested them my whole life for it, because they didn't dare to be pure, because they weren't daring enough to do anything truly beautiful. When I look at Knut's life, I'm afraid. I don't want to degrade him in front of you, but I have to say that it would kill me if I had to live a life like his. What do you think it means for him to live? Nothing but to wake up in the morning, read the paper, drink a cup of coffee, go to work, repair a chair, eat breakfast, repair a table, go home, buy a newspaper, eat dinner, take a nap, listen to the radio, go to the bathroom, tell a story (preferably a filthy one), go out—to the cinema, a bed, or a café and watch a film, undress a woman, or drink a beer—go home, get undressed, snore, wake up again, drink a cup of coffee, read the paper, and go to work. The worst part isn't that he thinks this is living; the worst part of his life is that he's satisfied with it. Most appalling is that he thinks this is how it should be, and he can't understand anyone who thinks differently. Whenever he doesn't understand something, he says, I'm sorry; I'm just a simple carpenter. And he's forced to accept that I study literary history and Scandinavian languages. He accepts it not because it makes me intellectually richer, but because he thinks it will give me the chance to live an easier life than he had. *Easier but not different.* Essentially, he wants to provide me with exactly the same life. Only I should have more expensive underwear, wake up a couple hours later, read a different paper, sit at an instructor's desk instead of stand at a workbench, eat a better breakfast, eat a more expensive dinner, go to the opera instead of the cinema, have four rooms instead of two, maids and a gramophone. Can't you see how that disgusts me? My whole life I have searched, more or less consciously, for a way to support myself in a way that is different from his—one that is purer, more reckless, and more exciting. One that demands more, that burns more dangerously, that affords everything but the easy life.

It's important for me to say this, but above all it's important for me to say this to you. Why? Because it's through you that I have the chance to live purely. Now I want to sacrifice everything: my studies, my mourning for Mama, my father's trust, and my fiancée's devotion for the only thing I consider worth living for: my love for you.

You're wondering whether I have tried this before. You ask why I've waited so long. I have tried, but I didn't succeed, and I can tell you why. But first I'll tell you what I have tried. When I was seventeen, Knut took me with him to a socialist meeting. When the group sang "International," tears came to my eyes. I thought I had found a boundless and thoroughly overwhelming sense of solidarity and fighting spirit with everyone who was singing. Of course, it was an illusion. My own emotions had made me idealize the whole scene, but I didn't realize this until much later. The singing continued inside me the whole way home. Then outside the front door, Knut asked me, Do you want to be a socialist like me and Alma? I did become one— but not like them. After all, what do you think they sacrificed for their beliefs? Nothing! They may have gone to a meeting instead of a movie a few evenings, and they subscribed to a different paper from that of our neighbors. On Swedish Flag Day they didn't buy any flags, but on the first of May they did buy a red May Day flower. This is what they called conviction. I call it dirty fraud against what they said they believed in and against the ones who claimed to share the same convictions. When I told them this, they did not understand. They were just "simple people," so they didn't need to understand. But when I started to neglect my schoolwork for my principles, they asked me to think about the future. That's what I couldn't understand. Then they told me that everyone has to consider their future and, as a matter of fact, everyone did. Then I realized that they were right. I looked around at everyone who believed like we did and found nobody who was willing to sacrifice everything for his beliefs. Maybe they were willing to sacrifice something for a little while, but when their personal dream of the future came into conflict with their beliefs, they chose the dream. The ones who had the fortune to become officials had it best: they didn't have to give up their convictions; they may have grown a little cold, but they didn't need to give them up. Nor did they have to give up their dream of personal happiness, because officials with cold convictions can climb as high as possible. So I quit sacrificing everything for my beliefs because anyone who abandons everything by himself is just stupid.

The other time was when I was drafted. As you know, we were supposed to be prepared to defend democracy. I wanted to do everything I could to defend it, but nobody would let me do it. I once told this to a captain who was a Nazi. Then I got six days of probation for slandering a superior in the office. So I started playing dice, and I lost. I played poker, too, and lost. But it was harmless since I didn't have a lot to lose. From the office, where we played dice when the master sergeant was outside drinking, we had a view of the real war. Of course, we were happy when the right side won, even if they weren't as right as I had hoped.

I think I've learned that before you attempt to sacrifice everything for a just cause, you should always keep in mind that no one is willing to give up as much as you are. Because of that, it's no longer right but, rather, very wrong, many times over. Therefore, it's a matter of finding a cause that only a few people are willing to renounce everything for. The fewer there are, the surer you can be that your sacrifice is not in vain. It's best when there are only two. Love, you see, requires two and sacrifices everything to continue being love.

By now you must be tired of this long letter, and maybe even a little afraid. You shouldn't be afraid. There's nothing to be afraid of. You shouldn't be afraid of morality, because there's no one who believes in morality as strongly as we believe in each other. There is no one who could sacrifice for morality a thousandth of what we sacrifice for what we believe in. And by the way, is there anything more virtuous than giving up everything for something you know is right?

My darling! On Friday night we'll finally be alone together, more alone than anyone before us and perhaps even after us. I'm coming on the ten o'clock bus, and you can wait with the boat by the jetty. I'm arriving late so that no one will see us. I'm only bringing along a small suitcase with essentials, since you don't really need a lot of personal belongings when you're called in for service—or when you're in love. Then, you only need each other. There are three days left. Do you think I can wait that long?

Yours,
Bengt

P.S. Something silly happened this evening. Berit found a button in my bed, which must have come loose from your dress. I don't know if she recognized it, but she started crying all the same. When I asked her why, she asked whether I thought she was ugly. So I told her that I thought she was sweet. Of course, I think she's ugly, but it's senseless to let her know that. Then she asked me whether I had been unfaithful to her. I jokingly answered, Yes, several times. She didn't realize it was a joke, so I had a hard time trying to convince her that the button was Aunt Ida's. She finally believed me, because you can convince her of anything if you just keep at it long enough. Knut's very pleased that she's around a lot nowadays, and I keep her here as late as I can. It isn't necessary, of course, to raise any suspicions. We have to be very careful. That's why I think the island is an excellent choice. There will be some problems with the address. A conscript eventually does need a station address. I pretended to find out that I'd be placed in the vicinity of Norrtälje and gave both Knut and Berit *poste restante Norrtälje* as the temporary address. It's no longer a military address, but neither of them has been drafted, so there shouldn't be any risk. Good night, my darling. I should hurry and post the letter before Knut comes home.

A TIGER AND A GAZELLE

THE SEA IS HIGH AND GREEN during the day and black with flashes of white at night. But the water is clear as it usually is in fall. The six broadleaf trees around the inlet are shedding their leaves, which blow freshly onto the porch every morning. At night, the cool September moon gleams red. When it drifts out of the night's dark clouds it has blood on its lips. The sailboat season is over, and now colliers sway sluggishly along the horizon. Their smoke sinks black and heavily into the sea. Twice a week a train of barges drifts across the bay, and during that hour Bengt and Gun stay inside, thinking that someone might see them. When they kiss each other, their lips taste like salt. In fact, wherever they put their lips tastes like salt. So after ten days they know the taste of salt all too well.

They stay on the island for two weeks. And during that time they only see each other and no one else. Sometimes they might see people on the barges, but it's from several hundred feet away. No faces, just black shadows huddled up against the rudders—maybe only smoke from the pipes. Though this is true, they also see the dog. At first he hates the dog, but after the first week he is happy to have it along. But eventually he starts to hate it again.

The first few days are probably the best, the days before they really know each other. It's harder when they get to know each other, because it's hard to love the one we know really well. To be in love is to be curious. Therefore, only what we aren't accustomed to is beautiful. And maybe only that which is new is beautiful. In any case, we're only capable of loving what is new. So in order to love someone we know well, it's necessary to forget her first, not entirely but significantly.

This is what they learn in fourteen days. But they don't admit it to each other. They are cautious and even untruthful. To be able to love someone for long, you have to lie, largely to yourself but mostly to the one you love. One form of lying is refinement, and soon they are also refined. They give each other new names, find new places to kiss, new places to fall asleep. It makes them happy for a while, but it cannot hide the truth, so they find other ways to hide it. One way to prolong their love is to combine it with hate; this is the best way but perhaps also the most dangerous. Love and hate are the cat and mouse of emotions. Sometimes the cat chases the mouse, and sometimes the mouse chases the cat. But once the cat and mouse are both tired of the chase, there isn't much else for them to do. The only thing left is to acknowledge the most painful truth of all, the most painful but also the most honest: that two people in love cannot be alone together on an island without falling out of love, that they cannot be an island. They need contact with the mainland. They need all the other people they know. It's a horrible consolation for anyone who believes that love is an island in the sea, but once we weary of islands, it's actually quite comforting. Because when a person grows tired of loving, he is relieved to find there are still so many people to love besides the one he has loved.

The first few days are wonderful for them. The sun shines, there is a fresh breeze, and they are alone. They drink each other up, sleep, and rouse again. The dog often wakes them up, and when they put it outside, it barks in front of the door, slams its heavy body against it, and raps the doorknob with its paws. If the dog is inside, they jerk from their sleep, awakened from a dream about rain or some waves. The dog is hovering over them and licking their shoulders.

Gun pulls it down to her, lays it between them, and pets it. Bengt is a tad jealous of the dog, afraid of it, even—afraid in an absurd kind of way. But he doesn't dare admit it. He's afraid the dog is a witness. He's afraid the dog will understand.

Otherwise he isn't afraid at all. He simply thinks it's all very nice. They found a fur rug in a closet and spread it out in front of the fireplace, where they make large fires several times a day, lie naked in the flickering light, and play with each other's bodies. For the first time he isn't ashamed of his body. It's because Gun says his body is beautiful and because he knows he is strong. She makes him strong. They make each other strong. They aren't calm like the first time, but much stronger. They lie close to the fire, which nearly burns them. The sides braving the fire grow hot, but they wrap the rug around their cold parts. For the most part, they lie quietly with only their fingers playing. They constantly find new places to linger on, each softer than the previous. They don't move around much these days—just trips to the kitchen, to the alcove, to look for firewood, down to the sea. And they play innocent games. They pretend they're in paradise, the most innocent place of all. Lying naked at the bottom of the boat, they drift for hours and hours through paradise. The ocean crashes against the frame, water splashes inside—it is cold yet it burns. Sometimes he is her child, and he doesn't mind. And since she has never had a child, she enjoys it, too. Cleaving to her, he drinks her milk; he drinks and drinks and it never runs out. His lips only become sore.

Then they play games that spare their lips. She is his child, a little doll that he tenderly undresses for bed. They learn not to hurt each other. They pretend they're made of porcelain and that they have to be delicate with each other if they don't want to break. They are boundlessly imaginative. When they eat, they eat on the rug, lying on their stomachs like children on green grass. They close the shutters and play all night and throughout the thunder. They toast apples and roast potatoes in the crackling fire. They have wine, too, and they drink it but just a little. Because we never want to see the one we love drunk but only pure—pure, ardent, and beautiful. When they swim, they charge hand in hand into the highest swell, but the dog stays behind barking on the shore. When it finally does join them, they whirl around in the water, all three of them roaring with happiness. Sometimes he carries her under the water, and she is as light as a child. But he never dares carry her on land, because he's afraid he isn't strong enough and he's afraid to look foolish. And nobody in love can afford to look foolish. The first few times she asks why she is so light in the water, he says it's because she is a child or a bird that he is rescuing. But the day he responds with Archimedes's principle, she is pensive, though still not afraid.

They don't speak a lot about the future the first few days, perhaps not at all. Their bodies are so insatiable that no questions are needed, almost no thoughts either. Sometimes he wakes up at night. The ocean rushes through the night like an express train, and the dog snores in the kitchen. To avoid being alone, he delicately wakes her, and they lie in bed listening to the sea and the rain pecking like birds against the roof and the shutters. This may be when they are the happiest. They aren't fully awake, and they have no memories of yesterday to startle them. They only have each other's intimacy and warmth. In those moments, they are anonymous. There is no Bengt and no Gun, only one person next to the other, who could be anyone at all, and who is warm and in love. They even have to grope after each other's faces like blind people to recognize each other. But this is only a game, because they don't need to recognize each other. In fact, they shouldn't recognize each other. The darkness as well as the tenderness and warmth of the flesh are enough.

This, among other things, is why they keep the shutters closed all day. And they lie naked with their eyes closed at the bottom of the boat because their clothes carry memories with them. And even though it's harder for them, they can even be anonymous then— not for long periods of time but for a little while. But even in those moments they sense that the moment might be near, the moment when they are too familiar with each other, when their curiosity finally dies out. Then, every birthmark will be dangerously familiar; there won't be a single gesture they can make that won't remind the other of the gesture from yesterday or the day before. All of it is just a postponement.

One night, he wakes up and knows it is over. At the same time, he's unable to fathom it. As usual, he first lies there listening to the marching of the ocean and the mendacious whistling of the wind. Somewhere, a shutter is banging and the rain is pouring down. He's a little cold, has the urge to wake her, but suppresses it immediately without knowing why. Instead, he gets up very carefully. The floor is cold and damp. They were bathing in the dark just before they went to bed and their footprints haven't had the chance to dry yet. Standing there, he hears Gun turn in bed and mumble something, and finally he hears her breathing peacefully again.

As he lights the lamp, he wonders what the word was. He thinks he heard a name, but he isn't exactly sure. When he shines the light on her, she doesn't react to it. She is lying on her back with her hair over her face. Nothing would have to happen if she woke up, but she doesn't wake up. And he can't wake her up, because he's afraid she will recognize him. Instead, she just lies there, leaving him on his own. Yes, what he is feeling is loneliness. And her sleep is a shell that he cannot crack. He can only touch the shell and be terrified of its hardness. He tilts the lamp toward her and has the urge to twirl her hair around his finger. But he doesn't submit to this urge either, because he suddenly remembers the last time he did this. It was like watching a film. His hand slowly makes its way to her hair. Then he coils a lock around his finger, and Gun smiles. He must have done it a thousand times. But he cannot do it for the thousand and first time.

The thousand and first time he can only watch. It's the first time he has watched her while shining a light on her face. He sees that she is old. Then he realizes he will never be able to make her young, and this terrifies him. For the first time on the island, he sees for himself what he is doing and tears his eyes away. She has fine wrinkles under her eyes and her hair is dyed, with great care but not so well that he can't notice. He lowers the light even more, of course, in the hope that she will wake up and defend them both against everything awakening inside him. Unfortunately, she does not wake up. She sleeps heavily and peacefully. But he burns himself on the lamp chimney.

He puts the lamp down by the open fireplace, where the embers are still faintly glowing. The dog comes pattering from the kitchen. He lies down on the rug and spreads the dog over him like a blanket, but the dog must think he's going to hurt it and fiercely resists, clawing him on the shoulder. Then he has the overwhelming urge to be cruel to the dog, so he shoos it away. Of course, he is afraid to do any harm. He knows what it means. He knows how rotten people become when they hurt others. So he suffers alone and in silence, huddled up and musing in the glow of the fading embers.

Because when the desire within us starts to fade, we are struck with pangs of consciousness and a flood of questions. As long as our pleasure lasts, we can be happy—as long as we are also pure. But now he is lying there feeling filthy. It doesn't last long, but long enough for it to sting. And once it has sufficiently burned, he is no longer lying there filthy but standing at the porch railing, simply hating. He hates Gun.

It is raining and starless. With an almost invisible light, the moon wanders behind the thick clouds. The waves hiss against the rocks and fizzle out. He is naked but doesn't feel the cold. He grips the rail harder; he does this instead of hitting her. And he wants to hit her because she is able to sleep. It really is because she can sleep that he hates her, because she can sleep while he suffers. He simply cannot fathom such heartlessness. That she can be sleeping underneath warm blankets as he stands freezing in the dark rain.

So that's what she's like, his anger tells him, that's what the one I love is like. When she's had enough fun, she sleeps, and when she wakes up, she only does so to have more. This is why I, being pure, must hate her. Oh, purity is a terrible master and always wears a mask.

It is his passion and not his reason that hates her. His reason, which is now quite powerless, tells him he hates her because she is old and because he has just discovered it, not because she is any worse than he is. But what else is our reason but a young gazelle that comes down to drink at the watering hole? There, it suddenly sees the crystal clear surface darkened by a terrifying reflection. And the gazelle isn't much in the tiger's claws, a morsel at best. Its only salvation is that its flesh might be tough.

But his tiger has very strong teeth. And it's ferocious. It roars in his ears what he should do. He closes both doors in the kitchen so that he can't be caught by surprise. Her purse has a simple clasp— at least he's able to open it easily. Inside, there is a heavy cigarette case he has never seen before. It is also easy to open. It's empty, but engraved on the lid is "E.S." His instinct immediately tells him it's the name of a lover. There is a little notebook with yellow binders at the bottom of her purse. As he flips through it, his emotions tell him that he is right for doing it, because we have the right to know whether the one we love—that is, the one we give all our trust to— is deceiving us. In the book are some phone numbers next to insignificant names, the names of women. He doesn't even find their own number.

When he closes the purse again the clasp snaps much louder than he expected. When he looks at the dog, which is sprawled out on the rug, he sees that it is studying him with vigilant eyes. He throws the purse down as if it had burnt him and loudly opens up a cupboard door, so the dog would think he was looking for something—a glass or a fork. To find a fork, he pulls out a random drawer. There are no forks in it, but there is a pipe, which hasn't been smoked in ages. He sticks it between his teeth and inhales. It tastes bitter, as bitter as knowing you are being deceived. He carefully returns the pipe and slowly pushes in the drawer.

As he does this, the tiger swallows the gazelle in one gulp. Now he understands that everything is a lie. She had said that the island and the cottage on it belonged to a sick girlfriend who has been cared for by relatives in Norway for a long time now. But girlfriends don't smoke pipes. The house is a lover's. The boat, too. All the land he walks on during the day and all the skin he caresses at night belongs to a mysterious man, a man he hates but can do nothing about. He leans over and looks at the dog. This time with his tiger eyes. The dog is a man's dog, not a woman's. And with his tiger paws, he thrashes it on the back so that it yelps.

Then Gun wakes up. He hears her calling him through the

thin walls. He turns up the lamp's flame so that it's as bright as can be in the alcove, but he is instantly unable to look at her. What had just happened was too awful for that. When we ourselves deceive someone, we're able to understand it so well because every naked act we do is escorted by elaborate explanations. But that we ourselves might be deceived is inconceivable—just as inconceivable as the idea that we will one day die. We can only accept that other people will die and burn.

He puts the smoking lamp on a chair with some clothes on it, his and hers mixed together. He starts moving them because her clothes are defiled, but also because it takes up time and he can safely keep his back to her for a little while longer.

Bengt, she finally says in a voice almost bereft of softness, come to me.

He goes to her, but not like a lover does. The person hovering over her is a man deceived. His hair blackens his face, his lips are pursed, his breathing is heavy and tense. He is ugly. She wants to touch him as she always does when he looks that way, wants to stroke his hair, moisten his lips with hers—make him beautiful. But she doesn't. Partly because she is afraid of him, the unrecognizable stranger hovering over her. And we can only love strangers if they are beautiful. The other reason is that she is tired of constantly stroking his hair. It's too familiar to her.

When Bengt realizes she is afraid, he is afraid, too. He is afraid of being alone. When she was asleep he wasn't that afraid, because someone who is sleeping cannot leave another person as lonesome as someone who is awake. Like all other emotions, fear is contagious. With eyes full of despair, they gaze at each other in silence, a silence during which the ocean holds its breath and the rain ceases. They are both breathing heavily. Because she is stronger, she is the only one who can break the silence.

Why did you hit the dog? she whispers quietly and rather resigned, for she also knows in her own way that it's all over.

Then he topples over her. Sinks down with his hate, with his jealousy, and with his fear, but also with his love. His love makes him mute. If he only hated, he would have screamed, but now he can only cry—cry and forget himself. A woman is never afraid of a man who cries. Because a man who cries is merely a child. But when women cry they become very old.

Don't cry, she whispers and presses her mouth against his face.

The lamp is smoking, but it's very bright. His face is a child's face again, not a stranger's. He is no longer ugly, and when he himself forgets that he is and leaves his face alone, she thinks it is beautiful. But just when she thinks it's at its most beautiful, it hardens again. So she delicately rubs the ugly face to thaw it out, but her warmth is not enough. Hopelessly, she whispers:

Bengt! What happened?

She receives no answer. What had happened is something he can't confess. If he were a tiger, he would roar. But now he cannot roar, cannot even yell. He can only hurl his tiger body on top of her. *Don't cry,* she says to him. But the words aren't hers, nor can they ever be. They are his father's words or, more precisely, a father's words. What he now feels is something entirely new, something utterly absurd, something that only his instinct can comprehend—yet not entirely—or perhaps only express. The woman next to him, the woman he loves, is not just his father's or maybe another man's. She is his mother. This is what is so inconceivable to him.

We cannot fathom our own death or that someone is deceiving us, either. And we cannot imagine that someone else could sleep naked with the person we love. And if we could see it, our reason would not believe it. Only our heart would know it. Just as difficult to comprehend is the fact that we are capable of committing a crime ourselves. We can believe it of anyone else, but not ourselves. But when we do commit a crime, we still don't believe it, because we are the ones committing it. Our reason cannot process it and our feelings won't accept it. Our reason isn't strong enough, nor is our imagination. Our only real guarantee of happiness relies on the failure of our imagination.

He therefore doesn't spring from the bed, even though his heart knows that it's his mother he is holding. Instead, he grows only more excited than before, and he infects her with his passion.

As this is happening, they look into each other's eyes and this is when she finally has to understand, has to know that it is her son she loves, because she is afraid of what is happening, very afraid and very beautiful. The fear makes her beautiful but not him. But her beauty arouses him even more, and in the end it's not eyes they see, even though they are gazing into each other's eyes the whole time. Lust can transform everything. It is the deepest well, where all other feelings disappear. First, his fear disappears, then his jealousy drowns, and then his crime sinks down into it. Finally, his hate is swallowed up. The last thing he sees are her eyes, which are no longer eyes but a black, vertiginous well. Then his own body starts to sink down the well with all of his misery, courage, helplessness, and tears.

After he falls asleep, she rubs him dry with a sheet. She lays him gently on his side and watches him hour after hour, unable to take her eyes off him. She is no longer afraid, because he is her son. She is merely blissful and her body is throbbing as if she had just given birth to him. The only thing she still fears is that he might wake up. She loves him most when he is sleeping because then he is a child and his face is all alone, even his body is on its own. She has loved many men, but none like him. Before, she has only loved men, and men are never alone. Wherever they go, they drag their man with them.

She turns off the lamp without taking her eyes off him. The room smells like kerosene and sweat. It must be getting light out because the ocean sounds like it normally does at dawn. Birds are squawking high above the cottage, and the rain has stopped. When the dog comes up to her in the darkness and begs to be pet, she hits it. She doesn't feel bad afterward, but her hand hurts. Then she lays it on Bengt's heart, forgetting that she has done this a thousand times before.

Everything isn't the same in the morning though still very much the same. It isn't as though he forgot anything. When she woke him up with a bowl full of hot tea and rum, he recognizes her immediately. Not a single shadow on this face is foreign to him. He turns his face to the wall and drinks, and she is glad he turns away. The drink he is drinking tastes manly. Then he thinks of the pipe and the heavy cigarette case. He can't remember the initials, except that he didn't recognize them at all. But he is exhausted and quite satisfied and has a heavy, warm lump of gratification in his body. The tiger is full and satiated. It is sleeping. He also remembers his misdeed, but he can't comprehend it. So it doesn't upset him.

When they swim they now wear bathing suits. They used to run naked from the cottage—shivering in the morning cold—crash into the cold water with outstretched arms, and then dry off in front of the fire. Maybe it's just particularly cold that day. They walk down the steps cautiously. Jagged leaves cover the rocks, and a thousand little flies rise up from the seaweed. An empty box has floated into the inlet overnight. On the mainland there is a fire burning. It is very bright out and the flame is low, yet pure. When they wade into the water, they do not go together. It reminds him of the time when she and his father went out together. Now she is standing a short distance away and cupping water over her breasts. When Bengt tries pulling her strap down to see her shoulder he breaks the strap. She becomes irritated but doesn't say anything. She simply goes back to shore, but he doesn't follow her. Instead, he beckons the dog to him. Together they bob up and down in the sea of green, and together they sink to the bright bottom. His body fills with water and the dog mounts him, dragging him down. And they come up together—the dog, trembling, and he, coughing and spluttering. Smoke starts to rise from the chimney.

When he comes in, she is lying stretched out in front of the fire with her hands folded behind her head. She is looking up at the ceiling, and she is naked. When he lies next to her, she starts to get cold and tells him so. Sullenly, he gets up and sits at the table. Then she asks him if he wants to join her for another swim. He doesn't respond, nor does he go after her when she runs outside. Only the dog follows her.

Now he is the one lying on the skin rug when she comes back from swimming, and he has a pipe between his teeth. He watches her the whole time to see if she recognizes the pipe. But if she does, she doesn't show it. He slowly crumbles some cigarettes and fills the pipe—even then, waiting for a hint of recognition. When she still doesn't reveal anything, he grows discouraged and says that he feels cold. Then she says:

Don't be stupid.

But he is stupid—stupid and sulky. At the table he lights the pipe and then she sees it.

Have you started smoking pipes? she asks.

Yes, he says, as you can see.

She is a lot wiser than he is. Women are much wiser than men, not more intelligent but wiser. She is still lying in front of the fire. And she is still grinning. She feels the same pain he does, yet she still smiles. Smiling, she starts brushing her hair with the white comb. He cannot let her be. Indeed, he knows her much too well, but that's only when he is content or tired. But his lust can still transform her, make her almost unrecognizable. He leaves the pipe smoking on the table.

When he comes back it has gone out. As they eat breakfast—no longer on the rug but at the table—he keeps it next to his plate. They eat in silence. And Bengt gives most of his to the dog. It starts to rain. The fire goes out and it gets cold. To warm up, they drink tea with rum. As she clears the table, Gun tells him that he ought to write home and to Berit.

It helps to write. They are sitting on opposite sides of the table and thinking of things to say. They are playing a game, not committing a crime. And since it's only a game, they are able to do it. So they playfully think of things people do when they're drafted.

You have to write about girls, Gun says.

He looks up for a moment. Something occurs to him. And it makes him very upset. All of a sudden, he loses the desire to write the letter. He puts the pen down and looks at Gun. When she asks him why he isn't writing, he says he is thinking about all the girls he has had. Right when he says this, he tries to see if Gun looks jealous—she doesn't. She just laughs, leaving him disappointed. But not just disappointed. It also pains him to know that he cannot hurt her.

In the letter, however, he writes that there are plenty of girls. We have different ones every night, he continues, so life here is never boring. Father will laugh at that; Gun laughs at it, too. Then she signs his name at the bottom in her handwriting. This way it's more exciting. Now he feels he has to do something to get her to stop laughing. He crumples new cigarettes and stuffs them into the pipe. As he lights it, he senses that she recognizes it because she immediately seems bothered. Then he blows some smoke over her and says:

To think how little people know about each other.

She asks him what he means. He says that when his father gets the letter, he will believe it, believe that he has a new girl every night. Even Berit will believe hers, thinking that he is always alone. When she still doesn't understand, he elaborates and explains that whenever Gun says that she loves him, he, too, can't be sure if it's true.

Bengt, she says, with eyes as imploring as only a woman's can be when she is lying.

But then she agrees. It isn't what he wanted, of course. He wanted to have proof he was wrong. Now he feels utterly empty for a moment.

Gun, he says helplessly, can't we trust anyone?

She answers that we can trust the one we love.

And if she betrays you? he asks.

She replies that one should still trust her.

He cannot understand. So he wants to hurt her badly.

When I write letters to you, he whispers, you can never know if I'm lying.

Bengt, she says, are you jealous?

Some time goes by. He opens the window and rain sprinkles on his face. Outside, the clouds are low and drift slowly like black airships. The water is completely black. The dog is roaming around the rocks with its tail between its legs, head bowed, and tongue flapping.

Are you jealous of Knut? she asks.

For a very long time he searches deep down. Just as he closes the window and faces the room, she lights the fire on the hearth. Then she lies down and waits for him. When he comes to her, her lips are open but her eyes are closed. He unbuttons her blouse but leaves her lips untouched. Then he turns away. Quietly, he says:

Who is E.S.?

She says he has to kiss her first. When he kisses her, he has to keep going. Once he is tired and satisfied, he realizes that it doesn't matter who E.S. is; almost nothing matters. Nevertheless, she explains. Nestled in her warmth, he listens to her story. It might hurt to some extent but not much. But when she asks him if it hurts him to know, he says that it hurts a lot. And it's true. Everything he says is more or less true. That's what's so nice. It's also what is so frightening or what will become frightening.

Is it Erik's pipe? he asks afterward.

Yes, she answers and strokes his burning skin.

Then he snaps the pipe and throws the pieces in the fire. He doesn't feel anything as he does it, only that he is doing what he's supposed to be doing. And he usually feels nothing when he does what he has to. Although she seems to think he is affected.

Poor Bengt, she whispers.

He doesn't dislike sympathy, never has. It lets him know that he is suffering. And he enjoys suffering.

I've never thought that about you, he says, suffering.

But in reality, he has thought that. And now, to suffer more, he begins accusing her. He claims that she doesn't love him. This is a dangerous thing to say. If you want someone to love you, you don't ask her to see if she "really" does. Because, when all is said and done, there isn't much we "really" do. If you search deep down, you will find that the weight never reaches the bottom. Then you become terrified of the abyss within yourself. But you are never truly afraid until you discover that another name for this abyss is emptiness.

She walks in and sits on the bed. She lifts up the wet dog and starts petting it. When he can't think of anything else to say, she says:

I can't help it that I'm older than you. There were many before you. I can't help that. Can't you understand, Bengt?

Of course, he can't understand. A lover is like an actor. For him to perform really well, his heart has to believe that he's the first to play the role. If his heart isn't able to believe it, then his reason has to be convinced, at least, that no one has ever played the part as well as he. Once Bengt finally grows tired of suffering, he sits on the floor, beneath her, and asks:

Do you still love him?

No, she answers, I never have.

He asks to know why, so she explains. She explains what kind of man he was. She talks about him as if he were dead, but he is only in prison. She puts the dog down and pulls Bengt off the floor instead. She has to fill her emptiness, too, after all.

The man she talks about has been sitting in prison for a long time. He was a barber. When she met him, he was rich and happy. He was also pretentious and vain. He always combed his hair before going to bed. This makes them both laugh for the first time that day. He always tried to be funny, too. For instance, he always called the Swiss the Swisserists. He always tried to make her laugh, but she felt less inclined to do so as time went on. So he came up with new jokes that were even less funny. He used to put brilliantine in his hair before going to bed. He also bought her an island. When she asked him where he got his money, he didn't say, but he was very upset that she had asked. Then she realized that it was because of his uneasiness that he was with her. Just when she was about to break it off, he was caught. He had been selling counterfeit liquor ration coupons. He wanted her to hide him, but she didn't want to. She did not care for him enough.

After she explained everything, she asks him if he is satisfied. He says that he is because that's all he is. Satisfied that he was able to release his rage, satisfied that he had hurt her, satisfied that he was able to suffer. But when he kisses her, he notices that her body is still full of the other man. He wants to kiss him out of her; he wants to love him out of her. But when he tries, he cannot do it. Limp and crying, he falls next to her on the bed.

Poor Bengt, she says.

Then he leaps up, dashes out, and pushes the boat into the sea. By the time she reaches the shore, he is already drifting away. He is standing up in the boat, trying to get it to ride straight into the waves. They aren't high, but he is nevertheless powerless. The oars slip from his hands, he trips on the planked floor, crashes down, and doesn't pick himself up. She manages to pull the boat back to shore. When she turns him on his back, he pretends to be badly hurt.

Bengt, be sensible, she says as she tries helping him to his feet. Her dress is soaked up to her waist. When they get inside, she slings it over the damper to dry. He flings himself down on the ground, longing for her tenderness or maybe just one word. A single little word would save him. The word could even save her. As she packs up in the kitchen, she leaves the door open to hear the word. But all she hears is the creaking of the floorboards when he rolls over. As he rolls over, the dog comes up and sniffs him. He suddenly clutches it by the throat and starts to squeeze. When it tries to break loose, he becomes enraged and squeezes even tighter. Inside the kitchen, Gun drops whatever she was doing and comes running out. She pinches him to get him to stop.

Be sensible, Bengt! she yells.

But he doesn't want to be sensible. Anyone who fails with a woman doesn't feel like being sensible; he wants to be wild. But he isn't wild now, just very afraid, afraid as men usually are. Not afraid because he cannot love her the way she deserves, but because he might not be normal.

When he calms down, she asks him to explain himself. She is very gentle now, stroking his hair and kissing the salt from his face. He is lying down, silent and stiff. More than anything, he wants to humiliate her and to hurt her. He wouldn't be able to love her until he hurt her as much as she deserves. Not until then would he be fervent and strong. Therefore, the reason he gives her for trying to strangle the dog isn't true, or more precisely, it's as true as everything else.

It's his dog, isn't it?! he shouts.

Yes, she answers fatigued, he bought it for me.

In that moment, he knows what he is going to do to finally kill the mysterious man inside her, so that he himself could survive. He sits at the table, cool and collected, and they both drink a cup of rum before rowing out. Afterward, it's easier for them to accept each other. You can accept anything at all when you're a little intoxicated. They walk arm in arm down to shore, caressing each other's hands. Bengt leads the dog in the brown leash. She doesn't know what he's going to do, nor does she really care. She is tired and resigned. Then she sits in the stern with her hands on her lap. She looks very old.

This time he doesn't fail at getting the boat out. The sea is calmer, too. He doesn't look at her as he rows, and she wonders why but is too tired to ask. When she turns around to look back at the shore, she sees that he has tied the dog to the boat. It's trying to swim, but it's having too much trouble. When she tries to untie the leash, she feels his hard grip on her shoulder. Startled and a little afraid, she faces him. He is holding a rock in one hand. It is round and wet and quite heavy. A hard wave thrashes the side of the boat. She slips off the seat and, sitting on the floor of the boat, she finds him looming over her with the rock raised in the air. To avoid seeing any more, she squeezes her eyes shut. And to avoid hearing anything else, she plugs her ears.

When it's all over, he tosses the leash into the boat. He tries to help her up, but she won't let him. After rowing back to the inlet, he carries her ashore. She is very heavy, but he still manages. Gently yet forcibly, he lays her on the bed. Pale and feeble, she lies with her eyes closed, but she isn't covering her ears. So she hears what he says.

Don't you see? he whispers. It was his. So I had to do it. You got it from him because you were supposed to drag him around with you wherever you went. Can't you understand that? Can't you forgive me?

Maybe she does understand, maybe not. She is very tired and it is dark outside. She asks him to go and close all the shutters. When he comes back, he is naked. For a brief moment, he is standing just a step away from her bed, breathing heavily and fervently in the dark.

Bengt, she whispers, light the lamp.

When he shines it on her, she opens her eyes. Strong and aroused, he leans over her, stronger and more aroused than ever before. His eyes are black. His lips are open at first, but then he closes them. It doesn't matter to her. Indifferent, she lets herself be undressed by his strong, burning hands. When he is finished, she asks him to turn off the lamp, and she closes her eyes when he blows it out. Although it's dark and she cannot see him, she still closes her eyes. He finds her wrist in the dark. He grabs it firmly and forcibly and raises her up to him. He takes both of her hands and makes them feel his body. She has to feel how strong he is. And she does, but she doesn't care. She is indifferent to the fact that a man is getting into her bed.

Once he is asleep, she is not entirely indifferent. Because when he sleeps, he sleeps like a child. His knees are huddled up to his chin, and she feels how thin and bony his little boy knees are as she strokes them. And his shoulder blades are protruding from his back like wings. She caresses him dry. Then she kisses him wet. The whole time she fears waking him from his sleep. Because it's only when he sleeps that she is able love him.

Deep into the night, she has the urge to see him. Carefully, she gets up to light the lamp but can't find the matches at first. As she pads to the window where they usually are, she steps on the leash. She jerks her foot away as though an animal had bitten her. After lighting the lamp, she goes out to the other room and hangs the leash on the damper. Then she lingers there. She's afraid to go near him with the lamp. She is afraid of the dark. But she is even more afraid of his face. And when she finally does illuminate his face, she finds herself on the verge of screaming. But instead of screaming, she blows out the flame. As soon as she does, she lies down and starts crying. It doesn't wake him up. Because a woman's sobs do not wake any man. Yet the sobs of men keep women vigilant. She cries herself to sleep, but even in sleep she isn't free. She knows that she will have to love him the way some women love certain men: to give herself to him with lust but without pleasure; to let him believe she is everything to him because it would be too much trouble to let him think otherwise (besides, he would never believe it); to let herself be kissed when he wants, otherwise not bother; to accept a ring and be happy; to accept everything and be happy. This is more or less how she will love him. But she will never be able to love his face again.

Because the face she has lit up is the same face that loomed over her in the boat without seeing her, without seeing anything else but a dog doomed to death, nothing else but the tender prey needed to satiate the tiger in every man.

Even in her sleep, where a thousand seabirds are shrieking over a black sea, she sees the ugly, naked face of a young murderer.

A Letter to the Father from the Son

Dear Papa!

I'm writing this letter on Christmas morning. Berit has gone
to church with her parents. I had a headache, so I asked to
stay home. Besides, church ceremonies are hardly for me. I'm
doing very well here. The town is quite solitary, and we have a
few feet of snow. So the socks you gave me for Christmas are
being put to good use. I should also thank you for the razor.
I received a seemingly expensive shirt from Berit and two
wooden paper knives from her parents. They seem to think I
read an unbelievable amount of books. As you know, I read
frantically during the fall, but I still haven't managed to wear
out a paper knife. All joking aside, Berit's parents are very good
people. They live modestly and have very little contact with
the outside world, but they are still friendly and courteous.
They find me quite exceptional, though I'm just a philosophy
student. The other day I heard Berit's mother tell a neighbor
that her daughter's fiancé was a real philosopher. She stressed
the final *o* when she pronounced philosopher. I didn't correct

her, because I was afraid to offend her. The people up here are quite proud. When I tried to give her parents each ten *kronor* for the celebration expenses, they simply refused to take it.

I won't trouble you with all the details of my life here. But I did promise to write you as soon as I thought about what you told me before I left. As you so accurately stated, it's always easier to discuss something like this in writing than in person. What you told me naturally came as a shock. Not because it was completely unexpected, but it still would have been better if you had let me know before the first wedding announcement was published. Then, what you call "the scene" could have been avoided. On the other hand, I want you to know that I don't blame you in the least. Yes, I am my mother's son, but I am also yours. I'm aware that I'm not only obligated to my mother's memory but also to my loyalty to you. But that doesn't mean I will acquiesce in each and everything you do as if it were beyond criticism, even if, as you so rightly put it, I've become more reasonable lately. Reason is, as you realize, something quite relative. When a person is reasonable, we mean, as a rule, that she understands and consequently forgives all our actions. I don't mean to suggest that this is your attitude exactly—nor is it my own. I only mention it for the sake of balance, so to speak.

The reason I'm reacting differently to your marriage plans from how I did before is not that I'm suddenly more "reasonable" in December than I was in February, but that my initial pain has passed, and this has allowed me to develop a more dispassionate view of your behavior. Now I'm probably inclined to admit that love is something you can't control. My sentimental regard for Mama can no longer conceal the fact that this pertained to her just as much as to anyone else. Moreover, I feel it's my duty to tell you that I can confirm your suspicions about Erik and Mama's relationship. Besides, I think it's finally time we admit to ourselves that Mama was quite unbearable in her final years. There wasn't anything we could do that she didn't think was wrong or a failure. If we were kind to her, she suspected an ulterior motive. If we went shopping for her, we always came home with the wrong thing. On the other hand, if we didn't shop for her, we were cruel and wished for her death to come sooner. Of course, I know she was sick and therefore entitled to some indulgence, but it doesn't change the fact that her way of terrorizing us was simply unbearable.

Therefore, I can understand if you felt the need to run off to a less depressing environment. I would have done the same if I had been able to. So I understand quite well why you want to get married now. But I have nothing against your choice for a companion, so I have to disagree with you on that point. If I have shown your fiancée any "coldness," as you call it, it was probably because for a long time I was unsure of how I should behave in front of her. After all, it's still our first year of mourning (which you probably consider too conventional), and you can't blame me if this has caused me to keep some distance from her. But to conclude that I would somehow be cruel to her because of this is, without a doubt, to go too far. I wish you both happiness, and I think it's great the wedding is going to take place after the New Year; this way, no one can say that you remarried the same year Mama died.

I am a little hurt that you completely misunderstood my reaction to the news. Perhaps I should explain. It wasn't my intention to make a "scene," as you call it. And there were two reasons why I was a little harsh. The first and most important reason was that I was a little overwrought as a result of my studies being so demanding lately. As you know, I had to spend the majority of the fall term at the library into the wee hours of the night just to make up for what I lost during my military service. And this certainly wasn't beneficial to my nerves. The other and less significant reason was that, as I've already mentioned, I was a bit surprised by the sudden news, more precisely, not by the news itself but that it came so unexpectedly. Therefore, none of it was because of any resentment toward either of you, as you seem to think. You said yourself that you noticed Gun has been holding a slight grudge against me—ever since she found that stupid letter from that girl in my pocket when she was brushing my coat—and you therefore suspected that I had some reason to be upset with her, too. Yes, you might be right that it's really none of Gun's business if I'm unfaithful to Berit and that the scene she made when she found the letter was quite strange, but I think there's a natural explanation for her frustration. Women are very loyal to each other, and Gun must have felt very hurt on Berit's behalf. But she scarcely had any reason to be so upset for Berit in this situation. On the one hand, Berit didn't find out about it, of course. On the other hand, the affair was quite harmless. I simply met that girl while visiting a friend from school. She's one of those types who like falling for men, and rather often. You must have seen that cartoon with the woman who has a heart for a stomach? That's what she was like. Her lips were like a carnivorous flower. Kissing her was like sinking down into a swamp, and she didn't give me any pleasure. So I don't feel sorry about it, because you can't punish forbidden acts with regret, and we only feel remorse if we truly enjoyed it. The reason I "fell" for her was something deeper than mere lust. In my state of overexcitement I was seized by the suspicion that Berit was cheating on me. In retrospect, I agree that it was absurd, but you yourself know how absurd jealousy can be. Now, the best remedy for jealousy is to arouse jealousy yourself. This way, we achieve a comfortable balance. By the way, I think a Don Juan is a man who tries to keep his life in balance by not investing all of his affection into one object. A cowardly man? No. A wise man. Because for every disappointment, he can find solace in someone else. He knows how to economize his feelings. He is practical.

Not that I'm a Don Juan. It was just an observation, *nebenbei,* so to speak. Of course, I eventually realized that Berit was faithful to me. It was just tragic, or more precisely, tragicomical. So I burned up all my letters from the girl and asked her to burn all of mine. Unfortunately, I must have forgotten one in my coat, but that kind of thing happens, as you know. Yes, it was too bad that Gun happened to read it, but the fact is that no one asked her to. To make it up to her, I bought her that bracelet I showed you before I left. It was rather expensive, but it's worth the price if it can restore peace to our family. Don't you think?

Well, I've explained my point of view the best I could. If you speak with Gun about my letter, you can mention my explanation for my trivial relationship with that girl. It really doesn't concern her, but it might make her feel a little less offended for Berit's sake.

Wishing you a Merry Christmas
(what's left of it) and a
Happy New Year
from your son Bengt

P.S. Berit and her parents send their warm wishes.

THREE O'CLOCK

BERIT IS EVEN AFRAID OF THE ICE. Not just the ice that has formed overnight, but also the solid ice that has been freezing all winter. This is why she is so anxious as they travel across the ice to the island. She is sitting on the kicksled and Bengt is pushing her. She fears the whole time that the ice will give way. But it does not. It only creaks. The runners are screeching, and Gun is singing. She is sitting on the father's sled with a bag in her lap. She is wearing short white boots. Berit has high black ones that she has borrowed. But they are too big, so she wobbles when she walks.

Sunday morning is white and clear and three degrees Fahrenheit. A sheet of frost covers the ice, and tiny spruce trees are scattered about. A car rolls in slowly from across the frozen sea, and its snow chains rattle with fear, like chattering teeth. Farther out, a ship is frozen in the water; it looks like it's lying flat on the ice. Its contours are sharp and precise. The smoke rising from the funnel is thin and frigid. And large ivory spider webs seem to be hanging between the masts. The islands look a lot different from how they did in summer. The long, low island has sunk into the ice and snow. A single ski track goes into it but doesn't come back out. And the tall island is no longer as high as it was in the summer. The frozen crowns of the pine trees glisten in the sun. Gun puts on her sunglasses, the same ones from last summer. And Berit covers her eyes with one hand. Partly because of the sun and the ice, and partly because she is imagining things.

Bengt is also imagining things. They all are, for that matter. Gun stops singing. So now only the runners are singing. Up ahead, the ice is black, and they cross a stream. There, Bengt doesn't dare dig his spike too deep in the ice, so the father is able to catch up to him and even pass him. Then Gun leans to the side and looks back. Her stepson returns her glance. Neither of them smiles, but Bengt steers in behind the father. This relieves Berit, although she won't be truly at ease until they arrive.

The cliffs are covered by a deep layer of snow, and ice towers over all the rocks like little white volcanoes. An animal has apparently trudged across the island; the tracks could be from a dog. They leave the sleds on the ice and plod up to the house. But Bengt takes a different route. He climbs over the cleft, where the wind has packed the snow into solid drifts. He hardly leaves any tracks behind him. But in the hidden hollow, he sinks down to his knees. Then he stands up for a while, takes off his gloves, and fills his hands with snow. When he tastes it, it tastes like salt. Then someone calls out to him and he goes back.

Where have you been? the father asks.

Out, he says curtly.

The fire is burning on the hearth. The father has taken off his shoes and socks. Now his feet are propped up on the edge of the fireplace. They are not very clean.

What time is it? the son asks.

Ten, the father says as he curls his toes in a hideous way. They eat at eleven. And even though it's warm inside, Berit is cold.

It is four below zero outside. A skater on sails swooshes across the bay in a flash, like a darting mouse. They drink tea with rum after they eat. Gun lights a candle that she happens to have with her and places it in the center of the table. Then Bengt goes outside for a while and sits down on the steps and smokes. Berit comes out and sits next to him, doodling in the snow with the tips of her boots. The father and stepmother eventually come out, too. Gun is standing at the foot of the stairs and squinting into the sun. She wants to take some photographs. Bengt steps out of the frame.

Why? Gun asks as he takes the camera from her.

He doesn't answer; he just takes it. He has them stand on the steps and has them look straight ahead for a very long time, but it never turns out well. They are standing either too high or too low. But mostly they stand too far apart from each other.

Squeeze closer together, he says.

His voice is tense, so he can barely say it. But hiding behind the camera, he is able to see how Gun's eyes try to watch him. For the first time in a long time, she wants to look at him. The camera shakes and he never gets a good shot.

Closer, he says.

Then she puts her arm around the father's body, around his new dark blue coat. The father puts his around Berit's black coat.

That's good, Gun whispers.

But it's not good for her. It's good enough for Bengt, even though he is shaking. Behind the camera, his eyes are pleased, but he doesn't want anyone to notice.

Smile, he whispers.

They all hear him, but he said it only to Gun.

Afterward, only the father is smiling. The newlyweds go inside. They have been married for two weeks, and for fifteen days Bengt has been living with Berit. The back of the sofa is fixed, but they still aren't happy. They were especially unhappy the night the father got married. It was a small wedding, smaller than the father had anticipated. None of his friends came. They must have remembered that the first year of mourning hadn't quite passed, that there were more than fourteen days left. Fourteen days can be quite a lot of time for acquaintances; besides, it was a Thursday. Only the bridegroom's sisters came, dressed in Alma's clothes. They made coffee before the wedding and helped him with his shirt. But Berit was the only one who helped Gun with her dress. They took only one car to and from the courthouse. They ate dinner at the same restaurant, not in a private room though pretty close to the music. The sisters left first; they didn't have an appetite. Nor did they laugh a single time. They had merely been curious. Actually, the ugly sister did laugh once when the bridegroom dropped the ring as he was putting it on Gun's finger. She laughed then, but into her glove. The only time she laughs is at the mishaps of others. The only time she's alive is when someone else dies.

The bridal pair and Bengt and Berit left at the same time but in different directions. The newlyweds took a fancy car, and Bengt and Berit rode the streetcar to Berit's. She woke up in the middle of the night because Bengt was awake.

Are you asleep? she whispered.

He did not answer. Then she asked:

What are you thinking about?

He lay in endless silence. He was drenched in sweat. Suddenly, he shouted:

Do you know what they looked like?

Who? she whispered. She was afraid, partly because he had yelled and partly because someone might have heard it.

Of course, she knew whom he meant, and he knew that she knew.

Like dogs, he whispered. Like two satisfied little dogs.

Then something compelled her to say:

Why do you love her, Bengt?

As soon as she said it, but not before, she knew it was true. But she didn't know how she knew it. When Bengt told her that what she had said was a lie, she realized that he was lying, although he was unaware of it then.

I hate her, he whispered.

Then he became fervent and aroused. Fearful of the banjo player and the sleeping card players, she let him take her. When he had fallen asleep, she started to cry in silence. And even though the blankets were thick, she was cold. She knew that the one she loved had spent someone else's wedding night with her.

But in a sense it is true that he hated. Bengt hasn't been home for two weeks, nor has he called. One evening the father called him and he wasn't sober. It's our honeymoon, you understand, he said. The father sounded happy to be have been left alone. He sounded happy about everything, happy, too, to be drunk. Take Berit and come to the island early tomorrow morning, he said. There's ice now.

After the picture is taken, Bengt places Berit into the sled, fastens his spike, and pushes her gently into the inlet. He goes around the island three times with her—very slowly at first. The first time, they stop and look back at the island. Smoke is rising from the chimney; it is faint and delicate. The windowpanes are glinting in the dull sun. Heavy and tinged with blue, the snow covers the roof. The father comes out to the porch holding a pail, a shiny pail that he carries very carefully. He empties it over the snow beneath the railing. Now there is a large, ugly patch in the snow. He goes back inside without seeing them.

Nothing like that happens the second time they go around. Nothing happens at all, except that the smoke stops. They also hear a door slam, softly yet distinctly. Then Bengt turns the sled toward the sea. They stand up for a moment and look at the frozen-in ship. There is a granular trench behind it, filled with tall blocks of ice. The ship is deeply submerged and leaning slightly aport. They are too far away to be able to read its name. Ice encrusts the gunwale and the smokestack is frozen in ice, too. The flagpole is holding up a stiff pennant of ice. Next to the ship, there is a dark cloud of men gathered around a black horse and a sled. Its hooves aloft, the horse starts to gallop to shore. A man in a white fur is sitting in the sled, and its ringing bells slide across the ice. The hooves clatter, sometimes hollowly, as if over a bridge.

The third time, the shutter to the cabin is closed. Then he turns very sharply but proceeds very slowly to the island. They sit on the steps for ages before the father unlocks the door and steps outside. He laughs as soon as he sees them. In that moment he looks like a dog. He is more affectionate than ever on his honeymoon, so he takes Berit by the arm, and she goes sledding one more time. Bengt goes inside.

When he enters, Gun hasn't finished getting dressed. So she quickly wraps a fur around her when she hears him coming. Without touching, they move two chairs in front of the fireplace and feel totally lonesome as they sit there.

Thank you for the letter, Gun says after a while.

The fire is blazing again. In its light, Bengt suddenly sees the dog leash hanging on the damper. He takes it down and hides it in his pocket. The leash shouldn't hang there, since the dog had been run over on the way to Gun's brother's farm.

It wasn't for you, he answers. The letter was for Papa.

She doesn't respond but rips off the corner of a newspaper and throws it into the fire. Then she rips off an even bigger piece. Finally, she throws in the entire newspaper. The corners of the house creak in the coldness, and the sun is starting to set. It's fifteen below. Bengt moves his chair closer to the fire and closer to her, but he knows he can't get too close. They had promised this to each other after she got married. At the very most, they can get close but never too close. But when they aren't near each other, Bengt hates her because his tiger roars incessantly into his ear all the things she does when they're apart. And if it is lying—well, who would dare accuse a tiger of lying?

But once his chair is extremely close to hers, he realizes how short the distance between love and hate is; they are merely two sides of the same coin. We can only hate the one we truly love, and he does love her because he is close to her. She notices and becomes afraid, afraid of the severity of the law but also afraid of the longing of the flesh. Whenever she was alone in the new, unfamiliar home, she sometimes opened the bookcase and read about this crime as well as all the other crimes. But now she is mostly quivering because she wants him, because she has been longing for him, too.

They both want to, and though they try, they can't resist. And they can't resist because they no longer know each other so well. They are once again beautiful strangers to each other.

Your cheeks are so red, she whispers as she looks at him.

She is also red. But it's foolish of her to have said it, because once you mention something like that, you crave touching it. And to touch him, she had to move closer to him, but she is still a little afraid. Bengt strokes her fur.

Thank you for the bracelet, she whispers.

She isn't wearing it. He asks why. She says she is too afraid of Knut. Then she reaches for her purse. The bracelet is lying at the bottom of it, and the cigarette case is gone. For a split second, he is grazed by his own hatred. A hot wind strikes his cheek and vanishes in an instant, as wind usually does.

I threw it away, she whispers, for you. Now I have nothing left.

His reason tells him it's a lie, but he still accepts it as the truth. For we will gladly accept lies as long as they are presented as the truth.

He fastens the bracelet around her wrist. It is heavy and beautiful. And because he doesn't recognize her wrist, he strokes it. And when they kiss, they do not recognize their lips. Then, when she takes off the fur, they hear Knut's voice from outside and they go up to the window. Knut and Berit are climbing up the snow. The thermometer reads twenty below zero. They manage to kiss each other one more time before the other two arrive.

Berit is crying when she comes in. Tears, or maybe water, have frozen on her cheeks. Knut is laughing.

She started crying out in the middle of the ice, he says, placing his new hat on the table and taking off his earmuffs. It was different in my day. Then, girls had nothing against sledding. Now we need cars to keep them from crying.

Bengt goes out to the porch alone, and even though it's twenty below, it feels good to be on the porch. He isn't cold but simply refreshed. Now the sun is setting, and the glow of winter covers the ice like a thin sheet of red tissue paper. The giant webs of ice on the frozen-in ship are also red. The spider is bleeding and so are the flies. When Berit comes out, he takes her hand.

Poor Berit, he whispers.

She does not ask him why. He doesn't really know why he said it either. He is merely cheerful and gentle. When tears begin to cloud her eyes, he strokes her with his warm hands, but she continues to cry. Then he leads her to her bed. When they pass the father and Gun's alcove, he hears them murmuring quietly inside, even laughing a little. But it doesn't faze him. He only feels calm and peaceful.

As the twilight deepens and grows warm, they sit and talk on the edge of her bed—that is, he talks. She just lies there and listens, but as she listens, her face grows paler and paler. Finally, he asks her if she isn't feeling well. Then she says that she is *ill*. But he can tell that isn't all she has to say, so he asks her to tell the truth.

She asks him if he remembers what day it is. He remembers as soon as she asks. But he doesn't grow cold, at first. First, he just says that his mother was sweet, and when Berit isn't satisfied with hearing that, he adds that he had known what day it is. She grows paler.

At the table, the father asks her why she looks so pale. Bengt says it's because of the cold. Then the father gives her some alcohol to drink because he doesn't think pale cheeks are beautiful. Then Berit's cheeks turn a light shade of red, and the father caresses them. As he does this, Bengt and Gun gaze at each other from across the table—joyful and without shame. Their eyes are a little glossy from the alcohol but mostly from joy. Then they suddenly remember all the beautiful things that had happened in the room, but nothing of the ugly things. They also might be feeling a little remorse in front of the ones who don't have a clue, but this only makes their memories sweeter since remorse is, after all, the best spice of all.

It is all so pleasant for only a moment. On the table there is a candle that has some Christmas wrapping on its base. Gun tosses a box of matches on his lap.

Light the candle, Bengt, she cries.

When he lights the candle, he plans to light it for her and for himself. But that doesn't happen. It can never happen. Because an image of a candle is already within him, and that image is eternal. Now every time he lights a candle, it will always be this candle he lights. He looks away as soon as he lights it. The father is sitting behind the candle, and there is only *one* candle the father can sit behind. Bengt takes a sip from his glass, but it doesn't soothe him. He has to ask. It's a stupid question—a stupid statement, to be precise.

It's three o'clock, he says.

Then he feels more intoxicated than he really is. It isn't three o'clock at all, and he knows it. It is much later. It is six.

No, son, the father says, it's much later than that.

The father doesn't remember anything, because reminiscing doesn't really matter to him. He scarcely cares about what used to be. He only cares about what is.

Is the clock working? Bengt asks.

He didn't want to mention anything having to do with clocks, but he can't resist. Shame—or decency, rather—forces him to go on. But the father replies that the clock is certainly working. The key was underneath the armchair, whoever the hell put it there, and they put the head back in its place, freshly gilded. This would have been enough, but when Bengt looks at Berit, he can see that she still isn't satisfied. He grows irritated with her because he isn't satisfied himself. So he tells her that she ought to go and lie down, and he grabs her hard by the arm as he usually does when he wants her to understand. She understands and goes.

He feels happier once she is gone, but not entirely. To be as happy as he needs to be, he drinks another glass. They have wine, rum, and aquavit with them. The father is also drinking. And the more he drinks, the more affectionate he becomes. He moves his chair closer to Gun's and caresses her both above and underneath the table. Bengt moves his chair farther away. All of a sudden, he doesn't want to see or hear them anymore. But he is not jealous yet. He is only suffering. There is a soiled napkin under the table—scarlet from wine. He picks it up and plays with it for a while. If only everything would just end now, if the candle would go out, if the ice would break up, if Gun would only scream with disgust at the drunken voice that was defiling their stillness. But the candle is in the center of the table and it is burning. It is an ordinary candle yet very brazen.

Then he realizes the candle is not the worst part. Once he realized this, he turns cold. A giant hole emerges from his suffering, and it swells with a shameless chill. Then he gets the urge to torture, to smash things, to tear things down. He destroys all the bars caging his tiger. Then he sics the tiger on the gazelle. He stands up and looks at Gun and his father, but they don't seem to notice. They are merely carrying on with their endlessly abhorrent behavior. What he noticed then is that Gun, quite simply, isn't suffering as he is from his father's drunken caresses. And then what he notices is something dreadful: she actually likes them.

If it hadn't been too late, his reason would have told him what he already knew, the shocking truth that he himself experienced so many times: namely, that we are never so tender to the ones we are bound to as when we are certain that the stranger we love actually loves us in return. He can only understand this when he himself is tender to Berit because of Gun's love, yet he can't understand this about anyone else. This explains why he is so upset and why such filthy thoughts are flowing out of him, like a busted sewer. As he leans against the window post, he thinks: they're just like this when they're alone together. They sit at the kitchen table, drink, and fondle each other as they're doing now. They are just like dogs when they are alone together.

At the same time, it turns three o'clock. His already misty eyes fill with tears. The tiger is chewing the gazelle and considers it just. It's only right for him to think of his mother after a year has passed since she died. There isn't anyone who is more right than he. He knows it when he leaves the room, and he is more convinced of it when he goes outside. It is twenty-five degrees below and dark as it usually is in winter, a luminous darkness that reflects itself in the snow and ice. He walks a bit and then drops to the ground. Because he is so right and everyone else is so wrong, he lets himself lie there and even cries for a while. Then he is afraid of freezing to death. That's when he feels the weight of the leash inside his pocket. It makes him feel like hanging himself. And when they come out with their lantern, they will find him hanging from a tree. Now he is staggering around, feeling after branches. In his heart, he feels he is already hanging. His throat is so taut that he can scarcely swallow, and he's on the verge of vomiting. Finally, he finds a suitable branch, makes a noose in the leash, brushes the snow and ice off the branch, and ties the leash around it. When he sticks his head through the noose, the branch snaps.

He knew it would happen. But he is satisfied he tried. And because he had been saved, he doesn't try it again. He feels somewhat better, a little less miserable. But he is immediately sad again because no one opens the door and calls out to him. They have left him all alone in the snow and the darkness. He simply cannot fathom anything so inhumane. Some light trickles through the slits of a shutter. Laughter and loud voices are inside. But inside him is only darkness and silence. And the beginning of tears, too. The memory of his mother shoots up inside him like a smarting pain. Like an ache and a fever.

Silently, he opens the door. The alcove is empty. Berit has gone to visit the others. His fever escalates, but at the same time his mind becomes clear, as a fevered person's does. He turns on a flashlight and lays it down on Berit's bed. He looks for a pen and paper. Then he writes a letter. Not to himself but to the others. The whole time he writes he hopes that the door will open, that light and warmth from the main room will come rushing in, and that someone will carry him into the light and the warmth. But no one comes, and soon the letter is finished. When it's completely finished, he folds it up and puts it in his pocket.

The candle is almost burnt out when he joins the others. But none of them notices that it's burning down. Not even Berit, who has been given rum, a lot of rum. Therefore, she doesn't see the candle, doesn't see much of anything, really—maybe not even Bengt. Slowly, the room begins to spin, and she seems to be enjoying it. Gun and the father are sitting with their arms around each other. He stands for a long time and watches them, the whole time seeing what he expected to see: they look exactly as they did on their wedding night. There are yellow pears on their plates. The father frees his hands and starts paring with his razor; either there was nothing better, or he wants to be funny. Once it is peeled, he tosses the razor on the table and starts feeding Gun.

Then the son goes up to the father very closely and hits him lightly on the shoulder, but not as lightly as he wanted. The father asks him what he wants. He says that it's three o'clock. No one seems to understand.

No, it's not, the father says.

Then he shouts so they will understand:

Aren't you all happy now!

Gun chuckles, but he is far from finished.

Aren't you happy? he yells. It's Mama's anniversary. One year since she died!

The room grows silent except for the scraping of chairs. Bengt blows the candle out before the paper starts to burn. But it doesn't get dark, because Berit turns up the flame of the kerosene lamp and because her hand is so white. She gazes at Bengt, gazes so strangely at him that he has to look away.

My boy, the father says with beautiful, glistening eyes, don't you think I remember? Come here. Don't be sad. Don't cry, my boy.

But he doesn't move. Everything is as he expected. Now it's only confirmation that he's looking for, confirmation that everything is how his tiger said it would be. Enraged, he shouts:

Your year of mourning is over. Mine is just beginning!

The moon, the pale moon of winter, and a multitude of pointy stars shine outside. Sleds are waiting by the shore, and their runners are glistening. He kneels down; the skin around his throat tightens. One of the sleds is sturdy and new, and he ties the leash around its handles. When everything is ready, Gun calls out to him. He looks up at the cottage one last time. Because she stays there and continues to call out to him, he looks up one more time. When she still doesn't move, he runs toward the cottage, stumbles, falls down, and white with snow, rushes up the steps. She pulls him close to her so that she can hold him. She is afraid because she doesn't understand a thing. She can't understand why he doesn't see that she is glad to have found him again.

But love is just a game of misunderstanding. Instead of wrapping his arms around her and saving himself, he takes a step down. The leash hook glistens when he raises his hand. Then he strikes her across the face like a dog. But she doesn't cry out. She merely leaves him alone.

He stands alone, cold, and naked on the steps. Hitting a woman is like hitting an animal. Afterward, you feel dreadfully alone. Afterward, you cannot be forgiven. But without forgiveness, he is hopelessly lost. And it is precisely this hopelessness he was searching for. But now that he has found it, he is terribly afraid, so afraid that he can't even move. And when Berit comes out to him, he is still standing hopelessly still.

What's wrong, Bengt? she whispers.

She isn't aware of what has happened, she never is. When he doesn't answer, she looks at him as curiously as she had just done inside. After studying him for a while, she turns away to the door.

Do you know what you look like? she whispers.

No, he whispers back at her. And it's true: he couldn't know. All he knows is that it's over, and to realize this is more horrific than he ever imagined.

Like a dog, she answers.

Now everything is confirmed. There is nothing left. There is only one thing to do, and he does it. He pushes past her, flings open the door, and marches up to the table, up to the woman who hates him and up to the man he is indifferent to. He still might need a little courage to be able to do what he wants to do. Then the courage comes. As he stands behind the father's chair, Gun suddenly starts talking about a Negro. She had only seen him on the street and thought he was beautiful. But men cannot, without hatred, tolerate it when their women talk about Negroes being beautiful. There is a lyncher in every man, for lynchers are only men who are afraid of their own women.

As irretrievably lost as can be, he pulls back his sleeve from his left wrist. As though in a dream, he sees the father's razor sink into his flesh. Everything is so dreamlike that it doesn't even hurt. When he drops the razor, he stands there and watches with surreal surprise how the blood slowly fills the wound, runs over his wrist and down his hand, and then falls with heavy drops to the floor. Then Berit screams. Gun and the father see it almost immediately, but first they are just as surprised as he. He hears Berit slam the door behind him, a soft, quiet sound that he has never heard before. Then there's an almost comical bustle that he doesn't really understand. These three people are running in circles around each other. He is the only calm one. With a sensation of surprising serenity, he feels his life flowing out of him with every throb of his shredded artery. The onset of death feels so peaceful that he finds their commotion almost absurd. Step after step, he shuffles back toward the door and braces his back against the nook between the door and the wall. He is looking down at his hand the whole time. The back of it is white and beautiful. He is not afraid, because we are only afraid beforehand. Once it has happened, however, we are only filled with expectation.

He is smiling with expectation when they come up to him with towels. His legs start to weaken, but they still manage to carry him. He is gentle and happy, and he can't understand why the people approaching him are so worried. He has already been dying for an infinitely long time by the time they reach him. He has no sense of time anymore. Everything is happening in slow motion, although in reality it's happening at a blistering speed. In the dream, he hears someone calling his name, and he sedately stretches out his bleeding arm to the towel—not sensing that this is going save him. He thinks it's only nice that Gun has taken his hand in hers. His hatred has drained out of him. His tiger has died from loss of blood. Even the gazelle is dead now. The only thing left is a resigned tenderness. If he could, he would caress all three of them, as their hands support his feeble body and carry him back to the alcove and into Gun's bed. He is alone with Gun for a second. Smiling, he asks her:

Do you think I'm going to die?

Lie still, she whispers, holding the towel over him.

Then she kisses him. He just lies there with the towel pressed against his wound. Hour after hour passes. The blood begins to slowly seep through the thick towel. He hears the distant sound of frantic footsteps and the slamming of doors. He can't understand why they are in such a hurry.

People who witness an accident start to feel—once the initial alarm has subsided—a strange sensation of exhilaration that is closely related to joy. Laughter is the only thing missing. All three of them feel this curious joy as they prepare for the ride. They move around as though intoxicated, only without the drunken sluggishness; instead, their movements are quick and precise. When they are ready, they carry him with great strength through the snow and down to the sleds. As they place him gently into the new sled, the father finds the leash on the ground. Then he wraps it around the son's leg and the sled's handles so that he won't slip off.

Very weak yet still filled with the same joyous calm, Bengt can sense everything that is happening. Just before the sled begins to glide over the ice, he hears the father say:

Thirty-two below.

The words sound so familiar, but he forgot what they mean. He simply thinks it sounds beautiful. He quietly repeats the words to himself for as long as he can. Then he gazes out at the ice and the moon. The moon is white and beautiful, but strangely far away. The ice is also white. The air is very warm. Then he closes his eyes and listens to all the beautiful sounds of the night. The night sings with silence. It's the greatest sound of all. Then there are fainter sounds: the rhythmic slicing of the ice from the spikes; the soft singing of the runners as they race over the black ice; the slight creaking of the kicksled's wood; the harsh scraping as they pass over granular ice.

The journey goes by in a flash. The sleds glide neck and neck to shore. Gun is pushing Berit, who is not crying. She is very calm and very tired. The trip is endlessly long for her, endlessly beautiful and endlessly long. It lasts an eternity for him, too. He can't even comprehend distance anymore. To be dying is to be like a child. In the end, you don't understand a thing: nothing about death and nothing about life, only that all distances are the same and all words are unintelligible—yet beautiful.

The sleds stop below the tall jetty. They wait underneath its shadow as the father runs toward the village. From the shadow, Bengt has a view of the beautiful moonlight. Gun bends down and unties the leash.

Are you cold? she whispers.

No, he whispers back.

He doesn't really understand what she said; he only sensed it.

Bengt, Berit whispers respectfully, as one does to the sick.

She holds his right hand for a while. Then she leans over and kisses him with her cold lips. Immediately after, they hear the taxi rumbling downhill. Snow chains are wrapped clumsily around the tires. The two women lift him onto the jetty, and he sits between them in the car. They are driving very fast; he doesn't recognize where they are. The car skids into curbs and his body ricochets between the two women's bodies; between one soft body and one hard one; between the one that knows everything and the one that knows nothing. He loves them both equally, for he loves everything now. He even loves his father.

It's thirty-two below, he hears the father saying.

Thirty-one, corrects the driver.

The road is fringed by tall white borders with branches in them. In the beam of the headlights, one neighborhood after the other emerges from the snow and quickly sinks down again. The driver has put some red paper over one of the headlights. Gun dabs a drop of perfume onto Bengt's lips so that he won't smell like alcohol. When they near the city, his head begins to clear up a little without costing him any of his bliss. At the toll, he notices the car speeding over a safety island and onto the wrong side of the road to save time. Then he starts to suspect what is happening: he is going to be saved.

But he isn't sure of it until they swerve up to the foot of the tall lampposts in front of the hospital. When he steps out of the car, he can feel that it's very cold. It isn't until then that he is afraid—not so much of what is going to happen but of what he is going to say.

What will I say? he whispers helplessly as the doors open.

But nobody hears him. The corridor is warm and bright, and far ahead is an opened door. He goes through it by himself. The room is enormous and shiny. The cabinets glisten, the instruments glisten, and the operating table glistens. A nurse unbuttons his jacket and gently peels it off him. He manages to lay himself on the table. Then a white lamp hovers over him and shines into his eyes. The nurse takes his arm and gently unwraps the towel. He turns his head and looks at his wound. It is long and very deep. It is also hollow and almost white. The nurse gently turns his head away, so he looks down at his body instead. His shirt is stained brown with blood. He doesn't really understand why. Then he senses that she is cleaning his hand. It does not hurt.

When she asks him his name, he tells her, but he doesn't recognize it and is afraid he has said something wrong. He doesn't recognize his address either. He turns his head and looks at her. Her glasses are glistening, and behind the lenses her eyes are glistening, too. When she asks him how this happened, he answers that he was trying to split wood with a knife.

When the doctor comes in, he likes him immediately. While they are busy with his hand, he looks at it. Although he doesn't recognize it, he is still interested in seeing it. And after the local anesthetic, it belongs to him even less. The thread is thick like a violin string. The doctor sticks it in and out of the foreign wrist. Finally, he snips off the protruding ends with a small pair of shiny scissors. He is weak and blissful—blissful even though he knows he is saved. Even afterward, his joy persists, the same joy as before. After all, dying and being saved arouse the same mild joy.

As the nurse applies the bandage, the doctor stays put and stares at him. Suddenly, he says:

Why were you splitting wood in the middle of the night?

It was thirty-two below, he answers.

The doctor pulls the lamp away, nearly leaving him in darkness. And from the darkness, he hears the low, familiar voice again.

Why were you cutting wood with a razor? he asks.

He's unable to answer. But when he looks up from the darkness, he sees the doctor looking at his right hand.

I burnt myself, he whispers, burnt myself on a candle.

He climbs off the table by himself, and the nurse lifts his arm into a sling. When he reaches the door, he notices that the doctor has followed behind him. Just as he is about to walk out, he hears the doctor say, in a voice low enough so that only the two of them can hear:

Avoid the fire.

The door shuts behind him. He trudges down the hallway. The floor slants slightly. At the mouth of the hall, there is a waiting room with a table, chairs, and monthly newspapers. He sees them before they see him. No one is reading, even though they all have newspapers in their laps. As he gets closer, he realizes that he loves all three of them.

They take a taxi home. He is immensely tired and immensely happy. They are all immensely tired. When they enter the building, he recognizes the smell at once. Even the smell of the apartment is the same: linoleum, food, and fabric. He even loves the smell.

His room hasn't changed. They help him to bed. The father undresses him and puts on his nightshirt. As the son lies in bed, the father strokes his hair.

My boy, he says, you shouldn't study so hard. You should rest for a while.

Then the son strokes the father's hair with his right hand. Gun comes and says good night from the doorway. One of her cheeks is red. He has an incredible urge to touch her. When the father leaves, she comes in, too, but just for a second. She doesn't say a word; she only lets him caress her where it stings.

Berit stays the longest, pulls up a chair, sits there, and watches him.

You are not allowed to die, she whispers.

She does not cry. Never again will she cry as she used to cry before. He lets her give him a long kiss because he does love her, too. She will sleep overnight in the kitchen. As she is about to leave, he asks her to take out the letter from his jacket pocket. Then he asks her to rip it to shreds.

As he listens to her ripping it apart over his desk, he falls asleep. Deep and blissfully.

A Torn-up Suicide Note

You ask why. I will tell you why. It's because I'm tired of living.
Tired of living here in this world of little dogs, this dog world
of measly emotions, measly pleasures, and measly thoughts.
We're supposed to be content, but I don't want to be content.
I don't want to be satisfied like a little dog, because there's
nothing more loathsome than little dogs when they come home
frightened and pleased from their little dog adventures. I myself
have been a big dog. But I don't want to be a big dog either.
Even if it is better to be a big dog than a little one. So we have
no other choice but to be either a big dog or a little dog.

I've been a big dog because I have deceived all of you. But
I've also been a little dog because I've deceived myself, too. We
all deceive ourselves in the land of little dogs, and we can only
dream of having little dog adventures. But all of us are afraid of
the greatest adventure of all: to live purely. Little dogs have a
panic-stricken fear of this one great adventure, because for them
only truly filthy adventures are worth living for. In the land of
little dogs, indecency is worse than immorality. But they fail to
realize that only one thing is truly immoral: to consciously want

to hurt someone. Therefore, in the land of little dogs, passive malice is more esteemed than active goodness.

In the land of little dogs, we are all cheaters, and we do everything in fun. In fun, we feed all the little dogs with scraps of our emotions. In fun, we tell ourselves that we love every measly dog we meet. Therefore, no one can truly love in the land of the little dogs and nothing is genuine. Not even duplicity is real there. In the land of little dogs, even cheaters cheat at their own fixed game. And in the land of little dogs, you don't need any faith. So no one has any. But if anyone does happen to have any faith, they only have it in jest, because everything is a joke in the land of little dogs.

In the land of little dogs, the older dogs have nothing to say to the younger dogs. And if they did have something to say, they wouldn't dare say it, because nobody believes in anything they say themselves. Not even their lies are truly mendacious. Because in the land of little dogs, the truthful ones tell lies and the liars tell the truth, so everything is always true and always false. Everything can be proven, thesis as well as antithesis. And we'd believe in both in the land of little dogs if only anyone dared to believe at all.

No one is happy or unhappy in the land of little dogs. The prevailing pleasure is indifference, the only valid feelings are small ones, and the only thoughts are even smaller. And only the most insignificant of feelings are beautiful. In the land of little dogs, reason is never beautiful. In the land of little dogs, you can never understand that the only thing keeping the state of the little dogs from being completely unbearable is that the reason of the big dogs is able to analyze it.

In the land of little dogs, everyone could live how they pleased if only anyone knew what they wanted. But in the land of the little dogs, no one believes in their aspirations, because everyone knows that they themselves are lying cheats. There's only one wish in the land of little dogs, and that is to want to always be someone else. Everything is fluid in the land of little dogs, even stones. And the stone of dishonesty displaces the stone of honesty. There, even the masks wear masks. And to don yet another mask is called unmasking.

The land of little dogs is a place where it's considered shameful to live. And if it weren't considered shameful to die, too, then several would prefer that as well. Besides, it's even shameful to be ashamed in the land of little dogs.

Only he who is not at home in the land of little dogs will be left to become a big dog. And the only advantage of being a big dog in a world of little dogs is that you are no longer afraid to die. But a big dog—least of all a big dog—cannot escape the shame of living either.

This is why I'm doing what I'm doing.

WHEN THE DESERT BLOOMS

YOU WAKE UP HAPPILY, feel the wound aching mildly, and remember. You tug at the bandage and smile in the darkness at the unimaginable. It doesn't hurt, and you are glad. You are brave, too, daring to turn on the light with your good hand. This time, you aren't afraid when you look into your own eyes; there was never a time before when this didn't frighten you. Your suicide note is on the desk, ripped to shreds. And when you turn out the light, the pieces continue to glow. You also manage to keep looking at yourself without becoming afraid. Brave and serene, you rest in the arms of the world. And little by little, you are infused with a warm certainty: you didn't do it to die or to be saved either—but to have peace. Peace with everything inside of you that wanted to die, peace with everything outside of you that pressured you to live. Otherwise, nothing has happened, nothing but some loss of blood and the fact that you have become a little older. You also understand that in order to begin to live, you must have already begun to die.

The father comes in early, turns on the light, pulls a chair up to his bed—sitting down gently as one does at a sick person's bedside—and says nothing. The son is awakened by his silence. He rouses gently and quietly. They look at each other in prolonged silence. At first, the silence is frigid but then it starts to thaw out. At first, they are both alone, alone as they have always been in each other's company. The father sits there and plays with his yardstick: pulling it out, folding it up, measuring the loneliness and the silence. They hear Berit wake up in the kitchen, and the alarm clock rings in the other room.

My boy, the father whispers.

Then the unimaginable happens. A wave of warmth gushes through the room. The father drops his yardstick, holds the son's unwounded hand in his, and brushes the hair from his forehead.

My boy, he says once again.

And those words contain everything—all questions, all answers, all affection, and all worries. They infect each other with their joy, and the warmth turns into heat. But the hotter it becomes, the deeper the silence becomes. Words can no longer express what they are feeling. Only their eyes and their hands, which are in a tranquil embrace. Before the father leaves, he tucks the son in, wrapping the blanket tightly around his body. He has always wanted to do that, longed to be allowed to do it, but never dared. Then he turns out the light and walks out.

It's twenty-two below, he whispers in the darkness.

The yardstick clicks. The door closes. It's only fifteen below, but he is overjoyed.

When Berit sits down on his bed, he spreads the blanket over her lap. It makes her knees softer and even warms them up. She hasn't slept much, and she had absurd dreams. She doesn't ask him why. Nor does he tell her why. But a knot has come undone, so he asks her to retie it. As she ties it, he feels how cold her hands are, so he puts them underneath his blanket. They rest there like cold stones. Once they are warm, he pulls her up to him. Her body is tepid, like the masonry heater early in the morning.

Poor Berit, he says.

She starts to cry. It's good for her to cry because the tears release her joy. She starts to warm up once she finished crying, bashfully caressing him as the heat returns to her.

I'm going to buy some grapes for tonight, she whispers, a big cluster.

Then she gently parts from him. He strokes her thighs, which are now softer than they have ever been before. He also fondles her breasts, and they swell up.

Don't be afraid, he whispers. And don't be cold. It's only five below outside. That's what Papa said.

It's already light by the time Gun comes. The air is crisp and clear, and the window is covered with roses. It's very warm underneath the blanket. She rests on his good arm, untroubled and unafraid. Her pink robe lies on the floor like a poor, broken soul. But they themselves are whole, and the brighter it becomes the more whole they become—and more pure. Hour after hour passes in silence. They don't speak much because there isn't a lot to say. And whatever could be said, they already know. They know that they are mother and son, and they know it with open eyes. And they aren't afraid of it, because we are never afraid of what we truly know. We are only afraid before we know it. But to know for certain costs us dearly. It costs us blood and tears, but it's worth the price.

To know also hurts. Her cheek still stings from the lashing, but the pain is strangely sweet. She knows that it has to be so. It has to hurt to gain a son. She tenderly strokes his aching wrist. Then he dares to caress her cheek, and she finds the courage to describe her joy—and her loneliness. She is bold enough to explain about the cold, lonely mornings when he isn't there. About the tepid heater, the cold bed, the frost on the windowpanes, and the snow that whirls down from the rooftops to the frozen cars below, about the room that peers at her with cold eyes, about all the things she refuses to touch because they belong to someone else, about her fear of the telephone and the receiver that always seems to be warm from someone else's ear, about the vase she smashed against the wall to be rid of its owner, and about the opera glasses she stole from the bookcase and used every night to peer down at the street and make people look big so that they would be closer to her and she would be less alone. She also explains about the husband, the cold husband, whose laughter is a frozen cry and who thinks that to comfort her means to grow cold. Regarding the furniture, he appeased her, saying that it cost nine hundred *kronor* in 1929. Soon, he would reassure her about the apartment, too, telling her that the rent happens to be the most affordable in the city. Then he would reassure her that that which is dead is dead. Lastly, she speaks of her own coldness, of life's great white icebox—she herself is twenty-two below. And of her yearning for something else. It writhes inside her like an imprisoned snake—which may be squirming inside us all.

Mama, he whispers, embracing her like a son.

Then their heat erupts. Their white desert begins to thaw. And look, the desert is blooming. Their desert is precious to them, and though they love each other very much, they mostly love their desert. They are not happier than before, not better either, but they are a lot less foolish. Warm and wise, they lie and look up at the white ceiling, the neighbor's floor, on top of which a sick child is dancing. Wise, because wisdom is to be in love with life, whereas foolishness is to be ashamed of love.

They are not only wise but silent, too, because our landscape is suffused with silence after a volcanic eruption. A moment ago, there was fire. Now the tepid ashes warm our feet. A moment ago, there was blinding light. But now a blessed twilight cools our eyes. Everything is calm again. The volcano is slumbering. Even our poor nerves are slumbering. We are not happy, but we feel momentary peace. We have just witnessed our life's desert in all its terrifying grandeur, and now the desert is blooming. The oases are few and far between, but they do exist. And although the desert is vast, we know that the greatest deserts hold the most oases. But to discover this, we have to pay dearly. The price is a volcanic eruption. Costly, but nothing less destructive exists. Therefore, we ought to bless the volcanoes, thank them because their light is dazzling and their fire is scorching. Thank them for blinding us, because only when we are blind can we gain our full sight. And thank them for burning us, because only as burnt children can we give others our warmth.

But the moments of peace are fleeting. All other moments are significantly longer. Understanding this is also wisdom. But because they are so short, we must live in these moments as if it were only then that we lived. They understand this, too.

Therefore, they do not answer when Berit calls.

They will not answer when Knut calls either.

And when the aunts call, they will let it ring.

STIG DAGERMAN (1923–1954) was regarded as the most talented writer of the Swedish postwar generation. Among the many books he wrote during his tragically short life are his classics *German Autumn* (Minnesota, 2011) and *Island of the Doomed* (Minnesota, 2012).

BENJAMIN MIER-CRUZ teaches Scandinavian literature and Swedish language courses at the University of California, Berkeley. He was awarded the Susan Sontag Prize for Translation in 2010 for his translation of the poetry and letters of Elmer Diktonius.

PER OLOV ENQUIST is a novelist, playwright, and poet. His works include *Lewi's Journey* and the international best-seller *The Royal Physician's Visit*. His awards include the August Prize, the Prix du Meilleur Livre Étranger, the Independent Foreign Fiction Prize, and the Swedish Academy's Nordic Prize.